MURDER AT A CAPE BOOKSTORE

"I just had a bit of Yvonne's freebie soup, but why not? I even brought my own spoon." I opened the container she handed me. "Mmm. Creamy and chock-full of clams. Delish."

"Thanks, Mac. Hey, are you surprised Wagner isn't out here schmoozing his way up and down town?"

"Yes, I guess I am. Who knows, maybe he's in the Rusty Anchor celebrating." I finished the chowder. "Thanks, Tulia. I'd better get back to my—" I broke off.

August pedaled furiously down the street past us and leapt off his bike at the Book Nook. Norland no longer sat on the bench outside the store. Police chief Victoria Laitinen sprinted there from the police station down the block. A siren wailed into action.

Uh-oh. "Something's up at the bookstore. I'm going to go see." I wasn't much of a runner since I blew out my knee cycling the mountains of New Zealand, but I could jog when I had to. This felt like one of those times.

I pulled open the door to the Book Nook. The bell dinged as I gasped.

One of the tall, heavy wood bookshelves lay toppled. I caught a glimpse of August kneeling behind the shelving unit. Something stuck out. My eyes widened. Was that a shoe? Victoria spoke into her police radio. A pale, somber Norland gave me a ghastly look.

"What . . ." I began.

Norland shook his head. "It's Lavoie. And he's dead."

Books by Maddie Day

Country Store Mysteries
FLIPPED FOR MURDER
GRILLED FOR MURDER
WHEN THE GRITS HIT THE FAN
BISCUITS AND SLASHED BROWNS
DEATH OVER EASY
STRANGLED EGGS AND HAM
NACHO AVERAGE MURDER
CANDY SLAIN MURDER
NO GRATER CRIME
BATTER OFF DEAD
FOUR LEAF CLEAVER
CHRISTMAS COCOA MURDER
(with Carlene O'Connor and Alex Erickson)
CHRISTMAS SCARF MURDER
(with Carlene O'Connor and Peggy Ehrhart)

Cozy Capers Book Group Mysteries
MURDER ON CAPE COD
MURDER AT THE TAFFY SHOP
MURDER AT THE LOBSTAH SHACK
MURDER IN A CAPE COTTAGE
MURDER AT A CAPE BOOKSTORE

Local Foods Mysteries
A TINE TO LIVE, A TINE TO DIE
'TIL DIRT DO US PART
FARMED AND DANGEROUS
MURDER MOST FOWL
MULCH ADO ABOUT MURDER

Published by Kensington Publishing Corp.

MURDER AT A CAPE BOOKSTORE

A Cozy Capers Book Group Mystery

Maddie Day

Kensington Publishing Corp.
www.kensingtonbooks.com

KENSINGTON BOOKS are published by

Kensington Publishing Corp.
119 West 40th Street
New York, NY 10018

First Printing: September 2023
ISBN: 978-1-4967-4055-7

ISBN: 978-1-4967-4056-4 (ebook)

10 9 8 7 6 5 4 3 2 1

Printed in the United States of America

For West Falmouth Friends Meeting, whose retreat cottage I run away to twice a year for intensive solo writing retreats as well as research for this series. Bless you for providing a quiet getaway.

Acknowledgments

Thanks to Phil DeCologero, the able and energetic director of the Amesbury, Massachusetts, Chamber of Commerce, for filling me in on how that organization operates.

I included Detective Penelope Johnson in *Murder in a Cape Cottage* after her twin sister, Pamela Fenner, won naming rights to a character in a charity auction. As I was writing Penelope's return in this book, the real Penelope Johnson passed away. I'm happy I can keep her memory alive on the page (even though Pam's sister was never a police detective).

Apologies to the actual Rosasharn Farm, which is in Rehoboth, MA, not Belleville. It's a lovely farm with adorable dwarf Nigerian goats and huge Great Pyrenees guard dogs, who are devoted and gentle—unless you're a coyote or a fox.

The vignette about the great Walter Mosley was something I witnessed at a New England Crime Bake banquet a few years ago and have never forgotten. In a gathering that year populated mostly by white people, he made sure to personally welcome every person of color.

Thanks, as ever, to my dear partner Hugh Lockhart, who always obliges me when I ask him to help me act out a physical attack scene. The man who doesn't read fiction is willing to pretend he's the villain and that the pencil in his hand is a weapon.

As I was writing this book, I was lucky to catch a presentation sponsored by Tufts University by linguist (and MacArthur genius grant recipient) Jessie

Little Doe Baird, who is working with many others to reclaim the Wampanoag language with the Wôpanâak Language Reclamation Project (wlrp.org). I was able to learn more about the People of the First Light as well as brush off my long-dusty doctorate in linguistics. *Kutâputush*, Ms. Baird. Thank you.

I am always grateful to my fellow blogmates—and friends—at the Wicked Authors blog: Jessie Crockett, Sherry Harris, Julie Hennrikus, Liz Mugavero, and Barbara Ross and all their pseudonyms. Come join us at WickedAuthors.com. And if you want a tasty recipe every day, stop by MysteryLoversKitchen.com and enjoy treats by my fellow foodie mystery authors and me.

Thank you, always, to John Scognamiglio, my editor at Kensington Publishing, publicist Larissa Ackerman and the other expert publicists, artists, production staff, salespeople, and everybody else at Kensington who makes the process of getting my books into print seem nearly seamless. Many thanks to my agent John Talbot for making it all possible.

To my sons John David and Allan and their wives, to my sisters Janet and Barbara, to Hugh: I'm deeply grateful for your support. This writer knows how lucky she is to have you.

And I'm always thankful for my enthusiastic readers and fans. Read on!

CHAPTER 1

The question, "What could possibly go wrong?" seemed custom-made for the Westham Spring Festival.

It's true, the businesses in our touristy town on Cape Cod's upper arm suffered in the cold months after the December holidays. March, otherwise known as Mud Season, wasn't any better. Sales and rentals were way down at my own business, Mac's Bikes.

But when I heard that Wagner Lavoie, the new director of the Chamber of Commerce, was proposing an outdoor festival on the spring equinox—March twentieth—I'd groaned. Out loud.

All the businesses decorated with flowers sounded lovely. A parade filled with flower-festooned bicycles? Great for my bottom line. But what if a cold rain poured down? Or worse, a late, wet snowstorm could blow in. Either was more than possible here in the Northeast. Everyone's organizing and work would be ruined, not to mention the spirits of the children and families eager to get out and imagine gardens in bloom.

Now, on the Thursday before the Saturday festival, I gripped my box of flyers and glanced around the dining room and bar of the Rusty Anchor, my favorite pub on Main Street. Few diners sat in the rustic wooden booths, and only two customers perched on stools at the bar, one nursing a beer, the other sipping a glass of red wine. It was three in the afternoon, which meant the slow time between the lunch and dinner rushes. I expected chef and co-owner Yvonne Flora would have a minute to speak with me. We'd met only recently in my shop, but I liked her competent attitude, and the food she prepared was to die for.

"Hey, Mac." The bartender paused in her wiping. "Looking for Yvonne?"

"Yep."

"She's back there."

I waved my thanks and pushed through the swinging door to the kitchen. I froze as my breath rushed in.

I hadn't met him in person yet, but I'd seen the new director's picture. Wagner Lavoie faced Yvonne, hands on hips, neck flushed, leaning into her personal space. Yvonne's wide mouth was drawn down in a scowl. Her eyes glared. The knife she pointed at him looked lethally sharp.

Uh-oh.

"No, I won't," she snapped, her black chef's jacket reflecting her apparent mood.

"Everyone is." His voice was low, threatening. Clean-shaven, his dark hair was neatly parted on the side. He had to be in his fifties. Maybe hair dye was a regular purchase for him.

I cleared my throat. "Hey, Yvonne."

Lavoie whirled to face me. Yvonne exhaled and set the knife on the cutting board next to her, where a pile of whole mushrooms sat next to another pile already sliced.

"Mac, what's up?" she asked.

"Sorry to interrupt." I mustered a polite smile. "I can come back."

"No, it's fine," she said. "Have you met our new Chamber director yet?"

"I haven't. Mr. Lavoie, I'm Mackenzie Almeida." I extended my hand. "I own Mac's Bikes down the street."

He transformed his expression into that of a beaming, schmoozing ambassador of Westham's businesses. Or he must have thought that was what it looked like. The sudden switch made me want to back away, but I gave his hand a firm shake.

"Pleased to finally make your acquaintance, Mackenzie. You must call me Wagner." He flashed an extra-white smile.

"Thanks, Wagner." I withdrew my hand. I barely avoided wiping it on my jeans. "And I'm Mac."

"Wagner here was trying to convince me to give away free food on Saturday." Yvonne crossed her arms over her chest. "I told him free food isn't part of our business model."

"Well, speaking of the festival." I opened the box. "I'm a bit late with these flyers about the bike parade,

Yvonne, but is it okay if I leave a pile out front?" I'd been nearly commanded—via email—to produce publicity about the parade, a flyer separate from the posters the Chamber had plastered the town with.

Wagner's pleasant expression slid away. "That's pushing it, Mac. The festival is Saturday."

"Thank you, Wagner." I gave him a smile I hoped didn't look as cold as I wanted it to be. "I was informed only two days ago I was expected to produce this. Life gets in the way, you know?"

"Very well," he said. "And what will your shop be giving away?"

I pointed to the flyers. "These, plus encouragement to the kids and their families. As you know, they're going to assemble in my parking lot to kick off the parades. Plus, we'll pump up any tires needing air." In fact, I had planned to hand out a small token giveaway. I'd ordered a hundred red keychains featuring a locked bicycle and the store brand. Somewhat perversely, I decided not to tell Wagner about it. Businesses shouldn't be strong-armed into distributing freebies.

"You both know I'm only trying to help out the Main Street businesses. Will you be at the pre-festival meeting tomorrow night?" He lifted his eyebrows, gazing first at Yvonne, then me.

"Tim Brunelle and I will be there." Tim being my delicious husband of three months, also the proprietor and head baker at Greta's Grains.

"Ah, Brunelle," Wagner said. "He's been most welcoming."

What was this, bro power? I'd ask Tim tonight. I expected he had a different story, but maybe not.

Tim had the biggest heart and most tolerant soul of anyone I'd ever met, with the possible exception of my father. I was one lucky woman, and I knew it.

"Can't make the meeting. I'll be cooking, as you might expect." Yvonne returned to her slicing, wielding the knife with perhaps extra relish.

"Good day, ladies." Wagner left via the swinging doors I'd come in through.

"Wow." I stared at the door as it whooshed back inward and then stayed shut.

"Creepy much?" Yvonne straightened. She was about as tall as my five foot seven, but was at least ten years older, which meant she was pushing fifty. She faced me. "I mean, if he hadn't pressured the businesses into this freebie nonsense, I might have considered giving out cups of chowder. Now? I doubt it." She tucked a strand of dirty-blond hair behind her ear. Usually her multicolored cap contained her ear-length do.

"I don't blame you. It's super short notice." I inhaled. "Man, it smells amazing in here. What are you cooking, Yvonne?" I didn't cook, to speak of, but I was the first to appreciate those who did, my Tim among them.

Yvonne uttered a low laugh. "I'm doing a mushroom and shallot risotto for our vegetarian and gluten-free clientele."

"Those who won't order the double cheeseburger with onions?"

"Exactly."

"Both those ideas are making me hungry."

"I can whip you up a quick slider if you want. On

the house." She pointed. "You're a skinny girl. Pull up a stool. I'm hungry, too."

"Girl, I'm not. But who am I to say no to an afternoon snack? My crew has the shop covered."

I sat. She cooked. We chatted and munched, with not another word said about smarmy Wagner Lavoie.

CHAPTER 2

Outside the Rusty Anchor, I tightened my scarf and tugged my hat down. A damp wind smelling of salt blew in off the bay, which lay only a mile away. I checked my list of Main Street businesses, otherwise known as destinations for my flyers. I glanced up to see Wagner stomp out of Cape King Liquors across the street. Zane King—proprietor—stood in the doorway, arms folded, staring after him.

Uh-oh. I checked for traffic and hurried across when it was clear.

"What's going on, Zane?"

"Come into the store, Mac." He shivered. "It's cold out here." He held the door for me, his cheeks as rosy as the pink flowers on his yellow bow tie.

"Thanks." I gazed up at my tall, lean friend after we were inside with the door closed. His signature bow tie went perfectly with a pale pink Oxford button-down shirt, the sleeves carefully rolled up as was his habit. His jeans were pressed, which never made sense to me, but Zane was nothing if not fastidious. "You're looking springy."

He gave a little eye roll. "I just finished putting away all the St. Patrick's Day decorations, and now we have to go all floral for Saturday."

"Your tie is a good start."

"Do you like it?" He patted the tie as he smiled. "Stephen gave it to me for Valentine's Day."

"It's perfect." I fished a stack of flyers out of the box. "Can I leave these by your register? They're about the bike parade."

"Sure." His smile disappeared as he stared at the door. "That dude is a piece of work."

"Wagner Lavoie?"

"Yes."

"Was he telling you to give out freebies Saturday?"

"Yeah." Zane faced me. "Can you imagine, Mac? I can't give away alcohol. What if a bunch of teenagers got hold of it? Lavoie is an idiot to even suggest it."

"I hear you."

"But instead I'm going to print up a recipe for a spring cocktail and hand out copies. I'm thinking gin or vodka, a few drops of orange bitters, some tonic or bubbly, garnished with strawberries and mint? How does that combo sound?"

"It sounds fabulous. And everyone will want to buy the ingredients from you. Plus, I want one right this minute."

"That's the plan." He straightened a couple of bottles of his own King's Bounty Rum on an end cap. "How are you enjoying *Homicide and Halo-Halo*?"

I wrinkled my nose. "I haven't had a chance to start it yet. But we have until Tuesday." Zane and I were both in the Cozy Capers book group. This week's cozy mystery featured a Filipino-American protagonist and her cooking family.

"You're going to love it. The book gives you a peek into a culture lots of us aren't familiar with."

"Cool." I took a step toward the door but turned back. "I forgot. Can you pick out a nice red wine for me? Tim's making meatballs tonight."

"You bet."

Wine purchased and in hand a couple of minutes later, I said, "You know, Wagner kind of rubbed me the wrong way, too. But I think he's really trying to help out Westham's businesses. We should give him a chance."

"You're a good person, Mac. Of course, we should. We don't have much choice, do we?"

I decided to make one more quick stop, but this time I'd try not to stop and schmooze. The Book Nook was only two doors down and it was on the way back to my shop. I waved at Norland Gifford in the front window as he tweaked an arrangement of gardening books. A fellow book group member and Westham's former police chief, Norland had taken over managing the bookstore for the winter months while the owner was away somewhere warm.

"The windows look great, Norland," I said after I was inside.

"Thanks." He turned to me, beaming. "Who knew

decorating a window display could be so satisfying?" He'd kept his trim midsection, but his former police-short salt-and-pepper hair now hit collar and ears, and his sweater had a moth hole near the shoulder. He'd gotten over the worst of the grief of losing his wife a couple of years ago and seemed to be happily settling into his role of relaxed, mostly retired grandpa.

"I'm glad. Hey, I just want to leave these flyers about the bike parade. Okay to put them here?" I pointed to the counter next to a donation can for the local cat shelter. A picture of a darling kitten stuck up behind it. Adorable, yes, but it made me feel like sneezing just to look at it. I had serious allergies to cats and nearly all dogs.

"Be my guest." He made his way behind the counter and fished something out of a box. "Check this out, Mac. It'll be the bookstore's freebie for the festival." He handed me a purple pencil.

I read the words on the side out loud. "Spring into a great book!" On the other side was thebooknook.com. "This is brilliant, Norland."

"Look, I ordered them in pink, yellow, and green, too." He fanned out the array of colors.

"Nice. Are you getting along okay with Wagner?"

Norland rotated a flat hand back and forth. "Mostly. He's trying."

"I'll say."

He snorted.

"See you tomorrow night at the meeting?" I asked.

"Be there or be square."

I groaned as I smiled. "Yes, Chief." I ignored the shelf after shelf of books calling to me. Mysteries, biographies, women's fiction, historical novels. They whispered in a chorus of, "Slow down. Stay and browse. Check out our back covers. Read our first pages."

Except this was not a relaxed read-on-the-couch kind of day. With any luck, Sunday would be, if all went well on Saturday. Nothing would go wrong with the festival. Would it?

CHAPTER 3

I was surprised by how many customers were in Mac's Bikes the next morning at ten. My mechanic, Orlean Brown, had a line out the door of people wanting a tire fixed, handlebars straightened, or the seat on a growing child's bike raised. Her younger sister Sandy McKean, my newest employee, was methodically ringing up purchases of bike shirts and helmets. And I had already rented out all our tandems plus another eight cycles.

Maybe the bright sunshine was the impetus for all this excitement about the parade. Yesterday's bone-chilling damp wind had blown off the Atlantic and kept right on going. It was only fifty degrees out today, but twelve hours of sunlight could make the air a lot warmer. And one's spirits, too.

In the door came two more spots of light. My

abo—Cape Verdean for grandmother—Reba bustled in, followed by my mom, Astra Almeida. Tiny Reba's cheeks were as pink as her ubiquitous tracksuit. Mom unbuckled her bike helmet but left it atop her fly-away blond-and-gray curls.

"It looks like you two rode over here." I hurried over.

"We did," Mom said. "We haven't been riding all winter, and we wanted to be sure our trikes were in good shape for tomorrow."

The two had bought adult tricycles last fall, one bright red, the other a brilliant yellow. They often rode together along the former rail bed now known as the Shining Sea Trail, a paved walking and biking path running from North Falmouth all the way to Woods Hole.

"I think my handlebars are a bit loose, querida," Reba—my father's mother—said. "Can you tighten them up for me?"

"Of course." I was perfectly capable of doing all aspects of bicycle repair and maintenance. Still, I'd gladly hired Orlean as a full-time mechanic when I opened my shop two years ago after I moved back to my hometown. She freed me up to run all the other parts of the business. "Let me grab a wrench."

When I joined the two ladies outside, Abo Reba was poking her extra-large senior-citizen cell phone. She might've been eighty-one, but nothing stopped the little powerhouse, and she'd recently become quite the texting machine.

I tightened the nut holding the handlebars in place. While I was at it, I checked to make sure the cushioned seat was secure, too. "There you go, Abo Ree. Mom, does yours need any adjusting?"

"No, dear. It's all tip-top. I'm glad I switched my order from a bicycle to a tricycle last summer. The trike isn't as likely to keel over sideways with me on it."

Wagner Lavoie trudged up with a heavy step as if every merchant had pushed back about handing out freebies. Maybe they had.

"Good morning, Wagner," I said. "Everything in good shape for tomorrow?"

He opened his mouth to speak, but my grandma preempted him.

"They're forecasting a fast-moving spring snowstorm." She glanced up from her phone.

A snowstorm? Bad weather was exactly what I'd been afraid of, even though I'd completely forgotten to check the weather report last night or this morning. Having his festival snowed out could be what had put lead in Wagner's gait.

"A storm will throw the proverbial wrench in the works, won't it, Wagner?" Abo Reba prodded.

"Yes, Mrs. Almeida." He didn't disguise his sigh.

"Now, didn't I tell you to call me Reba, sonny?"

"Yes, ma'am, you did." He cleared his throat. "Back to this weather event, I'm sure you know how it always is on the Cape. The impact depends entirely on how the storm tracks."

"Maybe it won't hit until the afternoon or evening." Mom smiled. "Mr. Lavoie, I gather? I'm Astra Almeida, Mac's mother." She extended her hand to Wagner. "I'm also a business owner in town and have been receiving your emails, but we haven't yet had the opportunity to meet."

He blinked. "Ah, yes. The fortune-teller."

"Not exactly." Mom tilted her head. "Have you never heard of astrology, Mr. Lavoie?"

"Yes, yes, of course. I'm sure it's all well and good, but it's not as if you have a storefront, is it?"

"Does it matter?" Mom sounded genuinely curious. "I have an office open to the public, a dedicated entrance, and a shingle, so to speak."

Her office was a few doors down and part of the parsonage where she and Pa, a Unitarian Universalist Church minister, lived. She was right. Her business had a separate entrance to the outside. Her tasteful sign reading "Astra Almeida, Professional Astrologer" had been expertly carved by a sign maker in town.

"Excellent." He rubbed the back of his neck, which had been growing redder in the last couple of minutes. "I'd better get along to my next stop. Mac, I trust you got all your flyers distributed?"

"Yes." I didn't need to say more.

Sandy stepped through the door. "Mac," she began. "There's something wrong with the . . ." Her voice trailed off and her nostrils flared as her gaze fell on Lavoie. She took a step back.

"Sandy." I jumped into the breach. "Have you met Wagner Lavoie, Westham's new Chamber of Commerce director? Wagner, this is my newest employee, Sandy McKean."

"Ms. McKean." Wagner didn't look at her as he spoke. "Have a nice day, ladies." He turned and nearly fled. His step no longer heavy, he hurried down the sidewalk toward the Chamber office, which sat just beyond the library.

"Yes, I've met Wagner Lavoie," Sandy muttered. "It was one of the worst days of my life." She ran a hand through a head full of bottle-blond hair grazing her shoulders as she headed back inside.

"My, my," Reba murmured. "She's got bad history with that man, mark my words."

"Kind of seems like it," I said. "I'll see what I can find out." She could have had a personal run-in with him, or something in a workplace. I couldn't pry too hard, though. I did my best to stay out of my employees' personal lives unless they offered information.

Mom stared after Wagner. "If he isn't a Leo, I'll eat my professionally made shingle. In his eyes, the world is all about him, all the time."

"He's not the easiest guy to get along with, from the little I've seen so far," I agreed. "But he's trying to do a good thing for Westham, and I hope it doesn't snow on his parade tomorrow. For starters, Cokey and the other children will be so disappointed." My five-year-old niece was beside herself with plans to deck out her pink two-wheeler, which she'd only recently learned to ride. She'd practiced so long without the pedals on, she understood the balancing act right away after I'd attached them. I loved that some kids now skipped the training-wheels stage entirely.

"Let's go ride while the sun shines, Astra," Reba said. "Thanks, Mac, honey."

I watched the two ride off toward the trail, then straightened the somewhat garish display of plastic flowers Sandy had added to the window boxes in front of my shop. It was still too cold even for spring pansies. *Whatever.* We were the parade staging ground and we had to be in with the floral program. And if we were, the display had to be tidy. I was the first to admit my slight obsession with neatness and order.

Now, what had Sandy come out here to ask me about, anyway?

CHAPTER 4

Wagner Lavoie's so-called important meeting that evening was already winding down at seven thirty. It hadn't started on time, with business owners slowly drifting into the large meeting room. A few latecomers had gone directly to the refreshments table and helped themselves to a bottle of beer or a plastic cup of wine before sitting. Wagner had said at the beginning the mixer portion of the meeting wouldn't start until the business had been conducted. The latecomers, who'd missed his announcement, earned a double glare from Wagner. And they proceeded to ignore him.

"Does anyone have any questions?" Wagner asked.

Next to me, Tim spoke up. "What's your plan if the snow starts in the morning?" His low voice was gentle, as always. And direct, as always.

Into the microphone, Wagner let out a noisy sigh.

"I've secured use of the high school gymnasium, if it comes to that. I'll make the decision by seven tomorrow. If we need to restage, tables will be set up around the perimeter of the gym, so you all can bring your freebies over there to hand out. There will be plenty of room for at least the children and their bicycles to parade through."

Grumbling echoing the word "freebies" popped up around the room. I'd initially had the same reaction. After I saw the bread flowers Tim planned to bake and the candy shop owner's flower-shaped lollipops, I was glad I'd ordered the keychains.

"We'll alert the radio stations and post the change on the Chamber website and social media pages," Wagner continued. "Right now it's looking like the weather might hold off until dinnertime tomorrow."

"What about postponing the whole thing?" a familiar voice asked.

I twisted to look behind me. Yep, Zane.

"You could announce it now for next weekend," he added.

"No can do." Wagner shook his head, his neck getting redder and redder above a pale blue shirt. "Too much publicity has gone out."

"He could have built in a rain date," Tim murmured to me.

"It's a shame he didn't," I replied. "But I agree. It's too late now."

"Why didn't you wait until it really feels like spring around here?" a woman asked.

I craned my neck again. Kassandra Jenkins was the speaker. A dark-haired woman in her early thirties, her usual broad smile was in hiding tonight. Her eyes were narrowed behind large dark-rimmed glasses.

"This is a ridiculous time of year to hold an outdoor event," she continued, her hands in the pockets of the flared tweed coat she hadn't removed. "You strong-armed the Main Street businesses to decorate and to give away merchandise. It could result in a net loss for many of them. What kind of a boost does losing money give our hardworking merchants?"

"Huh," I murmured. "She's not holding back."

A low roar of approval rose from the back of the room near where Kassandra stood.

"We both know how much she wanted Wagner's job," Tim said, almost so softly I didn't hear him.

She had. The daughter of our head selectperson, she'd thought she was a shoo-in for the Chamber position—until Wagner appeared on the scene. How had he landed the directorship, anyway? I couldn't remember. Kassandra worked in her mom's toy store, but I knew she had ambitions much higher than peddling teddy bears, plastic blocks, and board games.

Tulia Peters rose. "Hey, people." Proprietor of the Lobstah Shack, the ruddy-faced woman was a friend and a fellow Cozy Capers member. She held up both palms, facing the back and both sides before turning toward Wagner. She didn't speak until the room was quiet. "I think we should give Wagner a chance. No date is ever going to be perfect. Let's make the best of tomorrow, no matter the weather."

Norland, who'd been sitting beside her, also stood. "I agree with Tulia."

"Thank you, both of you," Wagner said. "Everyone, please check the Chamber website in the morning. Keep your fingers crossed. Sending out a prayer to the weather gods . . . I mean, goddesses, wouldn't hurt."

His words earned him a laugh, especially from some of the women present.

"Now, let's relax and get to know each other a bit." Wagner clicked off the mike.

Merchants stood and began moving toward the back. The buzz of conversation rose, too.

Tim suppressed a yawn. "A quick drink and then we head home? It's been a long day, and there'll be no sleeping in for this baker tomorrow morning."

"Sounds good." I squeezed his hand. "I'm going to grab a wine, and then I want to have a quick word with Gin."

We both headed to the drinks table. Two platters of cheese and crackers were going fast, maybe from Chamber members downing the snacks in lieu of dinner. I selected an already-poured plastic cup of Chardonnay, while Tim picked up a bottle of Pilsner beer. We'd had a bite to eat at home before heading over here.

"Shouldn't you be over running Breads and Brews?" Kassandra materialized at Tim's elbow.

"No, I'm still on my winter schedule of running it only on the first Friday of the month." Tim smiled at her. "I might keep it that way."

Breads and Brews was Tim's way of bringing in customers on Friday nights, when he transformed his bakery, Greta's Grains, into a bar with live music and fresh-baked savory snacks like mini-pizzas and tomato tortas. But it was a lot of work for him, and I'd supported him in his decision to go monthly with the event.

"Hey, Kassandra," I said. "I have to say, I agree with you. Tomorrow wasn't the best choice of date for this event. We need to run with it now, though."

"I guess." She shot her gaze toward Wagner on the other side of the room. "See you guys tomorrow." She pressed her lips into a line and turned away.

Tim greeted Norland. They started talking about the prospects for this year's Red Sox team. I grabbed a cookie and pointed myself toward the best candy maker on the Cape, my BFF Gin Malloy, who stood with Tulia and Zane.

"Thanks for keeping the peace, Tulia," I said.

"Somebody had to." She sipped from her water bottle. "I don't like to see the town divided like this." She gestured toward the clump of merchants surrounding Kassandra.

"I agree," Gin said. "Even though I'm not convinced Lavoie is a good fit, Kassandra needs to accept the fact she didn't get the job, and move on." She took a drink from her cup of red wine.

"I think she wanted the position so she could springboard into running for political office," Zane murmured.

"You think so?" I asked.

"That girl's ambitious."

"Plus, she grew up here." Gin tucked a lock of her reddish-brown hair behind her ear. "And Wagner is from the other side of the canal. A good portion of locals don't seem to like him being from away."

The canal being the 110-year-old Cape Cod Canal, which cut through the isthmus and divided the entire cape from the mainland.

"Oh?" I tilted my head. "Where did they recruit him from?"

"He lives in Belleville," Zane said. "But his parents own a cottage here in town, out near the point. I'm pretty sure he's staying there now."

"Did you know Kassandra growing up, Mac?" Tulia asked.

"She's a few years younger than I am, so not really." I watched her talking and laughing across the room. "And I don't think she went to Westham High. She might have attended boarding school somewhere or a private high school."

"Like Falmouth Academy?" Gin asked. "It's a pricey school."

"Maybe." I sipped my wine. "I can't remember."

Wagner sauntered up to us, beer bottle in hand. To my eye, his casual approach seemed too studied to be genuine, as if he was putting on an attitude he didn't really feel. Maybe he felt he had to, to counter the increasingly boisterous laughter coming from Kassandra's corner.

"Tulia, thank you for supporting me." He held up his bottle. "To a successful and snow-free morning tomorrow."

"You're welcome." Tulia tapped her water bottle against his beer.

"You're not drinking?" Wagner asked. "Let me get you something to toast with."

Bad move, Lavoie. I kept my thought to myself. Tulia was more than capable of sticking up for herself.

"Please don't." Tulia raised her chin. "Believe me, you don't want to see my Wampanoag blood mixing with alcohol. It's not a pretty sight."

She'd told the book group when we'd started up

she lacked the enzyme to digest alcohol and was better off simply avoiding it.

He cleared his throat. "I apologize."

"No worries," Tulia said. "Good luck tomorrow."

He thanked her and moved away.

"Anybody feel the teensiest bit sorry for that guy?" I asked. "I confess I do."

Zane nodded. "He's an adult, though. When you rub people the wrong way, you have to live with the consequences."

CHAPTER 5

By some stroke of luck—or maybe it was the blessings of the goddesses—the storm tracked farther out to sea and wasn't forecast to cycle back onto land until late Saturday afternoon. The parade was a go. As a consequence, by nine thirty Saturday morning the parking lot outside Mac's Bikes was full of, well, bikes.

"Titi Mac!" my niece called out, using the Cape Verdean word for "auntie." Cokey rode up on her flower-festooned bicycle, with my half-brother Derrick Searle directly behind. Her blond angel curls, inherited via Derrick from our common mother, Astra, stuck out from her purple helmet. A sprig of pink silk flowers was taped on the helmet sticking up from the top, making her look like a tiny Roman. "Do you like my bike? Daddy helped me decorate it."

Derrick worked for me part time, but I'd agreed he should have the day off to ride with his little girl.

"I love it." I leaned over to hug her. "And the flowers on your helmet are perfect." My nod to the theme was a multicolored artificial lei slung around my neck.

"They were my idea. 'Cause we're aposta look like springtime," she lisped.

"And you do." I smiled at Derrick, who also had silk flowers taped to his helmet. "Daddy looks like spring, too."

Cokey's eyes flew wide. She climbed off the bike and got the kickstand down after three tries. She raced into the shop, her words trailing after her, none of which I caught.

"Bathroom?" I asked Derrick.

"I'm sure of it." He smiled. "You saw how excited she is."

"Better now than mid-parade."

Orlean circulated among the bikes, a portable pump in one hand and her work apron loaded with wrenches. Sandy was handing out keychains and doing a great job directing traffic through the cones we'd set up for a shallow drop-off lane. Neither woman resided in Westham and had said they'd mind the shop for the day. When she'd started working for me, Orlean had moved from Orleans, the town she'd been named for, to a place in the Falmouth area. Now Sandy shared her apartment. Orlean told me her sister had been named for the Cape's many sandy beaches. The Brown parents had apparently been ultra-enthusiastic Cape Codders.

Sandy raised her voice. "No, ma'am." She leaned toward the open driver's-side window of a battered older sedan. "You can't park here. Please take a right to reach the public lot." She listened to the driver, then straightened and set fists on hips, her feet apart like a soldier. "I don't care who you are or who you know. You can't park here."

Oh, dear. I hurried over there. "Can I help?" I murmured to Sandy.

"Says she's Wagner's sister." Sandy pivoted away from the window to face me. "Tough toenails." She strode to the next car and helped a petite woman hoist a bicycle out of the trunk.

"I'm Mackenzie Almeida." I smiled at the woman behind the wheel of the Ford. "Is there a problem?"

The driver, whose face was weathered in the way of many sun-lovers, lit a cigarette and took a long drag before speaking. "My little brother is in charge, and he said I could park here." Her voice was low and throaty from the smoke damage.

I swore silently. "Mr. Lavoie is certainly running this event, ma'am, but I'm afraid he gave you the wrong information. As you can see, my lot is the staging ground for the parade, and we can't endanger any of our cyclists by allowing vehicles in here. If you take a right, you'll find the public parking area only two blocks down." Right was the only way she could turn. To the left, Main Street was already blocked off to traffic.

"There he is." Wagner's relative gestured with her cigarette.

Wagner, clipboard in hand, hurried toward them.

I preempted her. "Wagner, your sister says you told her she could park here, but we can't accommodate cars parking in my lot." I stepped back so he could speak with her.

"Faye, really?" He set his left hand above the door and leaned toward her. "I said you could park at the kite shop, not the bike shop."

Aha. That explained it. I was curious to see a gold band on his ring finger. I shouldn't have been surprised. I didn't know anything about his personal life. But was his wife living here in Westham with him, or had she stayed in Belleville?

"Well, where in heck is the kite shop?" Faye asked. "Can't you convince this girl to let me park here?"

"No, I can't. Drive out and turn right. The kite shop is a block down on the left, next to Shearlock Combs. You can't miss it. Kit's Kites has flags and kites out front, and they have a big parking lot they agreed to let parade-goers use."

Faye tossed her cigarette butt out the window. "Wonderful. Maybe I'll get my hair done instead of watching your silly parade." She drove off.

Wagner let out a long exhale. "Sorry about her, Mac. My sister can be, shall we say, a little unreliable at times." He extinguished the butt with the sole of his shoe and deposited it into his coat pocket.

"Don't worry about it."

He checked his watch, a flashy gold Rolex. "Ten minutes to go."

"We sure lucked out with the weather. I mean, it's not exactly warm, but it's not snowing, either."

"Right." His eyes narrowed as his gaze fell on Sandy, who was hoisting a tandem out of the back of a pickup truck as if it weighed nothing. "She's working for you, I gather."

"Yes. Sandy is my mechanic's sister. Where do you know her from?"

"You don't want to know, Mac."

Actually, I did. Maybe sometime later I could get Orlean to open up about the two.

He folded his arms, watching Sandy. As if feeling his focus, she whirled and strode toward us.

Uh-oh.

"What do you want, Wagner?" she demanded. "What are you doing here?" Her blue eyes smoldered under pale eyebrows.

"I have a job in Westham." He kept his voice low, although it shook. "Just like you, Sandy, from what I gather."

She gave her head a sharp shake. "I can't believe you have the nerve. After everything you . . . Oh, forget about it." She flung a hand in the air and stomped into the store.

Mom and Abo Reba arrived on their trikes, the baskets stuffed with pots full of flowering daffodils and narcissus. With a whir of gears, August Jenkins, Westham's bicycle cop, pedaled up on his police-issue hybrid right behind them. Even he had a small bouquet of plastic flowers taped to his handlebars.

"We ready to go, Mr. Lavoie?" August asked.

"Eight minutes," Wagner said. "Let's get these people lined up and ready." He gave only a quick glance toward the shop, then hurried toward the parking lot exit.

I helped August corral the kids, parents, grandparents, and other Westhamites into a rough line. August glanced around, looking worried.

"Is something wrong?" I asked him.

"Dad was supposed to be leading the parade. Walking, not riding," he said. "You know, as head of the select board."

I stared for a quick second. *Jenkins.* I should have

made the connection. August must be Kassandra Jenkins's younger brother, and their father was Park. I'd met the able August on a couple of cases last year. Now that I thought about it, I could see the resemblance between the siblings. August was younger enough that I hadn't known him in school, and he'd have been a kid when I moved away.

"Have you tried to reach him?" I asked.

"Yes. He's not answering."

Wagner blew a whistle. "Are we ready to celebrate spring, Westham?"

A shout of "Yes!" went up.

"All right, then." He gestured to August. "Officer Jenkins is going to lead you off. No racing, now, and no passing our able bicycle officer."

August pedaled to the head of the line and off they processed. Wagner hurried alongside, while I brought up the rear, walking. What in the world had happened to Park Jenkins?

CHAPTER 6

After the parade ended in front of the town hall, Wagner used a bullhorn to hold a kind of pep rally.

"I love the town spirit you all showed this morning." He beamed as he spoke. "We're not going to award prizes for the best decorated bike, because they were all great."

A few children let out disappointed cries, and the woman next to me muttered, "What is this? Nobody's allowed to be better than anyone else? My kid deserved to win."

Wagner pushed on. "It's fantastic how everybody got into the spirit. Happy spring, Westham!"

About half the crowd yelled out, "Happy spring."

"I can't hear you," Wagner said. "Say it louder and give your neighbor a happy spring high five while you're at it!"

"Happy spring!" I joined the roar as I smiled at my muttering neighbor and held up my palm. She relented with a slap and a smile.

"It is kind of nice to see everybody out," she acknowledged.

Most participants left their bicycles there and set out to peruse what the town had on offer. I did, too. In the crowds dispersing, I thought I spied Sandy riding along, bent low over the handlebars of a racing bike. It couldn't be. She was supposed to be at my shop. I must've been wrong. Everyone looked the same when bundled up against the cold.

Despite it being before lunchtime, children walked around licking Gin's flower-shaped suckers. I blew Tim a kiss as I passed him in front of his bakery, where he was handing out small paper sacks. I knew each included one flower-shaped sweet bun.

Yvonne seemed to have relented to the giveaway pressure. A table was set up in front of the Rusty Anchor, and one of the young waitstaff handed out half-cup-sized paper containers with lids and bamboo spoons. A giant electric pot had a ladle in it ready to dish up more servings.

"Curried chicken soup, ma'am?" the waiter offered.

I was going to decline. As a merchant, I knew the cost of freebies. But my stomach grumbled at the same time. I smiled, accepted the container, and thanked him. Hey, it was eleven thirty and breakfast had been hours ago.

The front door to the pub stood open. I peeked inside to see Kassandra and her father occupying barstools. Her mimosa was half empty and he cradled a glass holding what looked like the remnants of a Bloody Mary. The bar must have opened early for the parade. Did I want to venture in and ask why Park didn't show up to head up the parade? Inquire where he'd been? I did not. I expected he'd been right there on that bar stool.

But why? Why not lead the parade, as he'd been invited to do? His position was an elected one. Because Westham didn't have a mayor, the three select people were the closest we had to leaders, and he was the leader of the three.

I turned away before either Jenkins saw me. It wasn't my business to go over there and grill him. Somebody else could do that. I continued on my stroll. I spied Norland sitting on the bench in front of the Book Nook across the street. Crossing, I sank down next to him. He held a basket of his pencils on his lap.

"What do you have there?" he asked.

"Curried chicken soup." I pointed across the street. "Want me to get you one?"

"Thanks, but I'm fine. I brought a sandwich. Nice festival, isn't it?"

"It's turning out way better than I expected. No precipitation helps a lot." I pried the lid off my container and took a bite. "OMG, this is fabulous." I inhaled the aroma of curry, cumin, excellent chicken stock, and a hint of hot pepper.

"Pencil?" Norland handed pencils to a couple moseying by.

They thanked him but didn't go inside the store. I finished my soup.

"This is all fun," Norland said. "But it's not exactly good for business. Nobody has been in to shop all day."

"I hear you. I guess we're building good will, though." I gazed at the Rusty Anchor. "Did you notice Selectperson Jenkins didn't lead off the parade as he was supposed to?"

"Was he slated to? I didn't know."

"Yes. I just saw him at the bar with Kassandra. They weren't at the start of their drinks, either." I pointed. "Speak of the devil."

Kassandra ventured out, pulling on her gloves and tugging her cap low on her head but not going anywhere. After Park joined her, they made their way across and down the nearest side street. If they'd glanced up, I would have waved. But they didn't.

I stood. "I hope business picks up for you. I should get back to my shop."

"Take care, Mac. Want a pencil?"

I laughed. "Why not?" I slid it into my bag and made my way down to Zane's. He'd set his drink recipes in a plexiglass stand on a table out front, so I helped myself. With any luck, he was inside helping a customer. Across the street, Tulia also had a table in front of the Lobstah Shack and was handing out the same kind of containers the pub had. I crossed.

"Clam chowder?" I asked her.

"The very same. Want some?" She wore a warm sweater under her lobster-colored apron.

"I just had a bit of Yvonne's freebie soup, but why not? I even brought my own spoon." I opened the container she handed me. "Mmm. Creamy and chock-full of clams. Delish."

"Thanks, Mac. Hey, are you surprised Wagner isn't out here schmoozing his way up and down town?"

"Yes, I guess I am. Who knows, maybe he's in the Rusty Anchor celebrating." I finished the chowder. "Thanks, Tulia. I'd better get back to my—" I broke off.

August pedaled furiously down the street past us and leapt off his bike at the Book Nook. Norland no longer sat on the bench outside the store. Police Chief Victoria Laitinen sprinted there from the police station down the block. A siren wailed into action.

Uh-oh. "Something's up at the bookstore. I'm going to go see." I wasn't much of a runner since I blew out my knee cycling the mountains of New Zealand, but I could jog when I had to. This felt like one of those times.

I pulled open the door to the Book Nook. The bell dinged as my breath rushed in.

One of the tall, heavy wood bookshelves lay toppled. I caught a glimpse of August kneeling behind the shelving unit. Something stuck out. My eyes widened. Was that a shoe? Victoria spoke into her police radio. A pale, somber Norland gave me a ghastly look.

"What . . .?" I began.

Norland shook his head. "It's Lavoie. And he's dead."

CHAPTER 7

Dead? I brought my hand to my mouth. What was Wagner doing in the bookstore, and how had the shelving unit fallen like a giant domino on top of him? Had the crashing piece of book-laden furniture killed him, or was it a cover-up for murder? I—and the Cozy Capers book group—had become involved in four cases of homicide in the last year or two. Murder was a messy situation, and I didn't like messes. My brain couldn't help but ask the questions that might sort it all out.

On the other hand, it could have been a terrible accident. Wagner could have caught his toe on the edge of the bookshelf, tripped, and caused it to cascade on top of him. Maybe the shock had brought on a heart attack. But why was he in the store—alone or not—during the festival instead of networking with his public, as Tulia mentioned?

Whatever had happened, my heart was heavy for Wagner's premature death. He'd worn a wedding ring. A spouse would be grieving for him, and possibly children, too. Who else? He'd certainly rubbed a lot of people in the town the wrong way. Still, surely he had people in his life who cared for him.

Victoria finished her communiqué, during which I'd caught the name Haskins. She faced me, angling her gaze upward. "Mac?" She shook her head, her white-blond hair swinging. "What are you doing here?"

"I was only a couple of doors down, Victoria." I was careful not to call my former high school nemesis Vickie. I knew she hated it. "It looked like an emergency, and I thought maybe I could help."

"It's an emergency, all right." She blinked her pale Finnish-heritage eyes. "May I remind you, though, you are neither an EMT nor an officer of the peace?"

"Of course I'm not. But Norland is a good friend, so . . ." I took a second look at her as she turned to direct two actual EMTs who hurried through the back door, red bags in hand. Victoria was looking chunkier, carrying more weight on her petite frame than she usually did. I gave my head a shake. Her eating habits were none of my business.

I sidled closer to Norland. "What happened?"

"I don't know. I heard a noise and came inside to investigate." He stared at the toppled bookshelf.

"Was the shelving unit just sitting there unsecured?"

"I don't know. I'm the off-season manager, not the owner. How can he run a business where something so heavy can be tipped over so easily?"

"Yeah," I murmured. Or maybe it had been secured to the floor and a bad guy had loosened the bolts or screws or whatever. It bore looking into. Later. "Norland, you said nobody had been in to browse the books or buy anything."

As we spoke, the professional team was busy. August, looking a bit green, had backed away from the body to let the EMTs do what they had to. Our town's bike cop rarely encountered corpses. Usually his job involved keeping the peace at public events, reminding young cyclists to wear their helmets, and patrolling the high school grounds for illicit activity.

"Ma'am?" One of the EMTs spoke to Victoria. "The person is deceased. I assume you need us to wait to transport the remains?"

"Yes. The bookcase will need to be moved, but we'll wait for the SOC team."

"You didn't see Wagner go inside?" I asked Norland in a low voice.

"No." He blew out a breath. "I'd left the back door to the store unlocked. You know it opens onto the parking lot. I wanted to be sure customers weren't deterred from shopping and thought I would hear the bell from out front. I guess I didn't. It was a stupid move. I should have known better."

"Jenkins, until we get some crime scene tape out there, please guard the front door," Victoria directed. "Nobody comes in unless they're with us. From the looks of it, I'm thinking this wasn't an accident."

As I'd suspected. And anyway, it was an unattended death of a man in his prime. By now I knew the authorities always investigated such circumstances.

August looked relieved to get away from Wagner's body. He no sooner reached the door when the bell dinged. He held up his palm and opened his mouth to speak when he apparently realized who the newcomer was. "Detective Sergeant Haskins. Come in."

"Thank you, Jenkins." The state police detective made his way in. Lincoln Haskins stood six foot three and had a not-insignificant frame. At his doctor's urging, he'd lost some weight in the last six months, and it suited him. As always, he wore a flowered Hawaiian shirt, now nearly hidden by his winter jacket. His deep brown eyes were serious behind dark-rimmed glasses. August clicked the door locked behind him.

"Afternoon, Mac, Norland," Lincoln said, his voice pitched low and soft. Silver threaded his nearly black hair, which curled onto his collar. No military cut for him. "Chief, I understand you called for me?"

"Yes. How did you get here so fast?"

"I was in the area."

"Sorry about the civilian, Lincoln. She showed up just after Norland discovered the victim." Victoria gave me the side-eye. "Mac, you really have to leave."

I held up both hands. "On my way. Good luck. And may Wagner rest in peace."

"Wait, Mac." Lincoln pointed at me. "You're on a first-name basis with the deceased?"

"Wagner Lavoie is, I mean, *was* the new Chamber of Commerce director. We weren't best buds or anything, but I helped with today's festival. He and I had agreed to forgo the formalities."

Norland stepped forward. "Point of information, Lincoln. Most of the local merchants, plus folks like me, who work for Main Street businesses, were at a festival meeting last night. Wagner ran it."

"Okay. Good to know." Lincoln glanced at Victoria. "Sorry, but I don't mind if Mac sticks around. I've learned, a bit reluctantly, she has a pretty good eye for this kind of situation."

Victoria gave a slow nod. "Whatever you think, Lincoln." She turned her back, watching the EMTs behind the toppled bookshelf.

I knew she wasn't happy with his decision. That said, Westham was way too small to have a homicide division of its own. A state police detective, working out of the county district attorney's office, always investigated murders in the towns and small cities of the Commonwealth of Massachusetts. On Cape Cod and the islands off Barnstable County, someone like Lincoln was also assisted by the Bureau of Criminal Investigation, which helped local, state, and federal law enforcement agencies.

But it seemed there wasn't much more to say, for now. "Thanks, Lincoln, but I'll get going," I said. "I need to get back to my shop. You know where to find me."

"I do." He gazed at me from over the top of his glasses. "And you know not to speak of this until an official announcement has been made."

"Of course." I was well aware of the drill by now. "We'll be in touch," I whispered to Norland, getting only a somber nod in return.

This was their case, these uniformed and civvies-clad professionals. I didn't envy them the job.

CHAPTER 8

I plodded back to my shop at twelve thirty, with questions in my mind and sorrow in my heart. I barely saw the residents and visitors who were shopping, patronizing the Main Street restaurants, and apparently enjoying the spring-inspired floral decorations everywhere. They didn't have a clue a man lay dead in the bookstore.

"How did it all go?" Orlean asked from the repair area at the back of the shop.

"I think the parade and the festival were a success." I glanced around. "Where's Sandy?" I never liked to have only one person working in Mac's Bikes, for security reasons along with lots of other ones.

"She said she had something she needed to do," Orlean replied with an edge in her voice that made me take notice. She didn't meet my gaze, but she rarely made eye contact.

"She told me she could work all day." I waited, but Orlean kept her silence. "I'm sorry you had to be here alone."

"No problem." She tightened the nut on a wheel and spun it. "Nobody's been in."

"Regardless, it's my policy to always have at least two on staff." I began to turn away.

"Mac, my sister might not have told you, but she has a few issues she's working through."

Issues? "Thanks for letting me know. I'll talk with her." I made a beeline for the opposite side of the store before she could say anything else. I didn't want to negotiate a business relationship with Sandy through Orlean. I knew I could trust my mechanic. Her sister, who'd worked here only two months? Trust wasn't yet a given.

Customers flooded in. I kept busy for the next hour ringing up bike shirts, patch kits, and water bottles. In the fall we'd ordered a line of merchandise branded with "Mac's Bikes, Westham, MA" inside a stylized map of Cape Cod. The items had proved popular before the holidays, and I had high hopes for sales during the summer tourist season.

Sandy never showed. I texted her during a lull in shoppers. No response. Orlean kept glancing up, as if she expected her sister to appear. Maybe the cyclist I'd seen at the end of the parade had been her. Except I'd never seen Sandy on a bike before. Had she borrowed one of our rentals? No. We didn't offer a model with dropped handlebars like the one I'd seen after the parade.

Whatever. We were so busy, I was glad I'd had

those two small cups of soup. I wished I'd picked up one of Tim's rolls, too.

"Hey, hon." My mom breezed in, followed by Reba. Both ladies sported rosy cheeks and big smiles.

"Wasn't it a grand success?" Reba added. "That Lavoie fella knows what he's doing. I predict good things ahead for Westham's businesses."

My heart sank. Their blissful unawareness of Wagner's fate wouldn't last long. I wasn't allowed to be the one to tell them. but I hated having to keep the news secret.

"The festival was a great idea," I said. "And you two had a good time, it looks like."

"We did. Oh!" Mom proffered a paper bag she held. "These are from Tim for you and the girls."

I rolled my eyes but softened it with a smile. I was over thirty-five, and Orlean and Sandy were both older than I. Girls, we weren't.

"Thanks." I peeked inside to spy a half dozen of Tim's flower buns. "Perfect. I was just wishing I'd taken one of these while they lasted. Orlean," I called to her. "Baked treats from Tim when you have a chance."

She nodded her acknowledgment. I pulled out a baked flower and bit into it. Yeasty, light, with a touch of sweetness. Pure yum, just like its baker.

"He was closing up shop when we passed, don't you know?" Reba said. "He mentioned he'll stop by to walk you home if you're ready to leave at about two."

I swallowed what I'd been chewing. "We're short-handed, so I have to stay until closing. But I'll text him."

"Say, Mackenzie," Mom began. "We saw a quiet ambulance leaving the Book Nook. I hope Norland is okay."

"He is." How did I want to frame this? "Apparently a customer in the bookstore had an, um, health incident." I popped the rest of the roll in my mouth, and not a moment too soon.

Another wave of customers rolled in. A couple was returning a rented tandem. A family wanted souvenir shirts. A woman wanted to buy a repair kit. I set to work helping all of them. Mom and Reba waved their goodbyes.

By the time Tim strolled in at two thirty, I hadn't had a minute free to text him—or to think more about what had happened to Wagner Lavoie. The last customer had just left, happily wheeling a new bicycle for his ten-year-old granddaughter. I took a second look at my gorgeous man. The shoulders of his dark coat were dusted with white.

"Is it snowing already?" I asked, eyes wide.

"It is, my love." He kissed my forehead. "And the timing couldn't be better, at least for the festival and the Main Street businesses."

I leaned against his chest for a moment. I made a quick decision and straightened.

"Orlean, let's close up."

"You got it," she called from the repair area.

"And we're going to stay closed tomorrow," I added. "Nobody wants to ride a bike in a wet snow."

"I approve," Tim murmured. "What can I do to help?"

I smiled at him. "You can bring in the Open flag and any bikes out there. And you can letter a sign for the door." I handed him the key to the padlock that secured the cycles out front.

"A sign reading, *Gone Fishing*?"

"How about, *Gone Sledding, see you on Monday*?" One of my husband's many talents was an artistic bent that made him better than the average bear at lettering signs, birthday cards, you name it.

"Perfect." He headed back out.

I emptied the cash drawer into a bank bag, leaving only minimal starting change for Monday. The bag went into the safe in my tiny office. Orlean wiped her hands on a grease rag and scribbled on the repair ticket for the bike she'd been working on.

Tim brought in the furled flag and left it next to the door, then went back out. We usually kept a few types of bikes outside on display while we were open, locked together, of course, but they didn't stay out overnight. And definitely not in any kind of weather.

As Orlean shrugged into her jacket, I said, "I hope Sandy is okay. Please ask her to call me when you see her. I texted her, but she didn't answer."

She gave a curt nod. Tim wheeled in an adult tricycle with one hand and carried a child-sized one in the other.

"Thanks for the buns," Orlean murmured to him. "See you Monday, Mac." She stomped out, her shoulders sagging.

Tim gazed at the door after it shut. "She's even less cheery than usual."

"I know. Sandy has kind of disappeared. I think Orlean is worried. I know I am."

"Disappeared? Seriously?"

"I'm afraid so."

Tim wrapped me in his arms. "That's the last thing you need," he said into my hair.

I had to agree. I stepped back. "Let's lock up and get out of here." All I wanted was to be home snuggling with him, a cup of whiskey-laced hot cocoa in hand, as a pretty snow fell outside.

He uncapped a marker and wrote out the sign.

And then the door opened once more.

CHAPTER 9

I let out a long, low breath. "Hi, Lincoln. Come in."

Tim brought his light brows together and cocked his head, gazing at me.

The detective let the door shut behind him. "Sorry to intrude. How are you, Brunelle?" He extended his hand to Tim.

Tim shook it and faced me. "Did something happen I don't know about?"

I pointed at Lincoln. "Is it sharing time?"

"I'm afraid so. Could we sit down?"

"And here I was looking forward to enjoying a hot adult beverage at home and watching the snow come down." I sighed again. "Are you sure you don't want to join us at our house, Lincoln? More comfortable. Drinks."

"Food," Tim added.

Lincoln paused, then said, "You've convinced me. You two need a ride?"

"We'd love one," I said. "Give me one second to get my coat and lock the doors."

"I'll turn down the heat," Tim offered.

Fifteen minutes later I sat opposite Lincoln at our kitchen table. A steaming cup of cocoa waited in front of me, smelling like chocolate heaven, but I'd decided to save the whiskey until we were finished talking. Lincoln cradled a mug of black tea.

Belle, my African gray parrot, nattered away in the living room in her cage. She was always excited when I came home. I rose.

"Excuse me a minute," I said. "I'd better let her join us."

"Snacks, Mac?" The bird, always stylish in her smooth gray coat, red tail feathers, and white eye makeup, waddled into the kitchen after me. "Alexa, make a shopping list. Belle's a good girl. Snacks, Mac?" She gave a low wolf whistle. "Hey, handsome."

Lincoln nearly choked on his drink.

"Belle, we're not shopping right now." I gave the detective a "what can you do?" look, then poured a few chunks of frozen carrots into her bowl and set it on the floor.

Tim slid grilled cheddar-and-ham sandwiches onto three plates. He sliced each diagonally and brought them to the table. "Can you get out the pickles, Mac?"

"Sure."

"Pickles, Mac." Belle pitched her voice low and soft. Exactly like Tim's.

"Eat your carrots," I scolded. I was pretty sure briny pickles weren't on her foods list. And it still stunned me how she could reproduce different voices with uncanny accuracy.

After we'd eaten in silence for a couple of minutes, Lincoln swallowed and dabbed at his mouth with his napkin.

"To fill you in, Brunelle, today while Norland Gifford was outside in front of the Book Nook, Wagner Lavoie died inside."

Tim's hand went to his heart. "I'm sorry to hear that. Are you involved, Detective, because his death was suspicious?"

"We always investigate unattended deaths, unless the person was of advanced age and passed in their own bed," Lincoln said. "In this case, Lavoie appears to have been crushed by a heavy bookcase. What we don't yet know is if the unit hitting him was what killed him, or if he was a victim of homicide before that."

"What killed him," Belle began. "What killed him. What killed him."

"We're in trouble now," I said. "She just learned a new phrase."

"You knew about Lavoie, hon." Tim covered my hand with his. "Were you there?"

"Yes, but after it happened. I was in front of the Lobstah Shack when I saw Victoria run across the street to the bookstore at the same time August Jenkins raced past on his bike. I'd been talking with Norland only a few minutes earlier, so I jogged back. He'd just discovered poor Wagner."

"Was it awful?" Tim murmured.

Lincoln watched me as he finished his sandwich.

"Of course. I mean, I didn't go close enough to actually see Wagner. Only his foot." A shiver rippled through me. "But it was a big, heavy bookcase." I gazed at Lincoln. "Wouldn't Wagner have jumped out of the way when it started to fall?"

"That's one of our questions," Lincoln said. "I came by your shop, Mac, to ask about anyone you might have witnessed interacting with Lavoie in recent days. Having, shall we say, acrimonious interactions with him, to be specific."

Ugh. I'd witnessed exactly those interactions, but several of those instances were between Wagner and friends of mine. An employee, as well.

"I did." I took in a deep breath and let it out slowly. "For starters, anyone who was at the organizing meeting last evening can tell you Kassandra Jenkins wasn't happy with Wagner, and vice versa. She resented him securing the Chamber directorship and not her." I flashed back to what I'd seen in the pub. "I saw her and her father, Park, drinking in the Rusty Anchor at about eleven thirty this morning. They left and headed across Main Street to the nearest side street."

"The one leading to the lot behind the Book Nook?" Lincoln asked.

"Yes."

Tim pursed his lips and tapped the table. I was sure he was thinking about what he had seen, what he might be able to contribute to Lincoln's investigation.

"Anyone else?" the detective pressed.

"Well, a couple of merchants weren't happy about being pressured to give out freebies," I said.

"Who?"

I had to do it, but I didn't want to. "Zane King, for starters."

"The distiller."

"Yes." I gave a nod. "He was totally right. He couldn't be giving out free alcohol."

"Indeed not." Lincoln nodded. "I'm surprised Lavoie suggested it."

"I was, too. Instead, Zane made a bunch of copies of a cocktail recipe." I glanced at my crossbody bag on the counter. "I grabbed one. Do you want to see it?"

"No." Lincoln gazed at me, then checked the fifties-era red and white wall clock. "Who else?"

"Yvonne Flora wasn't happy with Wagner, either," I went on. "She's the chef at the Rusty Anchor. But she ended up giving out cups of soup, anyway."

"Was she at the meeting?" Lincoln asked.

"No. I saw them talking in the pub kitchen Thursday afternoon. Yvonne told him she'd be working Friday night. He didn't like her answer."

"Thank you. I need to get going." Lincoln stood. "Anyone else?"

I blew out a breath. I had to tell him about Sandy. I opened my mouth, but Tim spoke first.

"Sorry, Mac, but I saw Gin Malloy and Lavoie really get into it a couple of days ago."

My shoulders slumped as I swore silently. Gin was my walking buddy. My fellow book group member. My BFF. She never would have killed Wagner. No way.

"What were they arguing about?" Lincoln asked.

"I'm afraid I couldn't hear," Tim said. "I'd just come out of the bank, and they were a block away on the sidewalk. The body language was unmistakable. It was angry on both sides. You know what it looks like. Fists on hips. Arms folded. Leaning into the other person's space. Throwing hands in the air.

Turning away and turning back for one last jab or insult. It wasn't pretty."

"Was Ms. Malloy at the meeting?" Lincoln asked.

"Yes," I said. "I don't think she interacted with Wagner. She did tell me and a couple of others she wasn't sure if he was the best fit for the job."

"You haven't had your morning walk with her in a couple of days," Tim added.

"Right." I cleared my throat. "Lincoln, I know you need to leave, but I have one more thing to tell you. My mechanic's sister, Sandy, has been working for me since the end of January. She seems to have some history with Wagner, but I don't know what it is."

"Last name?" Lincoln asked.

"McKean. She was working this morning, but she went off somewhere after the parade started and never came back. Orlean didn't know where she was, and Sandy didn't answer my text. I just hope she's all right."

Lincoln looked over the top of his glasses at me. "I'll need her number." He pulled out his phone.

He hadn't taken a single note while we talked, but I knew he had a prodigious memory. Maybe not for numerals, though. I pulled up Sandy's contact on my own phone and read it out to him.

"Thank you both for lunch," Lincoln said. "Meals can get spotty at times like this."

Tim rose. The men shook hands.

"Let's hope we won't need any of these names." Lincoln shrugged into his large black pea jacket. "It's entirely possible Lavoie tripped on an unsecured shelving unit, fell, and brought it down on top of himself."

"One thing I know for certain," I began. "Neither Gin nor Zane would have tried to hurt Wagner."

"So noted," Lincoln said.

"Be in touch, okay?" I asked.

The detective gave me a little salute.

"Be in touch, okay?" Belle muttered. "Be in touch."

Lincoln snorted. "I promise, Belle."

Tim showed him out. I reheated my neglected cocoa as I cleared the table, rinsed the dishes, and loaded them into the dishwasher. I fetched the bottle of Cape King Bourbon—Zane's brand, of course—and added a couple of glugs to my again-warm mug.

What a tragic ending to a cheerful flower-bedecked festival. What a tangle of emotions and suspicious behavior. The whole thing was a mess. And I didn't like messes.

CHAPTER 10

Tim and I both fell asleep on the couch after Lincoln left, me stretched out with my feet in his lap. A little afternoon delight after we woke up was, well, delightful. We'd been married on New Year's Eve and were hoping to conceive a child sometime soon. The trying was thoroughly enjoyable.

At sometime after five, he headed upstairs to work on a software app he was developing, a lucrative side-gig he had in addition to baking. I sat with a cup of hot, milky chai. I stroked Belle's back, admiring the delicately scalloped feathers like a chic hijab covering her head and neck as I considered our conversation with Lincoln. What Tim had said about Gin and Wagner's argument had surprised and worried me. I tapped her number and greeted her after she picked up.

"Hey, Mac." Gin's voice was cold.

Uh-oh. "Did you hear about Wagner's death?"

"I sure did. Our detective friend paid me a little visit an hour ago."

I waited, but she didn't continue.

"So you know Lincoln came to see us," I said. "He asked me who I thought had had conflict with Wagner, and I mentioned Kassandra and a few other people. I was totally surprised when Tim said he'd seen you arguing with Wagner, and I immediately told Lincoln you would never have hurt Wagner or anyone else."

"Yeah, well, your detective pal apparently doesn't believe you."

Ouch. "I'm sorry. He should believe you." I sipped my tea. I didn't want her to be upset with me. But, if there was one thing I'd learned in my thirty-seven years, it was that I couldn't control other people's reactions.

The clink of ice cubes came over the line. "I shouldn't be mad, Mac. But, as you know, I've been a so-called person of interest in a murder once already, and it's no fun."

"Of course it isn't." The actual killer had planted evidence in Gin's unlocked garage. "At least you were cleared of any suspicion."

"Thanks to you, I was," she said. "But it's true. Lavoie and I really got into it a couple days ago, and on the sidewalk downtown, no less. The dude was full of, uh, cow-patty, as you're aware."

"Can you tell me what you two fought about?"

"It was stupid, really. He told me to change up my window displays more often. I told him go stuff it. I mean, I've owned Salty Taffy's for a decade. Shouldn't I know what works for my business and what doesn't?"

"You bet." I thought back to earlier. It'd been between eleven thirty and noon when Norland discovered Wagner's body. "Were you with anyone after the parade ended?"

She swore at me, and not silently. "Mac, are you asking me about my alibi?"

"I'm sorry." Apologizing twice in a row to my bestie wasn't a good pattern. "Can I assume Lincoln asked you where you'd been when he stopped by?"

"What do you think?" The ice cubes clinked again. "All I could say was I was in my shop. Alone. You know, I think we're done here."

"Gin, I'm on your side," I pleaded. I hoped she wouldn't hang up on me. "We're on the same team. We'll get the Cozy Capers onto solving this. Having an argument, even in public, about what you do with your store windows does not make you a murderer. Far from it."

Again I waited. I crossed my fingers, hoping she would hear my solidarity with her.

"I know." She blew out a noisy breath. "The whole thing just makes me want to uproot and move to Costa Rica or, like, anyplace else where no one knows me. Where I don't have a stake in what happens in town. Where ordinary people don't keep getting murdered."

"Don't leave town quite yet. Please?"

"You know I won't."

Whew. "I'll start a book group text going. We can meet here tomorrow afternoon. What do you say?"

"Fine." A door opened and someone spoke in the background. "Eli's here with our takeout dinner. Talk to you tomorrow, Mac."

"Sounds good."

Gin cleared her throat. "I shouldn't have gotten so upset with you."

"No one expects—"

"The Spanish Inquisition?" She laughed.

"That, too."

After we disconnected, I drained my mug. Lincoln was going to have to clear Gin, and soon. I doubted she would ever find a place to live where ordinary people didn't get murdered.

CHAPTER 11

I finished shoveling the sidewalk at Mac's Bikes the next morning at eleven, glad I'd remembered my sunglasses. The sun shone in full force and the snow was already melting, as was usual for spring storms. Still, the temperature was forecast to plummet tonight. The last thing any business owner wants is for a person to fall on the ice in front of their shop.

But where was my plow guy? I'd hired Corwin Germain, Orlean's ex-husband, to clear the parking lot. After a big breakfast with Tim, I'd walked over here to work on my books and pay bills. The lot was empty of vehicles, but six inches of white stuff covered it. No way did I want to shovel the whole thing.

I started removing snow from the walk leading around the side of the building. I paused, leaning on the shovel and gazing at the parcel in back of the parking lot. I owned the land, and it was where my tiny house sat for two years until I moved in with Tim just before our wedding in December.

I'd loved living with Belle in my super-efficient little abode. The 400-square-foot structure, which was built on a trailer, was now set up behind Tim's house. That is, our home. We'd hooked up the tiny house to water and electricity, so we could use it for guest quarters or as a retreat. The space was like a boat, with a place for everything and everything in its place, a kind of order I craved. I got antsy, verging on anxious, when life got messy.

Giving myself a shake, I returned to making sure this walkway wasn't messy with snow. A minute later a heavy truck, with its plow in place and lowered, turned into the parking lot.

Corwin hit the brakes and lowered his window. "Good morning, Mac. Sorry I'm later than expected." As he leaned his elbow on the window, the tattoo on his arm that snaked down onto the back of his gloveless hand was exposed.

"No worries. I decided not to open today, but I still want the snow cleared away so it doesn't freeze up tonight."

"A wise move. You been well?" When he smiled, a gap showed behind his eyetooth on the left side. He wasn't over fifty, but some rough experiences in his past showed in his worn face.

"Yes. You?"

"Can't complain. I'd better get to it. Hope this is the last snow of the season, but you never know."

I laughed. "Thanks, Corwin. The check'll be in the mail." I always said the same thing, but we both knew I paid him online.

He gave a little salute, raised his window, and

began pushing giant heaps of snow to the edges of the lot. Orlean hadn't had a problem with me hiring him, for which I was grateful. Corwin was a reliable guy, the kind any shop owner wants on retainer. It occurred to me he might know Sandy. I didn't want to interrupt his work to ask.

I finished my shoveling and headed inside to do my own work. My phone pinged as I was shedding outer garments. It was Derrick responding to the group text I'd sent this morning, inviting the Cozy Capers book group to my place this afternoon to talk through Wagner's death.

Can't do it this afternoon. Cokey already invited a friend over.

I thumbed a reply. **Gotcha. See you at dinner?**

We all had a standing invitation for Sunday dinner at the parsonage: Tim and I, Derrick and Cokey, and Abo Reba. Tim seemed to appreciate the tradition and usually accompanied me. Mom always scheduled it early so little girls—and early-riser bakers—could get home in time for a good night's sleep.

We'll be there.

Good, I replied.

I sat at my desk and organized the bills I needed to pay. Utilities were a biggie. I'd decided to shell out for solar panels. The power they generated would help with the electric bill after a while. I had the parts supplier to pay, plus the helmet manufacturer and the sport-clothing company where I ordered shirts, jackets, shorts, and pants.

Before I could start, my phone pinged again, this time with a text on the group thread from Norland.

Press conf going on now. Wagner's death ruled homicide.

I sat back, eyes wide. After I'd spoken with Gin yesterday, I'd shoved thoughts of the horrible scene in the bookstore into an imaginary box and firmly closed the lid. The box's lid was now open, and with a vengeance.

My thumbs flew as I searched for a way to watch on my phone. There it was. Lincoln spoke into a microphone on a stand in front of the Westham Police building down the street. Victoria, bundled up in a black coat and more than a foot shorter, stood at his right. I'd obviously missed the announcement itself. Lincoln was now taking questions.

"No, we have no one in custody at this time." The detective listened to a question I couldn't hear. "We do have several persons of interest with whom we are speaking."

Someone off camera shouted, "Why is there a rash of murders in Westham? Should the average citizen be worried?"

"I'll let Chief Laitinen answer that. Please be assured the state police of the Commonwealth, in cooperation with the Barnstable County Bureau of Criminal Investigation and, of course, Westham's finest, are bringing all possible resources to investigate this horrific crime and to bring the perpetrator to justice as soon as possible." Lincoln turned to Victoria. "Chief?" He stepped back.

"The people of Westham should always exercise caution with respect to locking doors of homes and vehicles," Victoria said. "That said, we have no reason to believe this was a random killing. Residents of town, and visitors, please go about your daily lives. Please note, we've opened a hotline for anyone who might have observed suspicious activity near the

Book Nook yesterday, especially in the parking lot behind the bookstore." She read out the number, which also appeared on the screen, then cast a glance at Lincoln. "Anything else, Detective?"

He shook his head.

Victoria ignored a barrage of questions. They included, "What was the murder weapon? When do you expect to make an arrest? Why would someone kill the Chamber of Commerce director?" And more.

"That will be all at this time." She turned away and preceded Lincoln up the wide steps and into the station.

I clicked away from the site and sat back in my chair. Wow. Just wow. I had the same questions as all those frustrated reporters. The group suddenly had a lot more to chew on this afternoon.

CHAPTER 12

"Some news, huh?" Tulia hurried in through my front door at ten after three.

"I know." I shut the door after her and joined everyone in the living room.

"Sorry I'm late," Tulia said. "I was just leaving the Shack when one more customer wanted a takeout lunch."

"It's fine. Help yourself." I had set out chunks of cheddar and gouda cheese, plus a round of Camembert, on a board on the coffee table. A basket of stoned wheat mini-crackers was next to them. Zane had brought two bottles of wine, and Gin had supplied lime and cranberry seltzer.

"Where's your better half?" Norland asked.

"Where's your better half?" Belle echoed from the kitchen in a voice sounding identical to Norland's. "Where's your better half? Belle's a good girl. Who killed him? Who killed him? Be in touch, okay?" She ended her litany with a wolf whistle.

Tulia burst out laughing. Gin rolled her eyes. Norland, smiling, shook his head.

I stood. "Excuse me a minute." I hurried to close the door to the kitchen. I'd put Belle in her traveling cage, but she didn't need to pick up any new words about murder. I sank onto my chair again. "Sorry about that. She was with us when Lincoln came by yesterday."

"Mac, you know we love her," Zane said.

"Thanks," I said. "Anyway, Tim is out for a run."

"With Eli," Gin added. She and Eli had been a couple since the summer, and he and Tim were running and drinking buddies. The four of us often hung out together.

"Speaking of Lincoln," I went on. "Thanks for sending the text this morning, Norland. I was in the shop and was able to watch the question period."

"Which obviously left everyone with a lot of questions." Norland frowned at his hands.

"Wait, what?" Tulia asked, holding her hand in front of her mouth, into which she had just popped a cheese-laden cracker. "What did I miss?"

"You know Wagner Lavoie died yesterday," I said. "The bookstore was where I dashed off to after I inhaled your delicious chowder."

"Yes, and his death is why we're here," Tulia said. "But did something else happen?"

"They decided he was murdered," Gin said.

"But not how," Zane added. "Or not that they shared, anyway."

"So, like, it might have been from more than being clobbered with a bookcase?" Tulia asked.

Norland gave a slow nod. "They didn't let me even watch yesterday. They must have lifted it off of his body. I feel entirely responsible."

"But you only work there," I said.

"Yes. Any responsible person would have made sure the place didn't have tippable heavy furniture, don't you think?"

"Norland, Barlow Swift owns the store. It's his responsibility, isn't it?" Gin asked.

"Yes, but . . ." His voice trailed off.

"Listen," I told him. "After they let you reopen, we'll all come over and make sure every single movable piece is secured. Okay?"

"I guess. But you're all busy. I think I'll hire someone to do it and bill Barlow."

"Good idea." Tulia glanced around. "Boy, this is when I miss Flo. She's always so organized with her yellow legal pad and her lists of action items."

"It's true." I gave a nod. Florence Wolanski, a group member and the head librarian at Westham Public Library, would be taking charge of the meeting right about now. Except she'd left on Wednesday for a library conference in California and planned to take a well-deserved vacation and do some sightseeing after it was over. She wouldn't be back for almost two weeks. "We're on our own."

Zane grinned. "I just happened to have brought a reasonable facsimile." He reached down and pulled out a yellow legal pad and pen from a messenger bag next to his chair. "I have entirely legible handwriting, too. I know it's a stereotype of gay men to have good penmanship. In my case, it's true and was even when I was a kid."

"So, who are the suspects?" Tulia asked.

"Not yet suspects, but here are the people I know of who had issues with Wagner." I listed the ones I'd spoken with Lincoln about. I left Gin off the list.

Zane jotted down Kassandra, Sandy, Yvonne. "Kassandra seems like the most obvious, and if it was her, maybe Park helped her. Dads do that kind of thing."

"Help their daughters commit murder?" Norland's eyebrows flew up. "Not in my universe, they don't."

"Well, I'm adding his name, anyway," Zane said.

"I saw Kassandra and Park leave the Rusty Anchor and walk down the side street next to the bookstore at around noon," I said.

"Old Mill Road?" Norland asked. "It leads to the parking lot behind the bookstore."

"Exactly."

"Don't forget me." Gin twisted her mouth and pointed at her chest. "Tim mentioned to Lincoln he'd seen me arguing with the victim."

Zane scrunched his nose. "We all know you didn't kill him, so just be quiet, girlfriend."

I hadn't included in my recited list what I'd told Lincoln about Zane's disagreement with Wagner, which now seemed entirely minor. I wished I'd never mentioned his name at all.

Tulia narrowed her eyes. "I think I've met Sandy McKean before. She's a vet, right? Strong woman?"

"She does look strong," I said. "I didn't know she was a veteran."

"She might have served in Afghanistan. My brother did, and I think he knows her. I'll ask him."

"She's staying with Orlean, but it's a new arrangement, I think," I said. "Maybe find out where she was living before, if you can."

"Good thought. Because that could be a clue as to how she knew Wagner," Gin said. "But can't you just ask Orlean?"

I hunched my shoulders. "It's tricky, right? I mean, Sandy is her sister. And they both work for me." Or did. I had no idea if Sandy would resurface or not.

"Action item for Tulia." Zane clicked the pen on and wrote on the pad in a flowing hand.

I gazed at our retired police chief. "Norland, how can we find out why they decided Wagner's death was a homicide? Would they have completed an autopsy so soon?"

"As I said, they didn't let me observe when they extracted his remains. Lavoie could have had a contusion on a different part of his head. A gunshot wound. A laceration on his neck."

I shuddered at the image of a garroted Wagner. Of his throat being slit or a gunshot wound to his torso or head. I wasn't alone. Zane hugged himself, and Gin grimaced.

"They might have detected evidence of his having ingested poison," Norland continued. "Any of those can be observed without doing an autopsy. Of course they will perform one when they can."

"You hear about the terrible backlogs," Tulia said. "How long do you think it'll take before they get him onto the slab?"

"Onto the slab?" I tilted my head. "When did you start talking like that?"

"It's how my cousin talks, you know, the forensic pathologist I told you guys about last fall. But saying 'slab' is nothing. You should hear my sister-in-law's nephew. He works in the morgue in Providence. Talk about grisly jokes."

"The police are not immune to their own gallows humor," Norland said. "Anyway, I'll make some inquires. Usually the victim of an unsolved homicide can jump the line, so to speak."

"Action item for Norland." Zane scribbled again. He looked up, eyes bright. "What else?"

"Does anybody know Park Jenkins?" I asked. "I don't even know what he does for work when he's not being a selectperson. Which can't pay much of anything, I expect."

Zane raised his hand. "He actually lives near us. He sells real estate. I'll see if I can have a little chat with him. A house near us is going on the market soon. I can use talking about properties as my pretense."

"Action item for Zane." Gin smiled.

"Oopsies." Zane laughed as he bent over the legal pad.

"How about Yvonne?" I asked. "I witnessed her fight with Wagner. I don't really want to press her on it." I sipped a most excellent Pinot Noir.

"I know the pastry chef there," Gin offered. "Which sounds fancy for a pub, but he's quite a good baker, and also helps out with other prep. I'll see what I can find out about his boss."

Zane wrote again.

"Which leaves me with . . . ?" I glanced around the group.

"Kassandra, herself," Norland said.

Great. She seemed like a prickly person, but I had to do my share. "Aye-aye, Captain." I made a mock salute.

Norland cleared his throat. "We all know to keep things low-key. Don't confront anyone. Be casual.

Murder is a real thing. And a killer is out there somewhere, hoping to evade arrest."

"What he said." I pointed at Norland. "With any luck, Wagner was killed because of a personal grudge, and this isn't a serial killer looking to pick off others in town."

Victoria had claimed as much when she ended the press conference. But did she or Lincoln actually know?

CHAPTER 13

After the group left at about four thirty, Tim called to say Eli had asked for his assistance with a software project.

"Do you mind if I skip family dinner, hon?" Tim asked. "Eli's wrestling down this program he needs to use so he can do his research, and I offered to help out."

I didn't speak for a moment. We'd been apart since late morning, on our day off, no less, and I loved my husband's company. I even loved saying "my husband." But I'd be with the rest of the family. And I'd be with Tim for the rest of my life, God willing.

"It's fine, of course," I murmured.

"You should drive over there."

"No, I'll be okay walking. I drank a glass of wine with the book group, and the sun won't set until nearly seven."

"Are you sure? There's the, um, murder thing going on."

"Yes, I'm sure. Whoever killed Wagner isn't out to get me. Anyway, Derrick can give me a ride home if I want one."

"The eternal designated driver." Tim gave a low laugh. "A good idea, my love. I'll see you before too long."

"Want me to bring you a doggie bag, so to speak?"

"No, we're going to have a couple of pizzas delivered. But thanks for offering."

We signed off, and I got ready to go. I fed Belle her dinner and got her situated for the night. She could use an extra-long sleep. I set out, carrying a public radio tote bag holding a box of the brownies Tim had baked to bring to dinner.

My feet slowed in front of the Toy Soldier. Could my action item, otherwise known as Kassandra, be working today? I peered in the window past a display of children's gardening tools and flower-bedecked stuffed animals posed as if enjoying a picnic—a spread set up for yesterday, no doubt—to see her behind the counter. I had a few minutes to spare.

She glanced up from her perch on a stool as the door whooshed shut behind me. "Let me know if I can help you with anything." She checked a phone sitting on the counter. "Just so you know, we close at five."

"Thanks." I browsed shelves of games ranging from Clue to cribbage, then wandered among boxes holding Tinkertoys and Tiddlywinks, Lincoln Logs and Legos. Another section was full of plush animals, and in a far alcove sat baby bath toys, pacifiers, and infant outfits. The store stocked toys and games of all kinds except electronic ones. I approved.

I selected a small unicorn and brought it to the counter. Cokey had been besotted with the imaginary creature lately.

"I'd like this, please."

She told me the price. I stuck my card into the reader. She must have read my name on her screen, because she looked up.

"You're the bike shop owner."

"I am. Mac Almeida." I extended my hand. "And you're Kassandra Jenkins, right?"

She shook hands, but it was the lukewarm grasp of someone not used to the practice. "Yes. My mom owns the store. I'm working here while . . . well, for now."

The machine dinged, telling me to extract my card.

"Terrible news about Wagner Lavoie, isn't it?" I asked. "And after what a success the festival was."

Kassandra blinked. "Yes, it was. On both counts. He sure had the weather on his side." She handed me my receipt and slid the toy into a paper sack with a handle.

"I heard you were hoping to land the Chamber job." I kept my voice casual.

"I was." She spoke to a spot over my right shoulder. "But I didn't get it."

"This place seems like a good fit. I love the window display."

"Thank you. I'm not sure about the fit, but we'll see." She straightened a box of pencils on the counter and a basket of tiny dinosaurs for sale.

"I need to get going," I said. "It was nice to meet you, Kassandra."

"Likewise, Mac. You know, I need to get the front tire on my bike fixed. Can I drop it off?"

"You bet." I smiled. "Have a nice evening."

"You too."

I slid out the door. Maybe I should have asked her a leading question about the bookstore. But questions could wait until later. Or never. Norland's caution still echoed in my brain. We needed to be very, very careful if we were going to poke the virtual hornet's nest by poking around into actual murder.

CHAPTER 14

"Mom, it smells heavenly in here." I'd barely unwrapped my scarf in the parsonage kitchen when I was rushed by an angel-haired child and an energetic dog. "Hi, sweetie." I squatted to give Cokey a hug.

"Tucker wants a hug, too," she said.

"I can always give hugs." I threw an arm around the pooch, who rewarded me with a slobbery lick. My parents had gotten Tucker, a barely full-grown Portuguese water dog, to make Cokey happy, with a side benefit that he was hypoallergenic. I could actually be in the same house with him and not sneeze my head off. I took another look at my niece, who sported white socks on her hands and a white tea towel tied cowboy-style around her neck like a bib. "What's with the mittens, Cokester?"

"I'm betending to be Tucker's sister."

"Good pretending." In fact, Tucker had white front feet and a white chest, contrasting nicely with his curly black coat. "You look just like him."

"Ruff, ruff!" She dropped to her hands and knees and crawled off, Tucker trotting next to her.

I hung my coat on a hook next to the door. "What magic have you wrought?" I kissed my mom's cheek.

"It's my seafood stew. This time I added orzo, not rice, and threw in a couple spoons of pesto from the freezer." She stirred a big pot on the stove, then replaced the lid. "Is your group working on the . . ." She glanced around. "Good. The little one is in the other room. Working on the murder? Terrible, isn't it?"

"It is. You must have seen the press conference."

"I saw it in person."

"You did?" I asked.

"I was walking by the station when they began, so I lurked in the back and listened."

"I caught part of it online. They didn't say much, did they?"

"No." She set down her wooden spoon. "I spied Orlean's sister hanging around the back like I was. She's kind of an odd bird, that one."

"Sandy was there?" I felt my eyebrows zoom up involuntarily.

"Yep." Mom lifted a jelly jar full of white wine and took a sip.

"I hired her, but I don't know her too well." Interesting learning Sandy was in town. She hadn't contacted me today and certainly hadn't dropped by the shop while I was there. I guess I'd discover tomorrow if she would show up for her shift or not. I pointed to Mom's makeshift wineglass, which was all anybody used here. "Okay if I help myself?"

"Of course, honey. I should have offered."

I grabbed another jelly jar off the shelf in the open-front cupboard and headed to the refrigerator. "Going for the boxed stuff now, are you?" I twisted the little spigot on the box labeled Chardonnay and filled my glass.

"Your father picked it up for some meeting. It's actually not bad, and it keeps forever."

I tasted the wine. "Not bad, at all. Have you heard from Pa?" He'd left last week to attend a Unitarian Universalist ministers' convention in Chicago.

"Yes. He's having a grand old time with his fellow pastors. They had a big service this morning, plus Joseph is heading up the Diversity, Equity, and Inclusion committee, along with a white lady minister from Newburyport."

I smiled. "Of course he is."

My gentle father—half American Black and half Cape Verdean—had inclusiveness in his genes, it seemed. He was the most welcoming and nonjudgmental person I'd ever met. He'd fallen in love with and married my mother, who, with her pale skin, blond hair, and green eyes, was as white as they come. He'd welcomed her little son Derrick as his own and raised him as his own, and then I'd come along, cementing the blend. Pa had only beamed when my mother changed her name from Edna to Astra and had hung out her shingle as an astrologer rather than letting the job of being a minister's wife take over her life. And he did the lion's share of caring for Cokey after school when single-dad Derrick was working or at one of the AA meetings he relied on to keep him sober. I had lucked out in fathers, big-time, and I knew it.

"Tim sends his regrets, but he'd already baked brownies to contribute." I pointed to the bag on the table.

"Lovely." She leaned closer and gave me a hopeful smile. "Any news?"

"No, Mom." I knew she meant if I was pregnant. "I'll tell you when there is. Um, could you possibly stop asking?"

She laid a hand on my cheek. "I'm sorry, Mackenzie. Of course, I'll stop. It was thoughtless of me to even bring it up."

"It's okay. It's just . . ." I shook my head. "I don't really want to talk about it right now."

Tim very much wanted children with me. I loved family and wanted to create one with him, and I'd committed to it when we decided to marry. But the thought of being pregnant and giving birth still gave me palpitations. Talk about messy.

"We won't say another word." The old-fashioned wind-up timer on the windowsill dinged. "Time to take out my bread. Go on in and sit with the others. We'll eat in about twenty minutes."

I grabbed the toy store bag and carried it and my wine into the family room. Slightly shabby but entirely comfortable and welcoming, the family room and the kitchen had been the center of my life for my first twenty years and still played a big part. I greeted my grandma, who also held a jar of wine, and my big brother, who was sticking to seltzer. Cokey lay in the far corner, her head on Tucker's back, paging through a picture book I'd gotten her for Christmas.

I sank onto the sofa next to my abo.

"Kind of a big news weekend, isn't it?" she asked in a soft voice.

"I'll say."

"Are the Cozy Capers on it?" Reba asked.

"Kind of," I said. "We met this afternoon. You lucked out, Derr. Nobody volunteered you for an action item."

"Good." He sounded relieved. "My coursework has really ramped up."

Derrick was taking an intensive course to retrain as a radiology technician. Despite not being Pa's blood relative, my half-brother had the same gentle spirit. It made him a good dad, and he would be a caring and careful person in the X-ray room, too. I'd hired Sandy after he embarked on his studies and cut way down on his hours in my shop. He'd had a rough patch in the past both with the law and with the drink. I was so happy to see him thriving and wanting a better job to be able to support his daughter.

"What's a caper?" Cokey piped up.

"It's somebody who lives on Cape Cod," I said.

"And a tiny pickled berry," Reba added.

"And an adventure," Derrick said.

"Hey, Cokey, I brought you something." I lifted the bag.

Cokey jumped up, ran over, and nestled onto my lap. "You did?"

I pulled out the little unicorn.

"She's so pretty!" Cokey stroked the horn. "Thank you, Titi Mac."

"You're welcome, sweetheart. What do you think her name is?"

"It's . . ." She frowned and cocked her head like a little scholar. "It's Cornelia."

Derrick and I exchanged a glance, meaning, "Where did that come from?"

"Do you mean, like Cornelia the Cornflower?" Abo Reba asked.

"Yes, Bizabo. Like the story you telled me." Cokey wriggled out of my lap and onto her great-grandmother's. "Tell me again."

Abo Reba gave me a look. "I have a different kind of story I want to tell you, Mackie, about the director. But later." She cleared her throat. "Once upon a time, there was a strong and brave blue princess named Cornelia Cornflower."

"And she was very smart, too, right?"

"Right." Reba squeezed Cokey. "Just like you. A unicorn came to visit her, and she named it Little Cornelia."

I stood and wandered back toward the kitchen. Sandy had been lurking around the police station this morning. Reba knew something. Kassandra had implied she would be moving on from her job at the toy store. To the Chamber directorship, perhaps? Who knew? What I did know was that the game was definitely afoot, as Mr. Shakespeare and Mr. Holmes after him had put it.

CHAPTER 15

Gin and I met to walk together the next morning at seven in front of Salty Taffy's, her candy shop, as was our habit. Often we talked about the Cozy Capers' book of the week as we strode along, but I doubted we would today.

"This might be slow going," she said, gesturing at the patches of ice dotting the sidewalk.

The temperature had dipped below freezing overnight, as forecast, and some of yesterday's snowmelt had become treacherous little skating rinks. I might have had to apply ice melt to my shop's walkways if they hadn't stayed clear.

"Slow is better than slipping." I tugged my fleece headband down over my earlobes. When your hair is two-inch-long curls, it doesn't do much to keep your head warm.

"Did you get a chance to talk to Kassandra yesterday?" Gin asked.

"In fact, I did. I walked by the Toy Soldier on my way to Mom's for Sunday dinner. I kept it super casual, and I bought a toy for Cokey so she wouldn't be suspicious."

"Good move."

"I kind of got the feeling she expects to move into the Chamber director's seat now Wagner's gone." I glanced up at the tall antique windows of the Quaker Meetinghouse as we passed. One of these Sundays I wanted to go sit in silence with the congregation of Friends. Their worship service might be a good way to settle my over-busy brain. I just hadn't gotten there yet.

"As long as she's not convicted of his murder," Gin said.

"Yeah." I gave a little snort. "A prison cell wouldn't make for much of an office."

"Who selects the director, anyway? Is it the Chamber of Commerce board? I mean, it's not a town department."

"Right, it isn't." I glanced over at her. "Don't you read the member emails?"

"Ugh, no. Not most of the time. I'm too busy, Mac, and I really don't care what goes on behind the curtain."

"Well, the directorship is a publicly advertised job. The board, or maybe a subset of them, holds interviews and makes a job offer. Just like in business, which is what the Chamber is. And it's how they operated when they hired Wagner."

"I'm obviously not on the board," Gin said. "Are you?"

"No. Neither are Zane or Tim."

"What about Tulia?"

"She's not, either," I said.

"Maybe because she lives in Mashpee? I don't know if you have to be a resident as well as a business owner to be on the board."

"Speaking of the director, last night Reba said she had something to tell me about him, but we never got a chance to talk in private."

"Your grandma knows everything." Gin gave a little laugh. "I hope I'm as sharp as she is at her age. Don't forget to pass along what she says."

"I promise."

As we discussed other business people in town, we swung left from the access path onto the Shining Sea Trail.

"What was your action item from yesterday?" I asked. "I can't remember."

"Talking to Uly Cabral, the pastry guy at the pub."

"Yuli?" I asked.

"U-L-Y," she spelled. "It's short for Ulysses."

"I see. Cabral," I mused. "He must be related to Al."

"Yep. His grandson. My daughter went to school with Uly. He's a good guy." She wrinkled her nose. "I think."

"What do you mean?"

"He never quite makes eye contact. I'm not sure what he was up to before this gig. But he knows me. He'll talk to me, if I can find him apart from Yvonne."

"Huh. I wonder if Tim knows him. I mean, because baking. I'll ask him."

We reached an open area, where the trail ran along a boardwalk stretching across a salty tidal marsh. I caught my breath and pointed up. "Bald eagle." The dark broad wingspan and white head were unmistakable.

"A late one," Gin said. "Usually they've gone north by now."

"Making way for the ospreys returning from the south."

The majestic bird flew off, appearing to take its time, but actually covering a lot of ground with those wide, strong wings. It somehow brought to mind the fateful tale of Icarus, and from there even more ancient myths.

"Do you know who Cassandra was in Greek mythology?" I asked.

"I can't remember."

"She was a Trojan princess, and Hector was her big brother. According to one version, Apollo wanted her for his own. She promised herself to him, and he gave her the gift of prophecy. But then she changed her mind. He couldn't withdraw the gift, so in his rage he added a curse, so no one would believe her truths about things that would happen. Or something like that."

"Interesting. I wonder if our modern-day Kassandra's parents knew that story when they named their little girl after a cursed princess."

We turned onto the extension that headed out to the bluff overlooking the beach and sped up our pace. Arms swinging and feet moving fast got the heart rate up in the best of ways but was still low impact, something my knees appreciated. Once in the parking lot, we each stretched a bit. I gazed out over the wide bay, spying New Bedford way across the water.

"The thing is," Gin began, "if Kassandra had foretold snow for Saturday, and it had happened, she'd be getting a lot of credit right now."

"Right. Instead she said she thought the festival should be postponed and would turn out to be a disaster for local merchants. But it wasn't. Did you end up doing well with sales?" We began retracing our steps.

"I did. I wouldn't have if it had snowed, and we'd had to be in the stinky gym. You know what a nice morning it was. Sure, I spent money on the free lollipops, but after the parade ended, I sold out of taffy, so I'll be spending the morning making a bunch of new batches of saltwater taffy. How about your bottom line?"

"Mac's Bikes did fine, too. We got super busy from midday until it finally started snowing." I laughed. "It's silly thinking Kassandra Jenkins is a Greek myth, anyway. She seems to have neither the gift nor the curse of her Trojan namesake."

"She still might be a murderer," Gin murmured after two silver-haired ladies passed us going the other way.

"She might."

CHAPTER 16

By nine thirty, Mac's Bikes was open for business. Orlean was reassembling a derailleur on her workbench. Sandy hadn't come in with her, and I'd been with an early customer when she'd arrived, so I hadn't asked. Derrick wouldn't be in until the afternoon, and I really wanted my new employee on the job.

I texted Sandy again, then wandered into the work area.

Orlean didn't glance up. "You want to know where Sandy is. Yeah. Me, too."

Oh, dear. "Has she been home since Saturday?"

"Yes. But she cleared out early this morning. I have no idea where she went, Mac, or why she's flipping you off." She finally looked up at me. "I'm sorry. I feel responsible for telling you she wanted work."

"Wait. Cleared out? Do you mean she moved out?"

"No. Her stuff is still there. But she left before I woke up."

"Did you see her yesterday? Or Saturday night?"

"She was mostly home. She came back after the snow started, but she went out yesterday for a while."

"How did she seem?" I asked.

"Like her own disturbed self. She mostly refused to speak to me." Orlean gave a gruff laugh. "We got takeout pizza and watched a stupid movie last night, which kind of relaxed her."

"Can you tell me what she has going on? You mentioned Saturday she has some issues."

Orlean opened her mouth to speak. After she glanced over my shoulder, she clamped it shut and bent over her work.

I turned. A Westham Police detective I'd met in December stood in the doorway.

Penelope Johnson held up her hand in greeting. "Ms. Almeida, may I have a word with you?"

"Sure. Be there in a sec." To Orlean I whispered, "Please tell me when you can."

Orlean nodded without saying a word.

I made my way toward the tall, fit-looking officer. All business, she wore a dark tweed blazer with black trousers and shoes. Her only nod to the temperature was a royal-blue cashmere scarf worn in a European loop around her neck.

"How can I help you, Detective?" I asked.

"I'd like to speak with you about the recent homicide." The skin crinkled at the edges of her brown eyes as she smiled. "Don't worry, you're not on our list of possible suspects."

"That's a relief." I didn't have any reason to be,

but it was always better not to be of interest in a murder investigation.

"And it's fine to call me Penelope. I think we got onto a first-name basis back in December."

"Right." I glanced around the shop. "We don't do a lot of sitting in here, unless on a bicycle seat, but I have a couple of stools behind the counter. Just so you know, though, I'm alone except for my mechanic. If a retail or rental customer comes in, I'll need to help them."

"It's fine, of course."

I led her behind the counter and perched on one stool. She took the other and pulled a small digital tablet out of her blazer pocket. Or maybe it was a big phone. I couldn't tell.

"Are you working with Lincoln?" I asked.

"Yes. I understand you sat with former Chief Gifford in front of the bookstore on Saturday. What time was that, Mac?"

"I think it was pretty close to eleven thirty. The pub across the street was already open, although they might have opened early for the parade goers."

"The Rusty Anchor?"

"Yes."

She tapped into her device, then glanced up. "How did Chief Gifford seem?"

"What do you mean, how did he seem?"

"Was he nervous? Antsy? Relaxed?"

"Wait a minute," I said. "You can't think Norland killed Wagner!"

"What we think is irrelevant." Penelope was no longer smiling. "We are simply gathering information at this time. I believe you're familiar with investigative methods by now. If you could answer the question, please?"

I let out a breath. "He was relaxed. Happily handing out Book Nook pencils to passersby. Not nervous in the least." She'd better be satisfied with my answer, because it was the truth.

"I understand you also witnessed conflict between Zane King and the deceased." She scrolled on the tablet. "On Thursday?"

"Yes, but it was minor, really. I already told Lincoln what went on."

She gave a single nod. "What about the altercation between Yvonne Flora and Lavoie? When did it happen, what exactly was it about, and how did they leave it?"

"Have you asked her?"

Penelope didn't speak as she waited for me to answer. Yeah, no. She wasn't going to tell me.

"Wagner was pressuring Yvonne to hand out freebies. Like he did all the merchants, by the way."

"So noted."

"She said she wasn't going to. As I told Lincoln, Wagner asked her if she'd be at the organizing meeting. She said no. She'd be right there in the kitchen cooking."

"And he didn't like her response."

I shook my head. "He didn't like any of it. Neither did she."

"Was it a peaceable disagreement?"

"No, not at all. When I walked in, she had a sharp knife pointed at him."

The detective's dark eyebrows flew up.

"In her defense, she'd been chopping mushrooms," I said. "But, really, they both seemed more upset than they should have been."

"How well do you know Ms. Flora?"

"Not well, although I like her. She and her partner own a tandem bike, and Yvonne has brought it into the shop a couple of times."

Penelope swiped at the tablet. "Has your friend Gin Malloy spoken with you about her own disagreement with the deceased?"

"Yes, and it was nothing. She told me Wagner wanted her to conduct her business differently, and she refused." I lifted my chin. Gin had spoken with Lincoln about her fight. "I wasn't there. I didn't witness it. I can't corroborate or contradict what she said. And, before you ask, my husband didn't hear what they were saying."

"Got it." Penelope gave me a look. "You know we're only trying to discover the truth, Mac. You don't need to get your back up."

"Gin Malloy is my best friend." I folded my arms. "She doesn't even swat mosquitoes. There's no way she killed Wagner Lavoie."

She consulted the device once more. "I understand you have a Sandy McKean on payroll. May I speak with her please?"

"She seems to be running late today."

"You said you were alone here except for your mechanic, who I understand is Sandy's sister."

I nodded without speaking. Orlean would very much not want to sit down for a cozy chat with Penelope.

"Was Sandy McKean working on Saturday?" the detective asked.

"Yes."

"All day?"

"Look, I don't know what's up with Sandy."

"Mac, please answer the question."

I shifted on my stool, unhappy to rat out my newest employee. "Sandy was here in the morning. When I got back after the parade—well, after Norland found Wagner—Sandy was gone. She didn't answer my text and still hasn't."

"When did she leave the shop?" Penelope asked.

I gave a quick glance toward the repair area. "I don't know. I kind of thought I saw her on a bike at the end of the parade, but I can't be sure." Orlean was going to hate me for this, but I had to answer the detective's questions.

The outer door began to open. *Whew.* Saved by a customer. Except . . . it wasn't someone looking for new bike shoes or a tire repair.

"Good morning, Sandy. I'm glad to see you." I stood, ignoring Penelope stirring next to me.

Sandy froze. Her eyes cast around like a trapped wild animal's, as if searching for escape. She started to turn away.

Penelope covered the ground to the door in a flash. "Detective Sergeant Johnson, Ms. McKean. I'm with the Westham Police Department. I'd like a word with you, if you don't mind." She slid herself between Sandy and the door.

"Do I have to?" Sandy bit off the words. Her face looked more lined than usual, and the corners of her mouth pulled down as if in anger.

"No." Penelope put on a perfunctory smile. "But otherwise we'll have to ask you to come down to the station for a formal interview."

Sandy's shoulders slumped as the verve seemed to drain out of her. I caught Orlean watching silently from the repair area, tire tool in hand.

"Okay. I'll talk here." Her voice low, barely above a whisper, Sandy gave Penelope a defeated look.

CHAPTER 17

Penelope Johnson emerged from my office, which I'd let her occupy to speak with Sandy, by ten fifteen. The detective thanked me, snugged her scarf around her neck, and made her way through the door with a brisk stride.

I waited for a moment to see if Sandy would follow her out. When she didn't, I headed into the office, leaving the door open so I could hear if a customer entered the store.

Sandy sat with her elbows on her knees and her head in her hands. I took the chair behind the desk. Again I waited, hoping she would offer an explanation. After a full minute, I opened my mouth to speak.

She straightened, palms on thighs, and cleared her throat. "I'm sorry, Mac. For deserting you here.

For not letting you know where I was. For you having to put up with a cop like her. For, well, whatever. I'm ready to work." Sandy did not look good. The skin under her eyes sagged, and the lines around her mouth seemed deeper. She'd pulled her hair back in a barrette, but limp strands had escaped and hung by her ears.

"Thank you." I thought quickly about what to say. Did I want to keep her on the payroll? I wasn't sure. But I felt I owed it to Orlean to give her sister one more chance. "I took you on because we were short-staffed, and because I respect Orlean. But I run a business, Sandy. I expect my employees to be here on time. I need them to be ready and able to do the work for the full shift. Where did you go on Saturday?"

She pressed her eyes shut. She took a long inhale and an equally long exhale, then opened her eyes. "I can't tell you."

"You can't, or you won't?" I hadn't noticed before what perfect teeth she had. They were straight and white and not worn down. And they contrasted sharply with the rest of her appearance.

"I can't tell you. But I didn't kill Wag."

Wag. "Where did you know him from?"

She only shook her head. "What I can say is, I'm ready and able to work for you. For the full shift, or what's left of it."

The outer door opened again. I leaned out of the office to see four fit twenty-somethings suited up in bike pants and windbreaker jackets. Following closely were a white middle-aged couple, with her arm tucked through his. After them bustled in my grandmother, bright-eyed as always, wearing her rainbow-striped Rasta hat and her pink tracksuit. Good. She hadn't gotten around to telling me last night what she knew about Wagner, and I was dying to know.

"All right." I couldn't deny I needed Sandy, at least for now. "You can work. Today. We'll need to talk more later, though."

She nodded. "Thank you, Mac." She tucked the stray hair behind her ears, rose, and headed out.

Had I made the right decision? I had no idea. I followed her into the retail area. As I passed Orlean, she muttered something.

I slowed. "I'm sorry, I missed what you said."

"Thank you," she repeated.

I nodded and kept going. "Hang on a minute, okay, Abo Ree?" I asked Reba.

"I have a while." She beamed up at me. "You go on ahead, hon." She set her huge bag behind the counter. She headed to the retail shelves and began straightening bike shirts, refolding a few suffering from being browsed through by customers and left less than tidy.

She was a woman after my own heart. Or, more accurately, I might have inherited my neat-freak genes from her. I shot Sandy a glance, but she seemed to be capably assisting the foursome with details about our rental policy.

I made my way to the couple. "I'm Mac. How can I help you today?"

"We just love your sweet town, Mac, don't we, Freddy?" she gushed in a lilting Southern accent. She continued, not giving him a chance to respond. "Your parade Saturday, with all the adorable little children, and the spring festival, was such a mood-lifter, especially with the snow you got later on."

"We lucked out on the morning weather, for sure." I smiled at her enthusiasm.

Her husband frowned. "We heard a man died in one of the stores on Saturday. A terrible tragedy."

"Yes, it was very sad," I agreed. At least he hadn't referred to it as murder.

Reba finished her tidying and perched on one of the stools behind the counter. She pulled out her phone and began poking at it.

"So, anyhoo," the woman went on. "Our grand-babies back in South Carolina are teenagers now, and they're *so* into cycling. We wanted to bring them a souvenir from your darling shop."

I ended up selling them three store-branded shirts and a map of the biking trails on Cape Cod. "Come back when it's warmer, and rent bikes." I handed her the handled paper bag.

"Bless your heart, hon." The woman laughed. "I'm no teenager. I would fall off the dang thing in a minute."

"Mac can rent you an adult trike," Reba piped up. "I ride mine every day. Or a tandem, if your man there is willing. All you have to do is pedal along in back."

"Why, thank you so much, ma'am." The customer beamed at Reba. "The tricycle sounds like just the ticket."

"My grandgirl, here," Reba continued. "She's fully equipped to help any customer's needs."

The woman's cheery demeanor slipped. She gazed from my tiny grandmother's dark skin to my mixed and frankly light complexion, which looked more Mediterranean than African. The South Carolinian gave herself a little shake.

"I'm sure she is. Thank you so very much, Mac. Have a great day, ma'am." She took her husband's arm again and steered him out the door.

"I shook up her tidy little snow globe of a world a bit, didn't I, then?" Reba said in a thoughtful tone.

"You did. I could almost hear her thinking, "Wait. What?"

"Maybe she thought I was the cleaning lady." Abo Reba tossed her head, wearing a bemused smile.

She—a decades-long and award-winning high school English teacher—didn't need some Southern woman's approval.

"Abo Ree, yesterday at dinner you said you wanted to tell me something about Wagner Lavoie." I kept my voice low. "I assume that's why you came in this morning, or one reason."

"Yes, indeedy. There's someone I'd like you to meet. I think we should—"

She was interrupted by the door opening to a dark-haired woman who ushered in nearly a dozen other women excitedly conversing in another language, complete with hands flying. I knew only a smattering of Spanish, but it was enough to pick out a few words in the language, and these folks sounded like they were from Spain and not Latin America. The woman who'd opened the door headed for where I stood behind the counter. The others began touching the new bikes for sale, fingering the retail items, pointing to the framed photographs and maps of the Cape hanging on the available wall space.

"Sorry, Abo Ree," I murmured. "Work calls."

"And I have to get myself off to aqua aerobics. But you and me? We need to take a little drive together. Later today, maybe?"

"Where to?"

"Just out to the cottage where Wagner's been staying. The neighbor is a friend of mine."

"I'll text you," I said, even as I smiled at the Spanish newcomer. I welcomed her as I watched Reba make her way out. As I wondered who Reba knew next door to Wagner's cottage.

CHAPTER 18

The morning rush of customers had slowed to a trickle by one o'clock. Sandy was still on the job. After her lunch break, I set her to work unpacking a couple of boxes of merchandise UPS had just delivered. After Orlean came back from her own lunch, I sat on one of the stools and popped in the last bite of my workday ham-and-cheese sandwich—Dijon mustard on one piece of bread, mayo on the other—which never varied. I saw no reason to shake up a good routine.

I'd always had a good appetite and a high metabolism, another handy gene inherited from Abo Reba. I glanced at my phone, but she hadn't texted me about this mystery neighbor she wanted to go visit. I checked the group thread, but nobody had posted anything since my text last night about speaking with

Kassandra. I supposed I could add a quick update outlining my visit from the detective.

Det Johnson stopped by this AM. Asked questions. Sandy finally surfaced. Johnson questioned her in my office. S won't tell me where she went Sat, claims she didn't kill Wagner, whom she called Wag. Some history there.

Norland almost immediately wrote back. **Johnson questioned me too. Hard to know what's happening. Anybody seen Haskins?**

Interesting. Lincoln was usually in the lead on this kind of case. I wrote back. **Not in person since Saturday PM.**

Zane popped into the thread. **Park Jenkins came by lobbying for K as next director. Too soon.**

Seriously? I added a reply. **Poor taste, much?**

No kidding.

I had my thumbs poised to respond more to Zane when the door opened to a gust of fresh air. Park Jenkins let it shut behind him. I tapped out a quick message.

Park's here. Making the rounds?

I sent the text and stuffed my phone in my back pocket. I'd met him only once, when I'd stopped into Tim's bakery and Park was there buying coffee and pastries.

"Good morning, Park." I didn't see any evidence he'd ridden a bicycle here. "Can I help you find a new bike, or do you have one outside you need work done on?"

"Me? Ride a bike?" He barked out a laugh. "No. Do I look like a bicyclist?"

In fact, he didn't. He had a soft body, thin dark

hair, and ruddy cheeks that might have come from alcohol, not fresh air. Plus he wore nice slacks and a sweater over a collared shirt and necktie. Not exactly biking togs.

"Anyone can ride." I lifted a shoulder and smiled, waiting. What did he want?

"As head of the select committee, I think it's important a new Chamber of Commerce director be hired with all due dispatch." He lifted his chin.

"Oh?" I pretended Zane hadn't given me the heads-up. "But the Chamber isn't a town department, and it's a private organization. What's the rush?" And why hadn't Park expressed any sympathy, even if superficial, about Wagner's death?

"Westham relies on its businesses thriving and attracting both tourists and new residents." Park's spiel was smooth, as if he'd practiced it. Which he probably had. "For Main Street to thrive, we need a vital Chamber with a competent leader. I assume you are a member."

"I pay my dues every year. But I don't serve on the board of directors, as you must know."

"Yes, I'm aware." He clasped his hands in front of his protruding stomach. "I've heard from a business owner all the members have a chance to offer input on potential new hires."

"We'll see. It's terribly sad there is an opening at all, don't you think? I feel terrible for Wagner's family."

"Yes, yes. Of course. We all do."

I waited. Would he really have the chutzpah to lobby for his own daughter being hired as the replacement?

Derrick hurried in, unfastening his bike helmet. "Hey, Mac." He was right on time for his afternoon shift.

"Derrick, have you met Park Jenkins, our head selectperson?" I asked. "Park, this is my brother, Derrick Searle."

The men said hello and shook hands. Derrick bent down to free his right pants leg from the clip keeping it out of the bike's chain.

Park squared his shoulders. "If you think Kassandra would be a good fit to fill Lavoie's shoes, I know she would appreciate your support with the board, Mac."

"Thank you." I left it at that. No smile. No commitment.

Park said goodbye and made his way out. I couldn't decide if it was with a scurrying waddle or a waddling scurry. I did feel like I needed a shower.

"What was that all about?" Derrick asked, looking from the door to me.

"Just a little veiled pressure from a coldhearted town official to slide his daughter into a noncritical job that's been empty for all of forty-eight hours." I let out a breath. "And not a speck of emotion about Wagner's passing."

"Am I ever glad I'm not involved in politics, local or otherwise." Derrick shook his head.

I wasn't sure if this was politics or something more sinister.

CHAPTER 19

After my grandma called, reiterating we had to go for a drive, I convinced Derrick to close the shop for me at five, our winter hours. I speed-walked home at four thirty and fired up Miss M, my red Miata convertible. She'd been my one big indulgence after I moved back to Westham. I lived a simple life and felt justified in a splurge. Plus, nothing was more fun to drive, especially with the top down.

But driving with fresh air ruffling my hair was for weather much warmer than today's. From the look of the clouds, I'd say we had rain coming later tonight.

Abo Reba was waiting at the curb in front of her Main Street apartment. She slid in and pulled the door shut, then buckled up and let out a contented sigh.

"You have the best wheels in town, you know that, Mackie?"

I laughed. "I know. Now, where to, and who are we visiting?" I idled in place.

"I thought we might call on my friend Helene Fadiman. As I said, she lives next door to the Lavoie cottage."

"Sounds good. How do I get there?"

Abo Reba directed me north, heading out of town. A quarter mile before the Westham town limits, she told me to take a left onto Salt Marsh Road. We cruised maybe a quarter of a mile down.

"There." She pointed a knobby finger. "Helene's is the blue Cape. Lavoie's is the cottage beyond."

"Did you call her? Is she going to be home?"

"Helene doesn't go much of anywhere. But yes, she's to home."

I pulled into the driveway of the tidy blue cottage. It had white shutters and window boxes sprouting red and yellow plastic tulips and daffodils. Helene must be dreaming of spring, too.

Reba rang the doorbell as I gazed at the house next door. Also a Cape, it wasn't so tidy nor in such good repair. Some of its naturally silvered cedar shingles, a classic near the coast where salt air wreaked havoc on house paint, were curled or missing. The front walk had buckled, and the shrubs in front of the windows were scraggly and overgrown. Maybe the family only paid attention to the cottage during the warmer months when they vacationed here.

A striking-looking woman opened the door. She had a deeply lined face indicating her age was near Reba's, but she was at least as tall as I. If she'd lost height with aging, she must have started out quite tall. Her silver-streaked hair, pulled back in a bun, was still mostly black. Intense green eyes focused on me over an aquiline nose. Her face became a ray of sunshine when she gazed down at Reba.

"Reba, dear." Helene's voice was low-pitched. "I'm glad you came by. And this must be Mackenzie. Please come in, girls." She led the way, walking with a lopsided gait, as if one leg was longer than the other, her hip-length purple tunic hitching over the higher hip as she went. We ended up in an airy, light-filled room at the back, which looked out over the eponymous salt marsh. Several framed movie posters hung in the spaces between the large windows.

We sat and got a few pleasantries out of the way. When Helene offered us a glass of sherry, neither Reba nor I refused.

"Cheers." Helene raised her small glass. "Now, what's on your mind, you two Almeidas?"

"I suppose you've learned about the unfortunate demise of your neighbor," Reba began.

"Of course, and I heard his death was purposeful. Murder. Poor Wagner. I've known him since he was a boy in short pants."

"It's very sad," I said. "Reba says the house next door is his family's summer home."

"I suppose you could call it such." Helene tilted her head. "The Lavoies lived there year-round until Wagner married. His mother died a few years later, and the life just went out of his father. He moved up to Belleville with Wagner and his wife, but he didn't last long. Wagner has only the one sister, who lives in Bourne, and he hasn't spent much time in Westham until recently."

The one sister must be Faye, the one who'd insisted she could park in my lot before the parade.

"Did Mr. Lavoie have children?" Reba asked.

"Yes, one child," Helene said. "But Belinda and their daughter didn't move down here with him. I suspect she and Wagner might have been estranged."

"What about recent visitors?" I took a sip of the very smooth, dry sherry. "Did Wagner have people coming to see him?"

Helene regarded me without blinking. "Your grandmother has told me you are a kind of amateur sleuth, Mackenzie. Is that right?"

"Well, a little. I mean, when someone I know personally is looked at suspiciously for a crime, I've tried in the past to sort out the truth."

"Who is it with this one?" Helene raised elegantly shaped eyebrows.

I swallowed. "I'm not sure it matters." I didn't want to entertain the thought of Zane or Yvonne being a killer. Or even Sandy, although I knew her much less well. I certainly didn't want to mention those names to Reba's friend.

"Very well," the tall woman acknowledged. "I suppose I should answer your question. I see everything that goes on on the street. A bit like my friend Reba, here." Helene frowned at her glass. "The thing is, my granddaughter stopped by to see Wagner more than once in the last two weeks."

"Oh? How did she know him?" I asked.

"You didn't tell her?" Helene asked Reba.

My grandmother blushed and shook her head.

From the front of the house came the sound of the outer door opening. "Nana?" a man's voice called.

"Back here, darling," Helene said.

August Jenkins appeared in the doorway, bike helmet in one hand and a pannier in the other. He moved toward Helene and kissed her forehead.

"Hey, Mac." He straightened and smiled. "Mrs. Almeida."

I must have been gaping. I shut my mouth.

"It appears you both know my grandson, August," Helene said to us, then addressed him. "Sit down, sweetheart."

"I brought you the new streaming device I ordered," he said. "I figured you'd want me to set it up for you." He headed for the large-screen television in the corner and pulled a box out of the modern version of a saddlebag.

"Thank you. Of course I do." Helene gave me a look. "I expect you now know who my granddaughter is."

"Kassandra," I murmured.

"The same." Helene nodded. "She and August are my daughter's splendid children."

Huh. No mention of Park. Maybe the parents were divorced. Or maybe Helene didn't like her son-in-law.

August looked over. "Why are you talking about Kassie?"

Helene waited. I wasn't going to tell him. I waited, too. Reba kept her mouth shut.

"I'll tell you later, dear," Helene said.

Reba drained her glass and stood. "Lovely to see you again, my friend." She smiled at Helene. "Catch you in the pool tomorrow?"

"I wouldn't miss it. Very nice to meet you at last, Mackenzie. I've never been into your shop. Bicycling is not something I do."

"It was my pleasure, Helene, and thank you for the sherry." I stood, too, leaving my glass half full.

Helene stayed seated. "Pardon me if I don't get up. Augie, see these ladies out, would you, please?"

"Sure, Nana." He walked us to the door. "Drive safely home. We're getting a pretty big storm later, but at least this one will be rain, not snow."

"I promise." I steered Reba to the car, with the wind threatening to blow my wisp of a grandmother out to sea. Once in the car, I faced her. "You knew Kassandra was her granddaughter."

"As a matter of fact, I did. What I didn't know was that she'd been stalking Wagner Lavoie."

"Stalking is a strong word."

"Maybe. The girl wanted his job, no two ways about it." She frowned out the window as I started driving. "I only pray she didn't kill the man."

CHAPTER 20

Tim and I sat finishing a delicious dinner of curried shrimp and veggies on rice. He'd whipped it up out of nowhere, or that was how it seemed to me when I arrived home after dropping off Abo Reba.

"Mmm." I swallowed my last bite. "So good, Tim. I seriously don't understand how you do it."

He laughed. "Oh, you know." He waved his hand generally in the direction of the stove.

"I don't, actually."

"We had a pound of frozen raw shrimp. We always have spices in the drawer, onions and garlic in the basket, ginger and carrots in the crisper, snap peas in the freezer, plus rice in the pantry. And we happened to have a can of coconut milk in the pantry. Voilà—dinner."

"I can't even." And I couldn't. Presented with all those things in the house, it would never occur to me to combine them. I would be calling for pizza delivery, instead. Was it a lack of imagination on my part? It didn't matter. Tim was an inventive cook who seemed more than willing to keep feeding me. "But I happily eat what you create with a wave of your magic wand. Thank you."

"My pleasure. So, where did you go off to in the car?"

I told him about my excursion with Reba. I didn't feel like talking about murder at the moment, so I omitted the part about Kassandra having visited Wagner at his cottage.

"It turns out Helene is the grandmother of Kassandra and Officer August Jenkins," I said. "She's a really striking woman. Do you know her?"

From the other room, Belle muttered in an exact reproduction of my voice and intonation, "Do you know her? Do you know her?"

"She sometimes comes in for coffee with Reba, after their swim class," Tim said.

"Aqua aerobics, I think Reba calls it."

"Right. Helene always buys a baguette to take home. And I agree. She's quite handsome, although I don't know why she limps."

"I asked Abo Ree the reason on our way home. She said Helene had polio as a child." Which was why she didn't ride a bike, I supposed.

Tim shook his head in sympathy. "Before the vaccine was available."

"Yes. Reba has talked about how, when the polio vaccination campaign was on, every single person got one, happily, eagerly."

"Because it was a matter of public health and the only way to stop the disease."

"Exactly. Everyone wanted to help the common good." I sighed, thinking about the last few years. "My grandpa had a brother who needed to sleep in an iron lung because of polio, and he died in his forties."

"Helene is lucky to be alive. Did you know she's a well-known filmmaker?"

I stared. "She is?"

"Absolutely." He reeled off the names of a couple of movies I'd heard of but not seen.

"Wow. I saw framed movie posters on the walls. I just thought she was a cinema buff."

"I can—" He broke off when his phone buzzed from the counter. He leaned over to grab it and looked at it, frowning. He thumbed a text, then glanced up. "I'm sorry, sweetheart. I have to head back to work."

"I'm sorry, sweetheart," Belle echoed Tim's deep voice. "I'm sorry, sweetheart." She ended with the wolf whistle she always associated with him.

I ignored her. "Is something wrong at the bakery?"

"We had a problem with one of the ovens today. I put in an urgent call to the repair guy hours ago. He only now got back to me, and he's willing to meet me there."

I glanced at the wall clock. It wasn't yet seven. "And you need the oven for tomorrow."

"We do. We have more than one, but we use all of them, every day." He stood and came around to kiss me. "I'll try not to be late. You should be able to find Helene's movies to watch, if you want. Streaming, or even online from the library. That was what I was going to suggest we do."

"Go on. I'll clean up, and maybe I'll take a look at one of them." I watched as he took our plates to the sink. "A raincoat might be good. I don't know when the storm is going to start."

"Good idea. I'm going to drive, too."

The house was within walking or biking distance to our Main Street businesses, but at night with a storm coming? Taking his older-model Volvo station wagon was the best plan.

Before I relaxed, I made the kitchen sparkling clean, with everything in its place, just how I liked it. I put Belle to bed, too, with her cage covered. I took out my contacts and donned my extra-thick glasses, then settled in on the couch with a second glass of wine and my phone. I wanted to update the group on what I'd learned and see if anyone else had shared information while I'd been otherwise occupied. Maybe then I'd look for a movie.

Zane had been able to talk with Park, ostensibly about real estate.

Park was a broken record, harping on how the Chamber needs to fill the director position. Insisted Kassandra would be best for the job.

Gin had written, too. **Asked Uly to stop by my shop if he had a chance. He did. Said he overhead something in rest. kitchen about Yvonne and Wagner.**

Interesting. Next was a message from Tulia. **Bro said Sandy came from Belleville. Saw her and Lavoie at vets' picnic there. Tension between them. He'll dig more.**

I tapped back. **Wagner lived in Belleville w/wife and kids. I met Helene Fadiman today. Grandma to August and Kassandra. Said Kassandra had been around Wagner's cottage lately—next door to Helene's.**

A new message pinged in from Zane. **Stephen reminds me special town meeting tomorrow pm. Group dinner at Rusty Anchor beforehand?**

I'd forgotten about the spring town meeting, where mid-year budget items were brought before the town. But dinner sounded good. I thumbed a response. **I'm in for dinner. We can walk from there.**

Zane added the time. **See you at six. I'll save a table.**

Derrick added a note. **Have to bow out of all this. Classes are busting my butt, plus Cokey. Will try to rejoin later in spring.**

I sent him a private message. **No worries, Derr. Do what you need to. Love you. Give my girl a goodnight smooch from Titi Mac.**

The group messages trailed off. *Huh.* Norland hadn't contributed. I hoped he was all right. I sent a quick message to him, but nothing came back. He spent a lot of time with his beloved grandkids, who lived locally. He was probably busy with one or more of them.

Did I want to search out one of Helene's films? Maybe later. Right now my brain was too full of this case to want to escape into something fictional, even a cozy mystery.

I grabbed my iPad from the coffee table and folded open the keypad, which made any considerable typing much easier to accomplish. Searching for background on one or more of the persons of interest seemed more urgent than watching a movie.

I started with Sandy. She was my employee—for the time being—and I should have done a background check on her before I'd hired her on. Instead, I'd accepted Orlean's vouching for her sister.

Sandra Brown McKean got me hits only for Sandy Brown McKean. Interesting. She'd filled out employee forms, but maybe I hadn't paid attention to Sandy being her legal name.

Sandy, as it turned out, was a US Army veteran, as Tulia said. She'd earned an undergraduate degree in biology. Most recently, it appeared she'd owned a house in Belleville and worked at a medical lab in Providence, Rhode Island. I dug into the address of the house, which she co-owned with a Lyle McKean. The couple still seemed to own it. But I didn't see any mention of divorce papers being filed.

I sat back. Something had caused Sandy to leave her job, her marriage, and her home. What had it been? Could it have involved Wagner? I searched for their names together, but no link appeared.

Next I hunted down Park Jenkins. Zane had said Park lived near him and sold real estate. I'd been to a Hanukkah party in December at Zane and Stephen's. It was outside of town a little, but in the opposite direction from where Helene lived. The book group didn't usually meet there, since it was farther than where anyone else lived. But it was a nice area. Park must've earned a tidy income from his home sales to afford that part of Westham.

I found his campaign site from when he ran for selectperson four years ago. One of the photographs showed him with Kassandra and August, but no wife was included. Instead of hunting down another set of divorce records, I sent a text to my grandma. She could find out the status of the marriage from Helene tomorrow.

See if you can ask Helene about status of her daughter's marriage to Park. I'm curious. Thx. Love you.

She texted back in less than a minute. **Will do. XXOO**

I smiled. Who knew eighty-something grandmothers would be texting maniacs? A wide yawn overtook me. I felt my eyes drifting shut, and I let them, tucking my feet up under me. I'd had a full day. A little couch snooze wouldn't hurt my night's sleep. Although I'd had one more person I'd wanted to research. Who was it?

I startled awake from a dream involving a black-clad figure in black-rimmed glasses creeping around the back of a small house.

A mighty crack sounded. *What?*

CHAPTER 21

I sat up straight, my heart thudding. What had that sound been? Was it a gunshot? Had someone broken a window? I cast a quick glance left and right. I didn't hear anything else. Now I was wide-awake and on full alert, with the dark figure from my dream lurking at the edges of my consciousness.

After investigating a previous homicide in Westham as a clumsy amateur, I'd been attacked in my own home. This time I hadn't been poking around at all. Or, hardly. Nobody would be after me for getting too close to them, at least not yet. The facts of the case were still as murky as my dream.

A deep rolling rumble started, followed by another crack. I let out a breath, shaking my head at how clueless I'd been. Rain began to beat at the windows on the west side. The predicted storm had arrived. Rain I'd warned Tim about. Silly me. I'd let my nerves take over for my common sense, which was never a wise plan.

My heart rate back to normal, I remembered I'd wanted to pursue one more idea online. I just couldn't think of what it was.

I ticked off the possibilities. I'd hit a dead end with Sandy. Reba was going to ask Helene tomorrow about the Jenkinses' offspring's mother. Yvonne had had a beef with Wagner, but arguing didn't mean she'd murdered him. I'd been assigned Kassandra, so I could dig further into her past.

But what about her father? Zane's conversation with him hadn't yielded anything useful. I mounted a search on Park Jenkins, learning right off the bat his legal name was Parkhurst. Well, la-di-dah. The name conjured up images of wealth, but why? Look at me. I had a family surname as my given name, albeit a Scottish one, not the British-sounding moniker Parkhurst.

So, did he come from money or not? It turned out he was Parkhurst Albert Jenkins, the third. *Gah.* How pretentious could you get? I scolded myself for these trite feelings. It wasn't Park's fault what his parents named him.

Park did seem to be a successful real estate agent. He'd sold several coastal homes valued at well over a million dollars in the last couple of years. He looked like he was in his fifties, and he must have lived in Westham for a while. I knew August had attended Westham High, even if Kassandra hadn't. But had Park grown up in town?

As I kept searching, my eyes widened. His unique name made it easy to find him. And what I found was one more connection to the small historic farming community to the northwest of Cape Cod. Parkhurst Albert Jenkins III had graduated from Belleville High School.

Wow. This was turning into quite a web. Now I wondered if his wife had lived there, too. Or ex-wife? That information had to wait for tomorrow, since I didn't even know her first name. I thought I might have to take a drive tomorrow or sometime soon.

I checked the weather forecast on my phone. The storm was slowing and circling. My buddy and I would not be walking in the morning. I texted Gin.

Rain is sticking around, so no walking in AM. After it clears, tomorrow or Weds, want to take a drive to Belleville with me late afternoon? #homicideresearch

She pinged back promptly. **Roger. Am on for #homicideresearch**

I smiled. I was so lucky to have made friends with her after I'd moved back to my hometown. We seemed to always be on the same wavelength. She'd been my only wedding attendant and had kept me on an even keel. I'd helped clear her name of murder and prodded her to keep walking with me.

Yawning, I switched off the iPad. With any luck, Lincoln and Penelope were making more progress than the Cozy Capers were, as was only appropriate.

I found one of Helene's movies and set it to play while I waited for my husband to come home safely.

CHAPTER 22

After I entered my shop the next morning at eight thirty, I shook the rain off my rain jacket. The brunt of the storm had passed, but clouds the color of a slate roof still sat low and heavy, leaking their drizzle as I walked. I'd barely hung up the hooded jacket when the door opened behind me. I whirled, shoulders tense, eyes wide. Nobody brought a bike in for repair early on a rainy Tuesday. I didn't expect Orlean and Sandy for another hour. Who—?

Aha. I relaxed at the sight of Lincoln Haskins. "Good morning, Detective. You surprised me." I smiled my relief.

"Sorry. Can we talk?" He did not smile.

"Sure. Let me put on a pot of coffee, okay?"

He nodded.

"Um, have a seat?" I gestured at the stools behind

the counter. “Hang up your coat if you want. I’m in no rush to fly the Open flag.”

Lincoln shifted, as if considering the offer. “All right.” He shed his own raincoat and sat after hanging it on a hook by the door.

“Cream, no sugar, right?”

He nodded. He kept his silence while the small pot dripped. So did I, puttering, getting started on the opening checklist while the coffee brewed.

A few minutes later I perched on the stool next to him, each of us grasping full mugs.

“What’s up?” I asked him.

He almost inhaled the coffee but stayed silent.

I peered at him, filled with sudden dread. “Lincoln, is my family all right? Please tell me something terrible didn’t happen.” I set my mug down so hard it sloshed onto the counter.

“What?” He gave me a frowny-smile, as if I’d said something ridiculous. “No, Mac, they’re fine, as far as I know. That’s not why I’m here.”

I let out a breath. “Good. So, what’s up?” I repeated.

“What do you know about June Jenkins?”

“Nothing. I don’t even know who June is. But Jenkins is Park’s last name, and his children’s. Is June his wife?”

“Ex-wife.”

“Helene Fadiman’s daughter.”

“Yes. How do you know her?” he asked.

“My grandmother introduced us yesterday.”

“Seriously?” His heavy eyebrows rose.

“Yes. Why?” I sipped my rich dark brew and snugged my scarf closer around my neck. Heat from the electric registers, which were on a timer, finally began to rise, but the damp cold seemed to penetrate everywhere.

"I suppose you already know Ms. Fadiman lives next door to the Lavoie cottage, as people around here refer to it."

"I do. Reba took me there to meet Helene. Wagner's house looks pretty run-down, unlike Helene's. What I didn't know when I went is that she's August and Kassandra's grandmother."

"Right." He frowned as he sipped his own coffee.

"After something Helene said, I wondered if her daughter was divorced from Park." I still wanted to know what news Lincoln had come with. Had something happened to June? Did she even live in Westham? For some reason, Lincoln was sitting on whatever brought him here. I didn't feel like asking a third time.

It was his turn to exhale through his lips. But he still didn't speak.

"Do August and Kassandra live with June or with their father?" I asked. "Or do they have their own places?" August was in his late twenties, and Kassandra in her early thirties, both of them well old enough to have an apartment or be married. With expenses the way they were, though, I knew adults who still lived with parents to save money for things like a down payment on a house or repaying student loans.

"I stopped by because we can't locate June or Kassandra."

"Oh?"

He nodded. "If you have any clue where they might be, I need to know. We would like to speak with both of them."

"Kassandra was working in the Toy Soldier on Sunday afternoon. She seemed perfectly normal. But I don't know where she lives. And I obviously don't know a thing about her mom."

"Unfortunate," Lincoln said.

"Have you asked Helene? Or August?"

"Ms. Fadiman is not interested in speaking with us at this time. We can't search her place without a warrant, for which we lack justification as yet. And Officer Jenkins seems honestly in the dark."

"What about Park?" I asked.

"All he'll say is Kassandra is staying with her mother."

"In Westham?"

"No, but close. June lives in a cabin on a pond in Mashpee."

"And I gather you can't find either woman there."

"We cannot." He finished his coffee and stood.

"Wait a second. I want to make sure you know about some connections I uncovered last night." At his glower, I hurried to add, "Online, Lincoln. I only did some internet searching. Nothing risky."

"Sorry, Mac." He rubbed his forehead. "This case is already getting to me. What do you have?'

I outlined the Belleville connections I'd discovered. Sandy, Wagner, Park.

"We're aware of Lavoie's residence in Belleville," Haskins said.

"Was there something up between him and his wife? She didn't come to Westham with him."

"I'm not sure."

"Sandy and Wagner are both veterans. Tulia's brother saw them at a veterans' picnic up there and said they weren't getting along."

He nodded slowly. "I know her brother."

Of course, he would. Lincoln was half Wampanoag, himself.

"And Park is from Belleville, too," I said. "I assume you know his full name?"

"Parkhurst Albert Jenkins the third." He did a little eye roll.

"Yes."

"Was there anything else?" Lincoln slipped on his coat. "I need to get going."

"No, I don't think so."

He had his hand on the door when he turned. "Thanks for the coffee. What time does Ms. McKean come in?"

"She's supposed to be here at nine thirty."

"Thank you. Please let me know if she doesn't appear."

"I will." She'd be in trouble with both of us if she didn't show up for work.

"I don't have to remind you to stay out of trouble, Mac. Correct?"

"Aye-aye, Captain."

He shook his head as he left.

I sat sipping and thinking. He never did say why he was looking for June. Maybe it was only as a way to find Kassandra. June lived in Mashpee. Did her address mean she was a member of the same tribe? Not everyone who lived in the town was Wampanoag, but the tribe's reservation and cultural center was there. I could ask Tulia about June later today. I drained my mug. Right now I had a business to run.

CHAPTER 23

By ten thirty, the shop was bustling. The drizzle seemed to have stopped. The latest customers to come in didn't hold umbrellas they needed to furl or have their hoods up. Orlean had come in an hour earlier at the same time as Sandy, both of them as scheduled. If things got quiet, I intended to ask Sandy how she'd known Wagner, but only if I could get her alone for a few minutes.

A man who'd just purchased a tube kit held the door open for a newcomer in a purple jacket and a pink ball cap with a dark ponytail threaded through the back. She thanked him and turned toward me. *Perfect.*

"Good morning, Kassandra," I said. "Did you bring your bike?"

"Yes. Can you help me get it out of the back of my car? It was kind of a tight fit."

"Sure. Has the rain stopped?" I'd slipped on a store-brand fleece hoodie this morning. I'd be fine outdoors without a coat as long as the precipitation had ended.

"Yes."

Kassandra held the door for me, and I followed her to a new-looking hybrid sedan. She'd laid the back seats flat, but she was right. The bike was wedged in with a handlebar hung up on a seat belt. We managed to extricate it. I held the bike, an older around-town kind of ride, while she shut the car doors and hatchback. As she did, I noticed for the first time how fit she looked, with strong arms and tight abs.

"Yep, it's pretty flat." I squeezed the front tire. The rubber was cracked, and it was as dusty as the rest of the bike. "When's the last time you rode it?"

"I don't know. Like, ten years ago? I used to run, but an injury put running out of the picture for now."

"We can tune it up, if you'd like. Oil and tighten and fix what needs fixing."

She wrinkled her nose. "How much will fixing it cost?"

Huh. She was concerned about the expense, but she drove a car like this? Maybe it had been a gift from Daddy after a luxury home sale. She couldn't make much at the toy store.

"I can have my mechanic look it over and give you a quote. We'll certainly fix the flat for you, but even that might require a new tire. This one is in pretty bad shape." I peered at the back wheel, which didn't look any better. The whole bike looked pretty beat-up. "You might need two."

"Okay. I kind of need the bike to get around."

I must have shifted my gaze to the vehicle.

"This is my father's car." She gave a nervous laugh. "I borrowed it."

"Is your mom working at the Toy Soldier today?"

"What?" Kassandra narrowed her eyes. "Why do you want to know about my mother?"

"I don't. You said she owned the store, is all." But now I wanted to know why Kassandra had reacted with what seemed like suspicion.

"Oh." She seemed to relax. "Yes, she is. I have the day off."

Should I tell her the detective was looking for her? Maybe not. She might disappear again.

"Let's get this inside," I said. "I'll write up a ticket but leave the specifics out. Orlean will text you after she gets a chance to check it out, and you can decide how much or how little you'd like us to do."

"Okay."

"Can you get the door?" I lifted the bike by the handlebars and seat tube and carried it into the shop.

Sandy stood behind the counter, ringing up the sale of a new tricycle for an older couple. She caught sight of Kassandra and blinked, a grim expression coming over her face. I kept on going toward the repair room. Sandy mustered a smile and focused on her customer. Kassandra didn't seem to react to seeing Sandy.

I introduced her to Orlean. "She wants to be able to ride the bike. Can you please give her a minimum quote, and also what it would be to tune it up?"

Orlean bobbed her head. "It'll be a couple of hours."

I picked up our repair pad and a pen and handed them to Kassandra. "Fill in your name and number." Our paper service tickets were entirely old-school, mostly because Orlean said her greasy fingers would trash whatever digital device she would have to use to keep records electronically. She had a point.

When we were done, I walked Kassandra to the door. "Have fun on your day off."

She laughed. "If you can call going back to Daddy's to do laundry fun, I guess I will."

I stepped outside after she'd gone. Lincoln needed to know where she would be, and her mother, too. I sent him a text. How hard had the police really looked, anyway? Or maybe June and Kassandra had just been hanging out with Helene. At least the Jenkins women seemed unharmed and weren't fugitives.

I gazed down Main Street. I might need to buy another toy later today.

CHAPTER 24

Things in the shop were mostly quiet by one thirty, and I'd never gotten to the bank yesterday to deposit the cash from the last few days. First, I took a minute to beckon Derrick outside.

"Derr, you get along well with Orlean. I wonder if you can find out from her why Sandy left Belleville. Or from Sandy, herself."

He gave me a quizzical look. "Why don't you just ask her?"

"I'm her boss. You know I try not to pry into my employees' personal lives."

"Except mine." He grinned.

If I'd been wearing my glasses, I would have looked at him from over the top of the frames.

"You know telling me what to do is fine," he added. "But, yeah, I'll see what I can find out for you."

"Thanks. The thing is, Orlean is such a private person, I don't want to pump her, either," I said. "But I kind of need to know."

"I'll try."

I thanked him, and we went back inside. "I'm heading out for a few minutes, gang," I called to my crew, suiting up in my jacket. I slung on my EpiPen bag and grabbed the zippered bank envelope. Orlean waved me on.

Now, banking accomplished, I had a little time to poke my nose into the Toy Soldier and meet June Jenkins.

I spied a woman perched on a stool behind the counter at the back, swiping and looking at her phone. She glanced up when the door shut behind me.

"Welcome to the Toy Soldier. Let me know if I can help you."

I smiled and nodded, then wandered the aisles as I had on Sunday. I examined the cooperative games. Which was fine, but I remembered the thrill of winning a game and the devastation of losing as being an integral part of childhood. The store also stocked classics like Candy Land and Parcheesi.

Cokey was almost old enough for a board game, if it was a simple one and didn't involve too many words. Her reading ability was picking up fast, but she was still a beginner. I picked up a brightly colored box. The age range started at six. The Cokester was five and a half and thriving in kindergarten. I supposed I shouldn't keep buying her gifts. But I was her auntie. Of course I should.

I brought the box to the cash register. "Do you think this would be okay for a girl who's five and a half?"

"It'll be fine. You can always help your daughter if she can't figure something out."

"It's for my niece, actually, but she lives here in town, and we're close." I extended my hand. "I'm Mac Almeida, by the way. I own Mac's Bikes down the street. I can't believe we haven't met yet."

"I'm June. Good to meet you, Mac." She shook my hand with a firm grip, gazing at me with chestnut-colored eyes. Broad-shouldered, she had Helene's nose but skin a shade darker. Her hair was pulled back into a braid streaked by only a few gray hairs. "I opened in December, and the holidays were nuts. You're a retailer. The season must have been busy for you, too."

"It was." I stuck my credit card into the reader. "After the holidays I was off on my honeymoon for half of January."

"Almeida. I think my mother is friends with your grandmother Reba."

"Yes. Reba actually took me to meet Helene yesterday." The minute I said the words, I wished I could take them back.

"Did she, now." It wasn't a question. "Any particular reason?"

I gave what I hoped was an innocent-looking shrug. "She thought I would like her, I guess. Your mother has had a fascinating career, June." I mentally crossed my fingers, hoping I had successfully changed the subject. The card reader dinged, and I retrieved my card.

"She certainly has." June slid the game into a handled bag.

"Your daughter brought her bike into my shop this morning."

June seemed to relax. "She's going to need it. Her old Toyota finally gave up the ghost."

"I met August last year, but I don't seem to remember seeing Kassandra around. Has she recently come back to town? I know she was interested in the Chamber director job."

"She still is. Or at least her father is interested in her having it."

I blinked. How much influence did Park have over Kassandra? At the festival meeting, she'd sure sounded like she wanted to run things.

"My August is a good boy, and landed a job with the Westham PD, as you're probably aware," June went on. "I understand you're some kind of amateur detective, Mac."

"What? Oh, not at all." I picked up the bag. "I mean, there have been several homicides in the area in the last year, which is how I met August. I somehow managed to get involved in the investigations. But seriously, I'm only a business owner, just like you."

"Right." She drew out the word as if she didn't believe me. She folded her arms. "Understand this. My girl had nothing to do with Lavoie's death. But Park might have."

Whoa. "In what way?" Was this an ex-wife's vendetta, or could she back up her accusation with facts?

June's gaze slid to the door.

I turned to see Lincoln closing the door behind him.

"Good afternoon, ladies."

"Detective," June muttered.

"Hi, Lincoln," I said. He hadn't responded to my text earlier, but he'd obviously read it. Had he already gone to visit Kassandra at Park's?

"Were you aware I've been looking for you, Ms. Jenkins?" he asked her. He didn't smile.

"Lincoln, you've known me my whole life." She kept her arms folded. "Just call me June and get it over with, will you? And besides, I never was Mrs. Jenkins, which you also know. If you need to be formal, you can use Fadiman."

"Regardless of how I addressed you, I'd like you to answer the question." His tone was low, serious.

I gazed from one to the other, pretty sure Lincoln wouldn't want me present for whatever conversation they were about to have. "I need to get back to my shop. Thanks, June." I smiled, bag in hand, and made my way out.

Before I started back to Mac's Bikes, I stood on the sidewalk, thinking. June hadn't answered my question about where Kassandra had been before this winter. I hoped the Internet would have some answers. I hadn't thought to poke into her history last night. June also hadn't responded to my query about Park, but when I'd asked was when Lincoln had arrived.

Judging from June's comment to Lincoln, I expected I was right about her being at least part Wampanoag. It must be June's father who had the tribal connection. Was he Fadiman, or did he have another name? Helene might have kept her maiden name and given it to her daughter to carry on.

I stepped off the curb, still immersed in my

thoughts. The driver of a pickup truck leaned on his horn. *Yikes!* I jumped back.

"Watch where you're going, sister!" he yelled out the passenger window as he whooshed by only feet away.

Excellent advice. I waited until my heart calmed before looking both ways—twice—and starting over.

CHAPTER 25

A thin woman in a bulky sweater stood smoking in front of the Rusty Anchor across the street from the Toy Soldier. I took a second look. I was pretty sure it was Wagner's sister, the one who'd demanded to park in my shop's lot on Saturday. What had he called her? It might have been Rae. Kay? Maybe Faye. There was no time like the present to cross over and greet her.

"Faye, right?"

Wagner's sister frowned and reared back. "Do I know you?" Her ear-length hair was a reddish hue, but a line of white peeked through at her scalp over a lined, leathery face.

"My name's Mac Almeida." I kept my voice gentle. "I met you briefly in the bike shop parking lot before the parade Saturday. I'm so sorry about the loss of your brother."

"Thanks." She sniffed, but her eyes weren't red, and she didn't appear particularly sad. She took a deep drag and peered at my face as she let out the smoke to the side. "Now I remember. You and your people wouldn't let me park at your business."

"My apologies." We didn't need to go into her refusal to cooperate again.

"This place any good?" She gestured with her thumb at the pub behind her.

"I like it. Decent simple food, good drinks, nice people."

"Huh. Not so nice." Faye dropped the cigarette on the ground but left it smoldering. "I was just in there applying for a job. That Flora lady, the cook, has a chip on her shoulder if I ever saw one."

"Yvonne?"

"That's the one. Thinks she's better than everyone else."

I'd never experienced that, personally. I kept my opinion to myself. "What kind of job were you applying for?"

"I told her I'd do anything. I've waitressed, done short order cooking, heck, I've even bussed tables and washed dishes." She lit up another cigarette and took a long inhale. "Thing is, I'm presently out of a job." She let out the breath. This time she didn't blow it away from me.

I took a step back. "Did Yvonne think she had an opening?"

"Nope. Negatory. She said they were 'fully staffed.' " Faye surrounded the last two words with finger quotes.

"Too bad. I hope you find something."

A man holding the hand of an identically clad toddler on each side approached.

"You and me both, hon." She took another puff, then coughed. Low and throaty, it sounded terrible, and she didn't cover her mouth.

The father looked horrified. He hurried the children past us and muttered, "Get a mask, lady."

I didn't blame him. Hers was probably a smoker's cough, but risking germ- or virus-laden airborne particles was never a safe bet, especially in the past few years.

"Do you have a place here in Westham?" I asked.

"Are you kidding? Who can afford to live in this chichi town? No, I got me an apartment up in Bourne, and not the fancy part of town, either."

I could tell her about Westham's affordable housing units but decided not to. I'd heard they weren't actually affordable for low-income people.

"Westham isn't like it was when we were kids." She gazed into the distance with a wistful smile as if conjuring up a long-ago era. Her face looked softer, her expression less jaded.

"You lived here then." I knew the answer, but I hoped she'd keep talking.

"Sure did. Me and Wag were happy, goofing around in the marsh, riding our bikes everywhere."

"Sounds nice. I had a happy childhood here, too."

She eyed me. "You have to be at least ten years younger than me, maybe more."

"Probably." I didn't remember her and Wagner at all.

"Bliss bubbles don't last forever, you know. Leastwise, mine sure didn't." Faye puffed on her smoke. "Everything went to hell and gone when . . . well, never mind."

Bliss bubbles. She was right. No bubble lasted forever, no matter what it was made of.

She lifted her chin. "Anyway, now Wag's gone, may he rest in peace, I might be moving into the family cottage. I'd love to be back in it."

"The one where he's been living?"

"Yep. Same one we grew up in. He told me he was leaving it to me. I bet I could sell it for a pretty penny, if I decide not to live there."

"I'm sure you could. I saw the cottage yesterday. It's in a nice area out by the salt marsh."

She coughed again, squinting at me. "Who are you, anyway, snooping around my late brother's house? Are you some kind of undercover cop?"

"Not a bit. I run a bike shop. It's just that yesterday my grandmother took me to see a friend of hers, who happens to live next door to where Wagner was staying." A chill breeze gusted by, and I shivered, snugging my jacket around me.

"Sure." She clipped off the word and pressed her lips into a skeptical line.

"Well, I'd better get back to work. Nice to see you, Faye. Good luck with finding a job."

"You know of any restaurants hiring?"

"I'm afraid I don't."

Her shoulders drooped. "See you around, Mac." She turned away, taking another drag on her smoke.

I watched her go. She wouldn't have murdered her own brother so she could have a place to live. Would she?

CHAPTER 26

Gin and I crossed the Cape Cod Canal northward on the Bourne Bridge, one of the two high-arching bridges letting tall-masted and tall marine vessels pass underneath. She'd picked me up at two thirty in her little red Honda, telling me I could navigate while she drove. We made our way along State Route 25 on the first leg toward Belleville. I checked the GPS on my phone.

"You want scenic and shorter or longer and faster?" I compared the mileage. "Actually, there's only a two-minute difference, even though going on 195 is ten miles longer. It's basically an hour either way." The two routes were like the top and bottom of a clamshell.

"They're both going to be scenic. Let's take 195, since it's highway all the way."

I directed her onto the lower curve.

"So, what's our agenda?" she asked. "We won't have very long, if we're going to eat with the group at six."

"Yeah. Maybe not the best planning. Do you want to turn around?"

"No. Let's go see what we can find out. The girl who works after school will close Salty Taffy's for me."

"So will my gang. I mean, Derrick." He was the only one of my employees who had the keys to Mac's Bikes. I'd asked him to do me an additional favor, if he could figure out how. He'd agreed to see what he could find out. "I looked up Wagner's wife's address, and where Sandy lived before she came to Westham."

"What was her husband's name?"

"Lyle McKean," I said. "I haven't had a chance to find out—or ask Orlean—if Sandy is divorced or what, but I did see both hers and the husband's names still on the deed to the house."

We now zipped through the former whaling city of New Bedford, where Gin grew up.

"How's your mom?" I asked. She'd helped us with some information on a case last fall.

"She and Dad are both good, but they've decided to become snowbirds. They're spending the winter in Destin, Florida. Eli and I are going down to visit next week, actually. It's one of those places with unbelievably blue water and white sand." She tapped the steering wheel. "You said Park was from Belleville, too."

"He graduated from the high school there. I don't know how long he stayed." I went on to tell her about talking with June earlier today, and how Lincoln had showed up to speak with her. "Lincoln stopped by my shop early this morning and said he couldn't find Kassandra or her mom."

"Is he slipping? If June was right there at her shop, how hard could it be to find her?"

"Yeah. And Kassandra brought her bike in to get a flat fixed today, too." As we drove, a little giggle escaped me. "Kassandra must be glad she wasn't named April, with a mother named June and a brother named August."

"No kidding. Or she could have been called May." Gin smiled. "Do you think anyone names their daughter November? Or February?"

"I can think of a few celebrities who might pull a stunt like that. Not regular people, though."

We passed through Fall River, leaving the interstate at Swansea and heading straight north on a state route. Soon we were wandering through bucolic countryside. A sign announcing the Belleville town limits included, "A Right To Farm Community."

"I wonder what that means," Gin mused.

I poked at my phone until I found it. "It basically means farms have rights. You can't move into a house in a development next to an existing farm and then complain about the smell of compost or pigs." We passed a sign reading, "Rosasharn Farm. Nigerian Dwarf Dairy Goats, Livestock Guardian Dogs." Two big white dogs loped toward the road but stopped short of the fence.

"Nigerian dwarf dairy goats? There's a whole world I know nothing about," Gin said. "I wonder if they hold yoga classes with little free-range goats climbing around on the yogis."

I smiled. "I've seen pictures of goat yoga. I wouldn't want one of those dogs on my back when I'm trying to do a cobra pose, though." I checked the map. "Go straight until the fork, then hang a left."

As we drove, I thought about what Faye had said. "What do you know about inheritances, Gin?"

"Estate law? Not much. Why?"

"I ran into Wagner's sister downtown a couple hours ago. Faye said she's going to be inheriting the cottage he was living in out on Salt Marsh Road. She's unemployed, and she seemed pretty happy about the prospect."

"I should think so. Those properties are valuable."

"But wouldn't it go to Wagner's wife?"

"No idea." Gin tapped the steering wheel. "Were you thinking this Faye killed her own brother? That's, like, horrible."

"Of course it is. But at this point? The suspect pool is wide-open." I glanced down at my phone. "Oh! Turn right, quick."

CHAPTER 27

We decided to park in the town's small center, which looked a bit down-at-the-heel. I spied several empty storefronts, plus faded paint on the Fowle's Drugstore sign. Still, the town center offered an old-fashioned hardware store, a small department store that had to date from the sixties, and a diner, along with a ubiquitous dollar-type chain store. After a quick bathroom break at a Dunkin's, Gin grabbed a cup of coffee. "Nothing for you?"

"No, thanks. Two cups of caffeine in the morning are all I get. You know I'm kind of wired as it is. The last thing I need in the afternoon is a boost of energy."

She laughed and agreed.

I consulted my phone again and led Gin down a side street filled with a mix of small two-story houses with brick foundations built in the late 1800s, a few foursquare homes with tiny garages from the dawn of the automobile age, and a handful of sixties-era ranch houses. I stopped at a ranch with the name McKean on the mailbox at the curb.

"This is the house Sandy apparently still owns with Lyle McKean." I peered down the driveway. The garage door was closed, and no cars were parked in front of it.

"What can we find out?" Gin sounded dubious. "Do you want to ring the doorbell?"

A silver sedan slowed and turned into the drive. The window lowered.

"Can I help you ladies?" the man behind the wheel asked.

Caught in the act, I mustered a smile. "Hi. My name is Nancy. I love your neighborhood. I wondered if you might be selling your house soon or know of others who're about to list theirs." I ignored Gin's snort at my alias. "This is my friend, Georgette."

She muffled a laugh with a cough.

The man looked from me to her and back. "I might be putting it on the market." He had acne-pocked cheeks and small eyes under sandy-colored hair slicked back with a touch too much hair gel. "Are you two a couple?" His eyes nearly disappeared when he narrowed them.

"No, not at all," I said. "We're just good friends. She said she'd come scout out the town with me. So you think you're going to sell?"

Now he frowned. "My wife is about to become my ex. She's leaning on me to buy her out. It's a real pain in the—" He broke off. "Well, you don't need to hear about my dirty linen."

"I'm sorry about your breakup." I spoke softly. Of course I wanted to hear all his sordid stories, if they involved Sandy.

"Say, do you know the Lavoies?" Gin piped up. "I've been trying to find Belinda. We're old friends."

"Of course I do." He pushed his lips out. "The poor woman is a widow now."

Gin's breath rushed in. "No. Wagner died?"

Lyle looked both ways, even though we three were the only people in sight. "He was murdered down Cape. Such a shame."

"Were you friends with him?" I asked.

"We'd go for pool and beers sometimes. Good man. Sorry he's gone." He tapped the steering wheel. "Well, Nancy, tell your real estate agent to contact me. I'll probably be ready to list before too long." He fished a business card out of a well in front of the gearshift and passed it through the window. "Nice meeting you both."

We stepped back while he put up the window and hit his garage door opener.

"I'm Georgette now?" Gin asked as we retraced our steps to her car.

"I was thinking Nancy Drew and her friend George, but it sounded too obvious."

"Mac, I'll bet you dinner at Yoshinoya our Lyle there has never read one word of a Nancy Drew mystery. Or possibly of any book with a female lead."

"I won't bet, because I'd lose." I read the card in my hand. "Lyle McKean, DDS. He's a dentist."

"Don't they make a lot of money? It was a pretty modest house for someone who's a dentist."

"You're right." And no wonder Sandy had such perfect teeth. She'd been married to a someone with expertise in the area. I slid into the car. "It would be interesting to go pay our condolences to your good friend Belinda. Except she must be grieving. I'd hate to bother her."

"Or maybe she's not. Didn't someone say their marriage was in trouble?"

"Yes. Helene suspected it was. Let's go find out for ourselves."

CHAPTER 28

As it turned out, we didn't drive anywhere. A phone search yielded the information that Belinda Lavoie was Belleville's town manager. Town Hall turned out to be the big white building across the street from where we were parked. In need of a paint job and with a rotting clapboard here and there, it looked historic but not particularly well preserved.

"You know we should leave in half an hour, Mac," Gin said as she trotted up the front steps.

"Yes. I sure hope they have a ramp around the side somewhere. This entrance is so not accessible to anyone with mobility issues."

"It's a municipal building." Gin held the door open for me. "They would have to."

Inside, over antique doors with glass windows, signs hung down indicating Town Clerk and Collector on left and right, with Public Works and Town Manager beyond.

Gin touched my arm. "Just so I know, are we Nancy and Georgette again?"

"I think we should be."

"But what are you going to say to her?"

"Huh." I thought for a second. "How about the same story I gave Lyle?"

"Whatever. After you, Detective."

I elbowed her and pulled open the door labeled Town Manager. Instead of a high reception counter, a desk faced the door, but no one sat at it. At a desk farther back, a woman with an impressive fall of tiny black braids tipped with small beads sat erect, her hands on a laptop keyboard.

She glanced up. "May I help you?"

Former English teacher Reba would approve, of the hairstyle as well as the grammar, using "may" instead of the more common "can."

"I'm looking for the town manager," I said.

"I'm the town manager. Please come in."

Interesting. Everyone we'd seen in town so far had been pale-skinned. Belinda was definitely Black. I approached the desk. "Thank you. My name is Nancy. I'm looking to buy property here in Belleville, and I had a few questions about the town."

She tilted her head, the beads clinking like little bells. "Have you spoken to the Chamber of Commerce?"

"Yes, of course," I said. "But I'm wondering about how the town operates and the schools, those kind of things. This is my friend, Georgette."

"Very well." She gestured toward two chairs. "Please

have a seat, ladies." She wheeled out from behind the desk to face us.

Her wheelchair fit her perfectly and, lacking armrests or handles sticking out of the back, it looked different from the kind I'd seen in hospitals. She didn't have a cast on her leg or foot, making me think she used the chair permanently.

"I'm Belinda Lavoie, by the way, but I'm afraid I avoid handshakes."

She was at work and didn't appear overtaken with grief, so I didn't hold back from my plan.

"Lavoie?" I asked "We drove here up from Westham on the Cape. A man by that name died in our town recently. I hope he wasn't a relative."

Belinda folded her hands in her lap as she blew out a long breath. "He was my husband."

Gin leaned forward. "I'm so very sorry, Ms. Lavoie."

"Thank you. Don't be." Her gaze was level. "As you can see, I'm not dissolved by sorrow nor wearing widow's weeds." She had on cream-colored slacks and a magenta cashmere sweater that made her skin glow. "Wagner and I were estranged. He is my child's father, and I once loved him. Any human loss of life is sad. And his appears to have had malicious causes."

I bobbed my head. "You and your child have my condolences, too."

"Did either of you know him personally?" Belinda asked.

"We're both local merchants," I said. "I'd met Wagner in his role as director of the Chamber. Gih . . . Georgette did, too." I caught myself right before calling her Gin and hoped it sounded like I was only stuttering.

Belinda blinked. "You have a retail business in Westham, and you want to buy a house in Belleville?" She quite rightly sounded as if she didn't believe me. "You already live in paradise."

"It is lovely there," I said. "But the taxes are high, and Belleville has its charms, too. Plus, salt air doesn't corrode siding inland here." I was grasping at how to bring up Wagner's cottage—and falling short.

"For sure," Gin said. "Your husband's cottage down there being a prime example."

"You went to his family's cottage?" The manager sounded suspicious.

I jumped in. "We know his neighbor, Helene Fadiman."

Belinda relaxed. "Helene is an inspiration."

"She is," Gin agreed.

"Now, what did you want to know about how Belleville operates?" Belinda asked me.

If she was on to my ruse, I ignored it. "My husband and I are hoping to start a family. What can you tell me about the schools?"

CHAPTER 29

I leaned over my plate and bit into a Rusty Anchor bacon cheeseburger with the works at six thirty. It was so thick I could barely get my mouth around it, and the juice dribbled down my cheek.

"I think I'm in heaven," I said after swallowing. I wiped my face with the napkin and took a sip from my glass of beer.

"You look like you are, Nancy." Gin grinned.

Zane frowned. "Nancy?"

"Yep." I smiled. "And this is George, whom I introduced this afternoon as Georgette."

Norland blinked. "Let me guess. You two went on a sleuthing jaunt, and you decided to masquerade as a freakishly old Nancy Drew and George Fayne."

"Would we pretend to be fictional girl sleuths?" Gin lowered her head and batted her eyelashes, faking innocence.

"Of course you would." Now Zane was smiling. "Okay, dish. Where'd you go, and what did you learn?"

I munched a lightly battered, perfectly crisp onion ring, holding up a finger as I savored it.

"I took Mac—I mean Nancy—on a little ride up to Belleville." Gin took a sip of her wine. "It's not far from Rehoboth."

"Belleville is where Wagner was from," Norland said. "And Park Jenkins, if memory serves."

"Exactly. And where Sandy's husband lives," I said. "As it happens, Georgette and I managed to speak with both spouses."

"And?" Zane asked.

I wrinkled my nose. "We didn't learn anything specific. Except Wagner's wife, Belinda, was the first to admit she's not shedding any tears over him."

"And Lyle McKean spoke of Sandy as his almost ex-wife," Gin added.

"Which must be why she moved in with Orlean, right?" Norland asked.

"She hasn't said as much, but I bet that's why." I spied Tim taking a seat at the bar. He and Eli were here for dinner, too, since all of us had to be at the meeting at seven thirty. Tim had said he didn't want to interfere with our group pow-wow, and he and Eli had race training to plan. They'd both qualified to run the Boston Marathon next month. He blew me a kiss, which I returned. "Lyle is apparently a dentist, according to the card he gave me."

"And Belinda is the Belleville town manager," Gin said. "We didn't manage to ask her what Wagner did before he came here. Does anyone know?"

"He was a supply manager at the base," Norland said.

"Otis?" I asked. The Otis Air National Guard base, formerly an Air Force base, was on our end of the Cape. "Otis is a trek from Belleville."

"It's an hour. Could be worse," Norland said. "You know, Mac, some people commute to Boston from here. At least Otis doesn't promise too many traffic jams."

"Did anyone else wonder about Wagner's gold Rolex?" I asked. "Those things are expensive."

"You're not going to buy a Rolex on a supply manager's salary," Zane said.

"It might have been a cheap knock-off," Norland pointed out.

Maybe. Or maybe he was getting money from elsewhere.

Yvonne emerged from the kitchen, wearing a black chef's tunic over a pair of the classic black-and-white houndstooth-checked chef's pants. She seemed to be looking for someone at our table, because she came straight over. She set fists on hips and glared at Gin.

"Why are you asking questions about me, Gin?" She kept her tone low, but it was a harsh one. "I know your little group thinks you can act like detectives. But you aren't real ones."

Whoa. Where had this come from?

Gin opened her mouth, then shut it. Yvonne must have overheard Gin speaking with the pastry chef. I wondered why she talked to him here and not away from the kitchen.

"Mac knows I wouldn't have hurt Lavoie," Yvonne went on. "I couldn't stand the man, but I didn't murder him."

"What makes you think I was talking with Uly about

murder, Yvonne?" Gin asked, keeping her voice casual.

"Because I saw you two with your heads together. When you saw me, you looked away fast, like you were guilty."

"Listen," Gin told her. "He's a friend of mine. We talk about sweet recipes. If I looked guilty, it's because I was taking away from his work time. It won't happen again."

"It had better not." Yvonne kept scowling.

"By the way," I butted in, hoping to redirect the chef's focus. "These onion rings are perfection, as usual."

She muttered her thanks, then glanced up. "Oh, great. Just what I don't need. Enjoy your dinner, folks." She turned on her heel and strode back into the kitchen.

I twisted to see Victoria with a man, being seated a few tables away. What beef did Yvonne have with our chief of police? Victoria turned to let the man help her off with her coat. I stared. Could it be?

"What is it, Mac?" Gin asked.

"I'll tell you later. Who's the dude with her?"

"He's her husband." Gin peered at me. "Haven't you ever met him?"

"I don't exactly socialize with Victoria, Gin."

"He's a pediatrician," Zane said. "Nice guy. Knows his whiskey, too."

And he plays a mean game of bocce," Norland added. "Don't look at me like that. We played at the last PD summer picnic before I retired. And yes, the police sometimes relax and have cookouts and beer just like the rest of you." He seemed to catch the attention of Victoria's husband and pointed his finger at him in greeting.

I looked again. Victoria had not turned to see whom her husband had recognized. By how stiff her spine was, I guessed she knew we were here and didn't want to interact with us. Or at least not with me. Which was fine. I still wondered why Yvonne was upset about seeing Victoria.

"Gin." I kept my voice soft enough for only those at our table to hear. I hoped. "What did Uly tell you? Did you find out why Yvonne hated Wagner?"

"Do you know she's retired from the Air Force?" Gin asked.

Zane and I shook our heads.

Norland gave a nod. "Yes."

"So she's a veteran, too, like Sandy and Wagner," I said.

"Uly said Yvonne knew Wagner at Otis," Gin began. "I got the feeling the two might have had an affair that went south."

"Seriously?" I asked. "But she's gay."

"Maybe I have it mixed up." Gin wrinkled her nose. "Maybe he'd been hanging out with someone else on base."

"Either way, he'd have been cheating on Belinda," I said, almost to myself. "I don't suppose we know why she uses a wheelchair."

"It could be for any number of reasons," Norland said. "MS, polio, an injury, a wasting disease. You name it." He checked his watch. "Gang, we'd better pay up and get over to Town Hall. It's seven fifteen."

I drained my glass while Norland hailed the waitperson. This case seemed to get more complicated at every turn. I hoped Lincoln and Penelope were having better luck than our little band of amateurs. Time was ticking by, giving the killer time to get far away. Which was always preferable to feeling cornered and killing again, but it didn't help with catching him—or her.

CHAPTER 30

The hall was full of the usual pre-meeting buzz of conversation. Small groups conferred around the edges and at the back. On the stage people delivered sheets of paper to Zane's husband, Stephen, the town clerk. Two of the five members of the finance committee were missing from their table, as was one from the school committee on the opposite side.

Despite it being seven forty-five, Park Jenkins still hadn't gaveled the meeting to order. They must be short of residents for the required quorum, which was the percentage of registered voters required on certain budget items. I sat with Tim on one side and Gin on the other. Eli was next to her. I spied Mom on the other side of the aisle with Reba. Too bad Pa was still out of town, in case the votes were close tonight.

It was also too bad he was away, because I missed him. His wise, steady presence had been a comfort to me my whole life. As befit any man of the cloth, he was an excellent listener. He always seemed to know what question to ask that would gently move me along to my own decision without telling me what to do. He'd even sensed how to defuse my teen rebellion. When I'd insisted on multiple ear piercings, he'd lit up and said, "I'll go with you and get them in my ear, too."

"How'd your investigations go today?" Tim asked in a low murmur.

"Peaceably, but we didn't get too far. Gin and I learned a couple of things up in Belleville this afternoon."

"You drove all the way up there?"

"I texted you we were taking a drive."

"You did." He smiled. "I'm not challenging you, Mac. Go on."

"Well, the whole thing is frankly getting more tangled and stickier the deeper I dig."

"Are you glad it's not your actual job?"

"Absolutely." I pointed my chin toward Lincoln and Penelope, who stood with Victoria at the right of the room. "They're the ones who have to solve it." Although, for people who didn't actually need to investigate, the Cozy Capers took it seriously, me among them.

A woman hurried up the central aisle and handed a slip of paper to Stephen, who conferred with Park.

Park stood and rapped the gavel on its base a couple of times. "Good evening, Westham." He waited until the room was mostly quiet. "The special town meeting will come to order. Welcome, everyone, and thank you for doing your part for democracy. This year's new Eagle Scouts will lead us in the Pledge of Allegiance. Please rise." He mentioned their names, then angled to face the American flag, which flew from a floor stand.

Two khaki-uniformed teens wearing scout sashes full of badges and pins stood next to the flag. One skinny and gawky, the other muscular with a short beard, the boys raised their right hands in the Boy Scout salute and recited the familiar words in chorus with the audience. We sat again with a communal creak of uncomfortable wooden chairs a century old.

"I'd like to begin by acknowledging the recent tragedy suffered here in Westham," Park said into the microphone. "Chamber of Commerce director Wagner Lavoie was brutally struck down in the prime of life Saturday, just after he'd staged a highly successful festival benefiting Westham's merchants and residents alike. We extend our sympathy to his family and loved ones. I'd like to ask Chief Laitinen to come forward and share any updates she might have on the case."

I looked over at her. She shook her head and whispered to Lincoln. He made his way to the microphone on a stand at the front of the center aisle, where residents sometimes offered reports or asked questions.

"Thank you, Mr. Jenkins and the other selectpeople. The chief has asked me to speak on the case."

"Go ahead," Park said.

Lincoln faced the residents, angling the microphone. "My name is Detective Sergeant Lincoln Haskins of Mashpee. I am the lead detective from the state police unit investigating the homicide of Mr. Lavoie. Detective Penelope Johnson of the Westham PD is assisting us. At this time, we are following several persons of interest but do not yet have sufficient evidence to make an arrest. As we mentioned two days ago, anyone with information is encouraged to come forward."

An older woman stood. "How do we know we're safe?" she called out.

"We have no reason to believe this was a random act, ma'am." Lincoln turned to go.

"What about the girl who wanted his job?" a scratchy male voice asked from the back. "Shouldn't you be looking at Kaycie? Or is she off limits because she's the selectman's little girl?"

Kaycie must be a nickname for Kassandra, maybe from her childhood. I twisted in my seat. I couldn't see who had spoken, but he'd sounded on the young side. A murmur went up around the room. I heard some expressions of shock, but others seemed to agree. Park's normally ruddy face paled. Lincoln faced the speaker.

"We are looking at all points of information, sir. If you witnessed a violent act or have evidence about a particular person, you are obliged to inform the police. That will be all." Lincoln swiveled the microphone again. "Thank you, Mr. Jenkins." He returned to the side where he'd been standing and stood, like the rock he was, hands at his sides, his steely gaze focused on the back of the room.

The chorus of commenters went silent. Park hit the gavel again. The meeting proceeded.

"Wow," Gin whispered. "Is Kassandra here?"

"I don't know." At a glare from a woman in front of us, I pressed my lips together. I hadn't seen Kassandra. If she was in the hall, I couldn't imagine how hot her cheeks must be right now.

CHAPTER 31

"Who were those guys last night, anyway?" Gin asked as we walked the next morning. "The ones who thought it was a good idea to tell Haskins how to do his job?"

"I never got a good look at them. I wouldn't be surprised if they slid out early, to avoid both Lincoln and Park." We'd all dispersed and gone home last night after the last item on the warrant was voted on. Our group hadn't talked about the disruption at all.

"Yeah. But they called her by a nickname, so they probably went to school with her."

"Right. The dude who spoke sounded youngish. Park sure looked shocked when he mentioned Kaycie," I said.

"I know. And Haskins totally shut them down."

A gust of wind nearly blew my ball cap off. But it was a warmer wind than in past days.

"I think spring might actually be getting close." A movement in the sky made me glance up. "Gin, look." I pointed to a large bird with both white and dark coloring beating its way toward the open water. "The ospreys are back."

"They're like a cross between a hawk and a seagull."

"Ospreys are birds of prey, for sure. They just hang out in the same places where seagulls do."

A bike bell dinged behind us. "On your left," a man's voice announced. He passed us, then braked to a stop, resting one foot on the path. We stopped, as well.

"'Morning, Mac, Gin," August Jenkins said.

"Hey, August." I smiled. "Out for an early sprint?"

"Yes. I like to get my cardio in before work." He didn't return the smile. His light eyes, which he must have gotten from Park, contrasted with skin more the tone of June's.

"Are you involved in the murder investigation at all?" Gin asked.

I shot her a quick glance. Her question was more blunt than she usually was.

He couldn't hide his wince. "No."

"Because it's a conflict of interest?" I kept my voice as gentle as I could.

"Yes. Both of you are in that book group, and Mac, I know you've had experience with past investigations. So you probably know they're looking closely at both my father and my sister. Which is completely ludicrous, but they are, both Haskins and Johnson."

August's own grandmother thought Park was guilty. The guys at the back of the town hall believed Kassandra might be. I'd seen her and her father head in the direction of the bookstore's back door in the hour before Norland found Wagner dead. I didn't blame Lincoln for keeping the two Jenkinses on the list. I had nothing to say in response.

"I'm going to get going," August said. "Have a nice walk."

"Thanks," I said. "Enjoy your ride."

Head down, he pedaled away, picking up speed.

"Interesting," I said as we resumed our own pace.

"Agree. I wonder if there's something more he knows but isn't saying."

"Because he seemed so serious?"

"Yes. I mean, it is his sister and his father. It would be terribly serious if either of them was the killer."

"Or both?" I asked. "What if they worked together to murder Wagner?"

"Ooh. Accomplices. Maybe one of them knocked him out."

"Or poisoned him."

"And the other, or both, pushed over the bookcase," Gin said.

"For August's sake, I hope neither was involved." I frowned. "I wish we knew more about if Wagner was attacked before the bookcase hit him. They should have done an autopsy by now."

"You kind of have an in with Lincoln. Can you ask him?"

"I'll try to." We swung onto the extension leading out to the bluff. An osprey with salt marsh hay in its predator's beak alit on the nesting platform twenty feet up. The shelf sat atop a pole and had been erected to encourage the birds to maintain a nest year after year. I pointed. "Look. I wonder if they're already laying eggs."

Gin shot me a look but didn't ask about my own eggs. She knew better. I appreciated her tact, but it didn't mean I couldn't bring up the topic.

"Speaking of babies—and no, not mine—do you think Victoria might be pregnant?" I asked. "It kind of looked that way at the Rusty Anchor last night."

"You know, when I saw her take off her coat, I wondered the same thing. Or maybe she's enjoying married life and just eating more."

"I didn't think she looked fatter all over. In someone as petite as her, a baby bump has nowhere to go but out."

"I guess we'll see." She smiled. "It won't be any different with you, Mac. Even though you're taller than Victoria, you're so slim. It'll be super obvious."

I laughed. "I'll cross that bridge when I come to it."

We reached the bluff where we usually stopped to take a breath before reversing course. I touched a hand to a pole for balance and pulled my left heel up behind me to stretch my quads.

"Do you know what Kassandra did for work before she moved back?" I asked. "Was she in town before this winter?"

"I don't remember seeing her around, but she wasn't on my radar, either. At least, not until the chamber job came open in the fall."

"June Jenkins opened the toy store only in December. But Park has been around for years."

"He has," she agreed.

"I'll run a search on her when I get home. Speaking of which, we should head back."

I gave one last look out at the broad bay. When the weather was calm, the water could be a lovely shade of green. Today, wind whipped up whitecaps in the dark sea. A tern made a dive-bomb into the water and came up with a wriggling fish in its sharp beak. I shivered. Wagner's killer needed to be caught, and soon, before he or she put an end to one more human fish.

CHAPTER 32

I'd just hung out the Open flag at a few minutes before nine when Derrick biked up. The child bike seat on the back was empty but held a small purple helmet clipped into the seat belt.

"Hey, Brother." I smiled at him, loving that he used his bike for transportation whenever weather permitted.

"I just dropped Cokey off at school." He set one foot on the ground.

"How's my girlie?"

"You know. Full of life and questions and opinions."

"I do know. And that's as it should be."

"Of course. For example, while we were talking about birds' wings and the principles of aerodynamics, she informed me she would be wearing mismatched socks for the rest of her life. 'Because they're more modeler.' When I asked what 'modeler' meant, she said, 'Like the ladies who do the fashions.' "

"So, she might end up working as an aeronautics engineer *and* a supermodel?"

"It wouldn't surprise me. Sure enough, she dressed herself this morning in a purple sweater, green skirt, yellow print leggings, and pink and blue socks—one each." He laughed. "I'm on my way to class, but I wanted to let you know what I learned yesterday."

My smile slipped away. "Please."

"Don't get your hopes up. It isn't much."

I waited.

"It seems Sandy worked at a lab in Providence," he said.

"That part I know."

"But she also did the books for her husband's business."

"The dental office."

"Right." He nodded. "She said she couldn't tolerate working with him any longer after their marriage fell apart, and she couldn't afford an apartment on the lab paycheck alone. Orlean offered Sandy the spare bedroom, and you agreed to hire her. So she's here."

"Thank you." I pressed my eyebrows down, thinking. "No hint about what happened between her and Lyle?"

"Nada."

The bell at Our Lady of the Sea, the Catholic church down the street, began to chime nine o'clock.

"Gotta run, Mackie. See you this afternoon." He blew me a kiss and pedaled off.

"Ride carefully." I watched him go. My phone pinged with an incoming text. It was from Norland to the Cozy Capers thread.

FYI. WPD granted permission to reopen Book Nook today. Carpenter will secure shelving before I do.

I tapped out a reply. **Glad to hear it.**

I added another, relaying what Sandy had told Derrick about doing the accounts for her husband's business. I sent it and added one more thought. **No idea what broke up marriage with Lyle McKean. Any info?**

I shoved the phone in my pocket and ignored further pinging as I finished my opening routine.

A pair of rental returns came in. I was processing them when Orlean arrived, lunch bag in hand. Sandy did not appear behind her. After I was finished with the rentals, I made my way to the repair area.

"Before you ask, Sandy says she's sorry," Orlean began. "She's not feeling well and has to take the day off."

I blinked. Was this a real sickness or a feigned one? "I'm sorry she's sick. I could stop by with some homemade chicken soup, if you think it would help."

"Mac." Orlean cocked her head. "You don't cook. Where are you going to buy this so-called chicken soup?"

I gave a sheepish smile, or maybe it was a helpless caught-in-a-lie smile.

"Anyway, I don't think it would help, and I doubt she'd appreciate a visit." Orlean took a deep breath and set down her wrench. "Look, Sandy's dealing with some crap right now. I'm sorry I suggested you hire her. If you need to start looking for someone more reliable, I understand. And she would, too." She cleared her throat. "I think."

"And I'm sorry your sister is going through a rough time. It can't be easy to get divorced and leave your home and job all at once."

"That's not all of it," Orlean muttered.

"What do you mean?"

She opened her mouth. Then clamped it shut again when the outer door opened.

I swore silently. She'd been so close to letting me in on Sandy's problems, which must have to do with Lyle and Wagner—and might have to do with murder.

"Tell you later." She picked up her tool, facing the bike on the repair stand.

But would she tell me later? Meanwhile, she and I were again the only two employees here until Derrick came back this afternoon. Well, the two of us had handled the shop before and we could handle it today. I turned toward the newcomer.

"Good morning, Kassandra." I approached her.

Her cheeks were flushed, and she looked like she'd hurried here. "Hi, Mac. I wondered if my bike was ready yet. I, um, I need to get somewhere."

Her "somewhere" must not be the toy store down the street. She could simply keep on walking and be there in five minutes.

"Come on in. Orlean can tell you." I gestured toward Orlean.

"Thanks," Kassandra said.

I realized I'd forgotten to run a search on her

after my walk. Maybe I could work in a way to ask her about her prior employment while she was here.

Orlean looked up with a scowl. "You confirmed you wanted a tune-up." She crossed her arms, still gripping the wrench. "I told you it wouldn't be ready until Thursday. Which is tomorrow." She focused on the bike in front of her again.

"All right. I just kind of hoped it'd be all set by now." Kassandra shoved her hands in her jacket pockets and turned away.

"Can't you grab a ride share?" I asked her.

"Ride shares cost money, Mac."

True. I followed her as she headed for the door.

"Somebody said you were living in California before you came back to town," I began, with no basis in fact. "You must have loved the winters there."

She whirled. "Who told you I lived in California?"

I flipped my hands open. "I can't remember."

"Huh." Her shoulders relaxed. "No, not California. But I lived in another warm-winter place. I had a position at the tropical research station in the Everglades."

"The Everglades? I've always wanted to visit there. It must have been a great place to work—and live."

"It was my dream job." Her tone turned wistful. "You wouldn't believe the diversity of plants, birds, and creatures."

"Are you a biologist?"

"Um, kind of."

Kind of? "So, why did you leave?"

She squared her shoulders. "Things didn't work out, okay? I'll be back tomorrow to pick up my bike." She let the door slam behind her.

I stared after her. Something hadn't worked out, and she'd left her dream job. My fingers were itching to explore an Everglades research station on my phone. Then three couples blew in, smiling and wearing athletic gear. My research would have to wait.

CHAPTER 33

When Derrick showed up at one o'clock—right on time—I nearly wept, I was so hungry. I had no idea why we were super busy at the end of March. I'd texted my brother we were shorthanded, but he couldn't get away early from his classes.

Orlean had gone out for her lunch break. She returned about the time Derrick arrived, just as the last customer in the place walked out wheeling a brand-new hybrid bicycle. It was all great for the bottom line. And hard when we were understaffed.

"Hey, guys? I'm going to wash my hands and hide out for a few minutes to eat." I didn't wait for a response. I headed into our sole restroom, then grabbed my lunch bag and closed the door to the office. Sitting had never felt so good.

After I cracked open a bottle of pink lemonade and took a long swig, I tore into the ham and cheese sandwich and was halfway through it when a tentative knock came at the door. I groaned.

The door cracked open. "Sorry, but Lincoln's here," Derrick said. "Do you want him to wait?"

I blew out a breath. "No, it's okay. Tell him he can come in. But say I'm eating."

A moment later Lincoln sank onto the chair on the other side of the desk. I swallowed a bite and motioned to the half sandwich now sitting on its wax paper bag.

"Sorry, but I have to keep eating. We were short a person all morning and this was my first chance to sit and get something into me."

"Don't let me stop you," he said. "I saw Orlean out there. Her sister isn't on today?"

"She was supposed to be. Orlean said she's not feeling well." I took another big bite.

"Interesting. I tried to reach her without success."

I raised my eyebrows, but my mouth was too full to talk.

"I dropped by to see if you might have picked up any pieces of information since we last spoke," he said. "I will say, we believe Lavoie might have been under the influence of something before he was hit with the bookshelf."

"Something?" I held my hand over my mouth, then finished swallowing. "Like what kind of something? Do you mean tequila? Or a narcotic?"

"Not alcohol. And probably not an opiate."

"But the autopsy is finished."

"Yes, although not officially. It's just that the toxicology tests take a lot longer, especially when they aren't sure what they're looking for. The pathologist can issue a preliminary report, but it won't be final until the lab results are in."

I thought about the timeline. "Have you nailed down when Wagner was last seen? I mean, after the end of the parade? It seems like it was about eleven thirty when he announced he wasn't giving out prizes for the bikes. It produced a bit of grumbling, but I have to say he jollied even those people into shouting, 'Happy Spring.' "

"No one seems to have seen him after the end of the parade. No one who has come forward, I mean."

"I wonder if he had a date to meet someone in the parking lot. Or even inside the bookstore. Do his phone records help?" I popped in the last bite of sandwich.

"Nothing." He shook his head, frowning. "No text, no phone message. I wish there was."

"So, someone could have slipped him a note. Or said something in person." I sipped my drink.

"Right."

"I have picked up a few bits. You probably already know Kassandra Jenkins worked in the Everglades before moving back to Westham."

"Yes."

"Orlean is tuning up her bike. This morning Kassandra was in looking for it, but it isn't ready yet. She described the work down there as her dream job. I asked her why she left, and she said something vague about things not working out."

"Curious." He blinked behind his glasses and crossed his legs. "Did she say what kind of work she was doing?"

"She was kind of vague about it. She said she had a

position at a research center in the Everglades, but when I asked if she was a biologist, she said, 'Sort of.' "

"Mmm. What else do you have?"

I told him about visiting Belleville with Gin and meeting both Lyle McKean and Belinda Lavoie. "And, let's see. At dinner before the town meeting yesterday, Yvonne chewed out Gin for asking questions about her. Yvonne, who apparently had worked at Otis with Wagner, said she hated him but never would have killed him."

"So she says."

Derrick rapped on the door and stuck his head in again. "Mac? Sorry, but we're already swamped."

"Be right there." I drained my drink bottle and stood. "Sorry, Lincoln."

"I have to go, myself. Thanks, Mac, and take good care." He gazed over the top of his glasses. "I mean it."

"I will."

He rose with his usual grace and faced the door.

"Lincoln?"

He twisted to face me.

"Good luck."

He nodded before slipping out. He was going to need it.

CHAPTER 34

Tim pulled a round loaf of cheese bread from a paper bag and passed it in front of my face as I sat at the store counter at two thirty. One of his many specialties, this was a yeasted bread laden with Double Gloucester cheese. The loaf was actually a mass of small buns, so you could pull one off and eat it without needing a knife. The loaf he held smelled like it had just come out of the oven. As in, minutes earlier. It also smelled how I imagined heaven must.

I inhaled and nearly took a bite midair. "You're torturing me. I finished lunch not very long ago, but I'm telling you, I could eat every one of those."

He beamed, sliding it back into the bag. "It's for you and your gang here. I made a bunch for the Free Dinner tonight." He set the bag on the counter.

My eyes went wide. "Man, I'm glad you mentioned the dinner. I almost forgot I'm scheduled to serve at four thirty." Pa's church hosted the Free Dinner for those in need several days a week in the UU church basement.

"I knew you were. Private dinner at home afterward?"

I smiled. "If you're cooking, I'm eating."

"See you there, sweetheart. I'm off to deliver these and then catch a few winks of beauty sleep." He leaned over to kiss me, then sauntered his sexy self out the door, a rear view I would never tire of.

I couldn't help myself. I ripped open the bag and spread it flat on the counter. "Fresh cheese bread for everybody," I called out. I tore off a hunk and bit into it. The cheese was soft and stretchy, the bread yeasty and tender inside a buttery crust. "Customers included."

A fit-looking woman browsing shirts turned, looking surprised. She sniffed. "OMG, I thought something smelled good. Thank you." She headed over and tore off her own piece. "Mmm."

"Right?"

"Does that hunk of a guy belong to you?" She pointed her chin toward the door. "If he doesn't, I want his number."

I extended my left hand, palm down, displaying my lovely Victorian knot engagement ring nestled into the gold wedding band. "In fact, he does."

"All the good ones are taken." The little beads at the ends of her dozens of black braids sounded like tiny bells. A bit younger than me, her skin looked similar to mine.

"Well, that one is."

She gave a little laugh. "I was kidding."

"I'm Mac Almeida, by the way. This is my shop. I'd shake hands but we're both eating."

"Nice to meet you, Mac." She pressed her palms together in front of her chest. "Namaste hands work better, anyway. I'm Neli Lavoie."

"Nelly?" And . . . *Lavoie?*

"N-E-L-I. Short for Nelinda." She gave a little eye roll. "My mom's brilliant idea."

My smile slipped away. "You're Belinda's daughter. And Wagner's." Thus the biracial look to her. Just like my own, although I'd never bothered with braids. My curls weren't very tight. Even if they were, I would have worn my hair in a super-short, no-maintenance do. Her hair looked great on her, and matched her mom's, come to think of it.

"I am." Her expression turned somber, too.

"I'm so very sorry about your father's passing, Neli."

"Thank you. He and I weren't, um, close."

Derrick headed our way.

"Hey, Derr, this is Nelinda Lavoie. Neli, my brother Derrick Searle."

"We actually know each other, Mac." Neli greeted him.

He smiled at her in return, and the two exchanged a look I couldn't quite figure out. Was it a secret smile? Maybe this was someone he'd met in AA. I knew those relationships were to be kept in confidence. Or maybe she was a new love he'd met at the college? That would be cool. He'd been without a relationship since things hadn't worked out with Cokey's mom.

Derrick tore off a piece of the bag and set a hunk of the bread on it, then tore off another piece of bread. "I'm going to take this to Orlean while it's still warm. Neli, come see me over in the rentals area after you're done with my little sis."

She gave him a sweet smile and a thumbs-up.

"Do you live around here, Neli, or up in Belleville?" I asked.

"I have an apartment in Falmouth. But, wait a sec." She knit her brow. "How did you know my mom's name?"

I swallowed. "My friend and I were on a drive yesterday. She wanted to know some stuff about property in the town, so we stopped into Town Hall."

She tilted her head as if she didn't believe me. "Let me get this straight. My dad was murdered here in Westham, and you just happened to go talk to his estranged wife—my mom? Are you a PI or something?"

"Not exactly." My heart sank. I was caught in my own web of lies by someone my brother seemed to like. I hadn't given Belinda my real name. Now what? I opened my mouth. And shut it again.

"Don't worry." She smiled as she dusted off her hands. "I'll weasel it out of Derrick. Now, I wanted to buy the pink-and-purple shirt over there. Tomorrow's my birthday and I'm treating myself." She headed over to grab the shirt off the stack.

I rang it up for her, then watched as she walked toward the rentals area with a fluid athletic gait. Like Belinda, she didn't seem to be in mourning for her father. What had he done to estrange both wife and daughter?

I might have to weasel information about Neli out of Derrick. If the two were dating, I'd also have to come clean about using an alias when I talked with Neli's mother. It would be worth it to see my brother happy in love.

CHAPTER 35

At four twenty-eight, I slid my green Cape Symphony ball cap around so the brim was in the back and slipped on the thin plastic gloves the Free Dinner servers were required to wear. I picked up the big spoon and stared into an enormous pan of steaming lasagna sitting in front of me.

"Everybody ready?" Norland asked me and two others also wearing red Our Neighbors' Table aprons.

"Yep." My stomach gurgled at the delicious smells, but this was not my dinner.

The two women on the other side of me nodded, and Norland gave the signal to a high school student at the door. A stream of people filed in and picked up plates from the stack at the start of the line. Men and women, old and young, single and in couples, plus families. It broke my heart to see children who might be going hungry if not for these dinners, as well as the Free Food Market I also volunteered at. But not being able to make ends meet was a fact of life for many, especially during the off season here on touristy Cape Cod.

Norland forked up thick slices of ham. I added a generous helping of lasagna, which the cooks kept meatless in case some diners were vegetarians. The woman next to me dished up a spoonful of slivered green beans. By some miracle, they were still bright green. The last stop was green salad and Tim's cheese bread, which someone had already pulled apart into individual rolls and set in a basket with a pair of tongs. Diners could come back for seconds on anything, and all were also welcome to have a takeout container filled for another meal at home.

After the more than eighty people were served and settled at tables eating, Norland leaned toward me.

"I learned something today," he murmured.

"About our, um, joint venture?" I wasn't about to say the word "murder" in here.

"Yes. One of our selectmen went to high school with the former director."

My eyebrows went up. "In Belleville?"

"Exactly."

"In the same class?"

"Yes." Norland smiled at a man who approached for another round.

"Hey, Chief." When the man smiled, it revealed a gap where the teeth behind his eyetooth would have been. "You're taking it easy these days, I hear."

"How's it going, Joe? You bet I am, although it's all I can do to keep up with the grands."

"Tell me about it." The man gestured with a knobby thumb over his shoulder. "I got my own brood of grand-brats to run around after."

I looked where he'd gestured to. A tired-looking young woman sat at a table with three children aged maybe five to eight. The kids were devouring their dinners, with the littlest holding a piece of ham in his hand and biting straight into it.

Norland's expression turned serious. "Joe, if those children are ever hungry, you come to me, you hear? The department has a fund."

"I surely appreciate it," Joe said. "They get them free breakfasts and lunches at school, even the little guy at kindergarten. But weekends can get tight, and vacation weeks are tough."

"Do your daughter and the little ones live with you?" Norland asked.

"They do, ever since her no-good husband deserted her."

"I mean it," Norland said. "You come to me. I might be retired from active duty, but now I manage the Benevolent Fund. We take care of our own, which includes you, Joe."

A woman waiting behind Joe cleared her throat.

"Excuse me, ma'am," Joe said. "I'm much obliged, Chief." He stepped in front of me.

I scooped from my pan, which was running low. "Do you want to wait for the next pan?"

"Nah, this is fine. Thank you kindly, miss." He moved on down.

Norland and I didn't get another quiet moment. The runners from the kitchen swapped out empty containers for full ones. Diners came back for more food, and more again to take home. Fat squares of brownies were brought out. It wasn't until an hour later that the last diner left. We tossed our serving gloves into the trash and our aprons into a box destined for a washing machine. I slipped on my jacket.

"Was Joe with the police department?" I asked Norland.

"He wasn't an officer of the peace, but he worked as the custodian for years. I hired him, myself. But then he hurt his back and couldn't do the job anymore, which is a shame. He was a hundred percent trustworthy."

"You would need someone you could trust in a police department, I'd guess."

"Absolutely." He held the door for me. "We have suspects' names and photographs on whiteboards. Someone is always on shift overnight when the cleaning happens, and calls come in. Discussions happen. Joe never divulged a single thing. Never leaked a story to the press. I wished I could have kept him on."

"I'm glad if you can help out with food money for the kids." For many people, a single medical emergency could mean the difference between self-sufficiency and disaster. Or, in Joe's daughter's case, perhaps, a breadwinner leaving the marriage and creating an overnight single mom with young children to provide for.

"I will make it happen, Mac. Without a doubt."

I zipped my jacket up to the neck. The sky was still light, but the wind sent its chilly fingers into any gap.

"I thought March was supposed to go out like a lamb," I said.

He laughed. "We have a few more days yet until April. Almost a week."

"Was there something else you were going to tell me about Park and Wagner?"

He checked his watch. "Uh-oh. I have to get going and fast. My oldest grandgirl has a basketball game at six and I said I'd drive her."

"Go, then."

"Super briefly, I think I dug something up, about a friend of Jenkins and Lavoie's dying in an accident when they were all seniors in high school. My keenly honed police intuition, otherwise known as my Spidey-sense, tells me it might not have been an accident."

CHAPTER 36

I stared as Norland hurried to his car in the church parking lot and drove off. "Thanks for the bombshell, Norland," I said aloud. It could be hours before he had time and space to text his thoughts. I swore silently. There was nothing I could do about the delay.

And my stomach was growling in earnest by now. I hurried away down the length of Main Street, eager for Tim, dinner, and an evening of research. Most of the retail shops were already closed and dark. The spring wind gusted, clanking chains that signs hung from. Even the Rusty Anchor, while lit from within, didn't have people coming and going. It emitted the aroma of fried food, though, which didn't help my hunger pangs. This was the kind of situation when I cursed my naturally high metabolism. Tim's cheese bread from this afternoon was a distant memory to my stomach.

When I turned onto Blacksmith Shop Road, the roar of the wind in the treetops seemed even more ominous. Back at the church, I could have called Tim for a ride. I'd be silly to do so now. Our house was less than a quarter of a mile along the street leading up the hill. The road was lined with oaks and maples, walnut trees and chestnuts, serviceberry trees and new, disease-resistant American elms. There were saplings planted by the Westham Tree Commission alongside grande dames gracing the street for many decades.

As I hurried, I thought about Park and Wagner attending Belleville High School together. Did Lincoln know that? I hoped so. It was his business to. But what had gone on, that a friend of theirs had died in an accident? Why did Norland think the death might not have been accidental?

If the two boys—now middle-aged men—had covered up a homicide, Wagner might have threatened to reveal the truth at last. Park had a lot at stake in his life. He owned a real estate business and held an influential position in town government. Had he killed Wagner to keep him quiet?

My own Spidey-sense suddenly flipped onto high alert. I could swear someone was watching me. Tailing my movement. I kept glancing over my shoulder, but no one lurked there. No car crept slowly after me. I hurried as fast as I could.

My insides froze at a sound behind me. Had it been a cough? A throat clearing? It wasn't a branch or an engine.

I gave a quick look backward. As I did, my toe caught on an uneven piece of pavement in the sidewalk. Arms flailing, I staggered forward and tripped again. I was reaching for the trunk of a street-side oak when someone grabbed my arm.

No! My breath rushed in. My throat thickened.

"Are you okay, Mac?" a woman asked.

I twisted to see Penelope Johnson peering at me. "Where did you come from?" I swallowed.

She laughed, letting go of my arm. "I live here." She made a motion at the cottage behind us. "I came out to see where my trash barrel had blown off to. Instead, I saw you trip."

"I had no idea you lived down the road from me. Thanks for the save." I let out a breath. "I have a knee that wouldn't have appreciated crashing into the sidewalk."

"You looked like someone was chasing you. Except . . ." Her voice trailed off and she wagged her head back and forth. "Nobody but the two of us is out here."

"Apparently." I cleared my throat, embarrassed to be caught in my paranoia.

Her smile vanished. "I'm sure you're concerned about Lavoie's killer. We think we're getting close. Please don't be investigating, Mac. You and your group. It's way too risky. Okay? I'm serious. It's much too dangerous."

I nodded my acknowledgment, thanked her again, and headed for home. More slowly this time, and with great care. She was right. A murderer at large in town was dangerous, to the extreme.

CHAPTER 37

"I don't know how you do it, Tim," I said after swallowing my first bite of spaghetti and meatballs at our kitchen table half an hour later. "They're so tender, and the sauce is fabulous."

"I'm glad you like them. A long, slow simmer in the sauce is key." He pointed to his plate. "Plus, my top-secret ingredient is in the sauce."

"Are you going to tell me what it is?"

"Then it wouldn't be top secret, would it? Savor the flavors on your tongue and see if you can figure it out."

I took a bite of pasta and sauce without a meatball and rolled it around in my mouth. "I have no idea. I mean, it tastes Italian, and rich. And yummy."

He leaned toward me. "If you tell anyone, I'll have to kill you."

"I promise to guard the secret with my life." Although the idea of anyone else being killed, even in jest, gave me the shivers.

"Pesto," Tim whispered in my ear.

That gave me an entirely different set of shivers, these of the delightful kind. He sat back, beaming.

"The basil pesto you mixed up last summer and froze?" I tasted the sauce again.

"The same, a big spoonful of it. The olive oil, pine nuts, and garlic meld with the fresh basil. You can't taste any of them separately, right?"

"Not at all. All I taste is heavenly deliciousness. Mom put pesto into her fish stew on Sunday with the same delicious result." I took another bite from my heaped plate. "When I was serving the Free Dinner, I was so hungry I wanted to serve myself a plate and eat it standing up."

"How did they like the cheese bread?"

"It went quickly, even with the sign a server added asking people to take only one roll each."

Belle waddled in from the other room. "Top secret, Mac. It wouldn't be top secret, would it?" She reproduced Tim's voice exactly. "Snacks, Mac?"

"Belle, you had your dinner. You'll have to wait for snacks."

"You had your dinner." Now her voice sounded like mine. "You had your dinner. Snacks, Mac?"

"Your bird is better than a comedy show." Tim smiled at me. "How was your day, hon?"

Belle waddled out, muttering, "How was your day, hon?" in Tim's voice. "Snacks, hon?" She capped it off with a wolf whistle.

I took a sip of my Chianti and kept my voice low so Belle didn't pick up any new words. "Norland told me something disturbing after the dinner. He said he'd learned Wagner Lavoie and Park Jenkins went to Belleville High together. And a friend of theirs had died in an accident at the time, but it might not have actually been accidental."

"Hmm." Tim lifted his beer glass and drank. "That sounds bad."

"I know. Norland had to run and do something with his granddaughter, so he couldn't finish telling the story. I hope he'll text the group later."

"What are you thinking?"

I told him my speculations. "It would have ruined Park's life to have a decades-old murder exposed."

"Wouldn't it have ruined Wagner's, as well, if he told the truth?"

"Yes, unless Park was the killer and Wagner only witnessed it."

"He'd still be an accomplice, or whatever they call it," Tim pointed out.

"True. I also met Wagner's daughter today. Neli—Nelinda—came into the shop. She bought a bike shirt, but she also seemed to know Derrick."

"From the college, do you think?"

"Maybe. She said she lives in Falmouth. They seemed pretty friendly, and I kind of wondered if they might be dating." I laughed. "Except, she was there when you brought the cheese bread in. She called you a hunk—which is true, of course—and said if you weren't mine, she wanted your number."

He blushed, hard, and shook his head. "It embarrasses me to say it, but I know I won the genetic lottery, at least as far as white people go. And I can't tell you how uncomfortable it makes me when people admire my looks, Mac."

"Well, I won the everything lottery when you fell

in love with me." I smiled fondly at this man. Yes, he was gorgeous. Far more important was how kind he was, how intelligent, how generous, and how much attention he paid to staying healthy with his beach runs and home-cooked meals for both of us. I forked in my last bite. "But wouldn't it be fun if Derrick and Neli were a couple? I really liked her, and I'd love to see my brother happy with a woman."

"You don't think she could have had anything to do with her father's murder?"

The corners of my mouth pulled down. "I hope not. She did say they weren't close. And her mom, Belinda, was estranged from Wagner. I'm not sure if Belinda and Wagner were officially separated or had just grown apart. But speaking of crime, when I was walking home, I tripped on a sidewalk." I decided not to tell him I tripped because I was freaked out someone might have been after me. "Did you know Detective Johnson lives down the road from us? Penelope caught me before I crash-landed."

"I didn't know. I'm glad you didn't hurt yourself." He tilted his head. "Was she following you or something?"

"No. She said she was out looking for where the wind had taken her barrel."

But had it been true? Maybe she'd been keeping an eye on me. No. I was sure my imagination had conjured up that Spidey-sense.

"By the way," Tim began. "A dude named Corwin Germaine stopped by while I was cooking. Said he'd like to speak with you."

"Corwin? I wonder why he didn't come to the store or call me." Why would he want to talk with me? I'd already paid him for the snowplowing.

"He's Orlean's ex, isn't he?"

I nodded.

"He probably didn't want to run into her there. Anyway, he said he texted, but you didn't reply."

Oops. "Right. I turned off my phone during the dinner."

I would wait to check it until after we were done here. We still had the salad to eat, and I always cleaned up, since I didn't cook. Plus, nothing could be that urgent.

CHAPTER 38

After I sank onto the couch with another glass of wine, Tim sat in the easy chair across from me and opened his library book, a history of surfing. Belle was down for the night, with her cage covered. African gray parrots need a lot of sleep. I glanced up. So did my hardworking husband, who now snored gently, open book on his lap. Wasn't falling asleep quickly the sign of a pure heart? Or maybe it was an unburdened soul. He had both, as far as I knew.

Feet up on the coffee table, I pulled out my phone and swiped open Corwin's text.

Pls call me. Might have info about Lavoie.

Oh? I placed the call, but it went to voice mail. I disconnected, because who listens to voice mail anymore? I tapped out a text, instead. **Tried to call. Interested in info. Pls call back before ten or tomorrow.**

There. This had to be something about Sandy. Didn't it? She was his former sister-in-law. But maybe Corwin had known Wagner. Or witnessed the killer going into the bookstore. I was antsy to find out, but I was going to have to wait.

Norland hadn't written or called, either. I thought about Wagner and Park's ages and subtracted back to when they would have been around eighteen. I grabbed my tablet and mounted a search including Belleville High School, "student accident," and the year.

I wrinkled my nose at the reports of a couple of non-fatal automobile fender-benders involving Belleville students. When I added Park Jenkins to the list, I found a much more interesting article and settled in to read. It said three Belleville senior boys had been on the bluffs above Cragshead Beach drinking and smoking late at night. One slipped and fell down the cliff to his death. Parkhust Jenkins III was quoted as saying how sad he and his buddy Wagner were, and that they'd warned their friend not to get so close to the edge. The Belleville High principal extended sympathies to the family and would be providing counseling to any classmates who requested it.

The reporter saved the intriguing bit for the end. The police chief mentioned an investigation was underway and reminded citizens to report accidents immediately after they occurred rather than the next morning.

I sat back and took a sip of wine. So the kids must not have called in their friend's death until the following day. But why? If one of them had pushed the friend, Wagner and Park would have been terrified and needed to get their stories straight. But what if the dude who went over had only been injured and could have been saved in the moment? And why kill a classmate, anyway?

This had to be the information Norland had come across. As a retired WPD chief himself, he might even know people formerly on the Belleville police force. I copied the link and texted it to the Cozy Capers.

Suspicious? Maybe. If P pushed the friend, was W threatening to go public after all this time?

I'd have to wait for Norland's response before going any further. If he had more information, surely he'd already relayed it to Lincoln or at least to Penelope.

Next I tapped in, "Kassandra Jenkins Everglades research center."

Her name didn't come up, but the research center did. They studied various endangered tropical species, such as the bonneted bat and the Stock Island tree snail, plus Cape Sable thoroughwort, whatever thoroughwort was. There was an avian department, with pictures of gorgeous black-and-white avocets, showy flamingos, and long-beaked glossy ibises standing knee-deep in the marshes. The center also studied mammals and provided pictures of fat manatees. Of course there were reptiles large and small. But the amphibian department really snagged my attention. One of the creatures occupying both water and land was a poisonous frog. *Whoa.*

I sent myself on an Internet tangent to look up a pretty little frog whose cerulean-blue skin with black spots signaled to predators it carried a lethal toxin. I shuddered at what I discovered. Even touching its skin would poison an adult human if they had a cut in their own skin. The frog wasn't native to Florida but had migrated north in recent years.

But why couldn't I find a record of Kassandra's employment with the research center? I thought of what the guy at the town meeting had called her and added Kaycie Jenkins to the search box. Zip. I hadn't seen that nickname written anywhere. I changed the spelling to Casey. Still nothing. A little light bulb lit up in my brain, and I changed my search to KC Jenkins, plus the Everglades information.

Bingo. My eyes widened. And double bingo. KC Jenkins had not only worked at the center, she'd also been employed in the department studying amphibians. I flipped through a few links until I reached a new article in the *Key West Citizen.*

The headline read, "Research Center Employee Leaves Under Cloud." The article went on to describe the death of a researcher in the amphibian department due to a biological toxin. The director described it as an unfortunate accident and stated new, stricter safety measures were being implemented. "Office Manager KC Jenkins has submitted her resignation papers. The center thanks her for several years of service and wishes her well in the future."

The police were quoted as saying they lacked evidence to pursue charges of homicide. I gave a soft whistle. It sounded like everybody thought Kassandra had poisoned the unfortunate researcher, but they couldn't pin it on her. The director could make sure she left, though.

No wonder she'd told me the job hadn't worked out. It was also no surprise she was working retail in her mom's toy store. Who else would hire her? Nobody in her field, for sure. Although . . . office manager? It wasn't exactly a career path. "Several" also didn't account for nearly ten years since she must have finished college.

The real question was if she'd brought some frog poison home with her to Westham. Lincoln had said Wagner had been under the influence of something before the shelving unit hit him. A lethal tropical toxin definitely would qualify.

CHAPTER 39

The next morning dawned much milder. Clouds gusted in the breeze as I walked to the shop at eight thirty, and the air felt like a kiss of spring. Gin had texted her regrets last night, saying she was a bit under the weather and wouldn't be up for speed walking this morning. I chose not to go alone, instead puttering at home, dancing with Belle to her favorite song, "Happy," and gearing up for the day. Between the song's toe-tapping beat and my parrot bobbing her head in time with it, I always ended up happier, too.

Norland still hadn't gotten in touch, I mused as I strolled. Not with me, not via the group text. I hoped he was all right. I'd try to carve out some time later to pop by the bookstore and ask what was up. I had taken a moment last evening to briefly let the group know what I'd learned. Everybody must have been busy. Not a single response came in reply.

As I walked by Penelope's house, I glanced at the cottage. I didn't know the first thing about her. Was she a married mom with a pack of kids? Did she live alone, or with a partner? I liked her intelligent, straightforward approach. Maybe she and I could be friends. Time would tell.

Walking back down Main Street was a different scene from last evening. Business owners were unlocking doors, and Greta's Grains emitted the most alluring aromas of yeast and sugar and brewing coffee.

My key was in my shop's door when I heard two bike bells ding behind me. I turned to see my mom and grandma on their matching tricycles.

"We have news," Astra said.

"And breakfast." Abo Reba pointed to the paper bag in her front basket.

"Then I've just won the grand prize." I smiled and held the door open for them as they unclipped helmets and left them hanging from handlebars. I'd already wolfed down a big bowl of granola, yogurt, and banana at home. So what? I was pretty much a bottomless pit when it came to eating.

Reba grabbed the bag and bustled in. Mom stopped to give my cheek a kiss.

"Your father sends his love and says he'll be home tomorrow." She headed inside.

I followed. "Good. Let me put on the coffee." Eight thirty was turning out to be my daily office hour, it appeared, with a rotating cast of visitors.

A few minutes later, they sat behind the retail

counter, coffees in hand, an array of Tim's pastries laid out on paper napkins. I stayed standing and selected a bear claw, one of my favorites from his bakery.

"Are you two headed out for an early ride?" I bit into the flaky, sweet, nut-studded crispness of the pastry and nearly swooned.

"Of course," Mom said. "Daily aerobic activity is important for heart health, especially when Mercury is in retrograde, like now."

I didn't roll my eyes, but I wanted to.

"Plus, we're celebrating this spring weather," Reba added. "We're going early because the rest of the day is busy for both of us."

"And don't forget Pluto is leaving Capricorn and entering Aquarius." Mom beamed. "We're all coming into a more egalitarian and progressive age. Life will be lighter."

"Really?" I asked. "For all of us?" *As if.*

"Yes." Mom nodded so hard I was afraid for her neck. She went on, "It's a slow process, but getting out of conservative Capricorn can't help but be a benefit to society. Pluto, as I'm sure you're aware, Mackenzie, rules the masses, the zeitgeist."

All I could do was smile. Not only was I not aware, I didn't believe in the power of the planet, which was possibly not a planet at all, to affect the actions of every person here on our rock called Earth.

Reba lifted her eyebrows. "Now, Mackie, have you heard about the wake?"

I swallowed my mouthful. "What wake?"

"Wagner Lavoie's, of course." Mom frowned at me. "You're a merchant. I thought you would have been notified."

"Why would Main Street merchants be involved?"

"Mackenzie." Reba sounded a touch exasperated. "Because it's the Chamber of Commerce who is throwing the party."

"She means the memorial gathering," Mom said. "Tonight at five-thirty in the bank's function room."

"Will his funeral be tomorrow?" I asked. That was how things were usually done.

"No," my grandma said. "This isn't an official wake. But the Chamber wanted to stage a gathering to honor poor Mr. Lavoie."

"The timing seems odd to me." I brushed the crumbs off my hands. "His homicide is still an open, unsolved case."

"Ooh, it'll be like an Agatha Christie story, with all the suspects in the drawing room." My mom's eyes sparkled.

"I like the way your mind works, Astra," Reba said.

"Hey, you two," I protested. "I'd like to remind you this is real life and not a work of crime fiction."

"Maybe Lincoln will show up and finger one of them," Mom added.

"Finger, Mom? Seriously?" A message came in on my phone. "Huh. Here's the notice from the Chamber." I glanced up. "They want all Main Street business owners and employees to attend, plus it's open to the public. I wonder who in heck is funding it?"

"His wife, maybe?" Reba asked.

"Or a deep-pocketed donor." Mom drained her coffee.

Like Park Jenkins, perhaps.

"Come on, Reba." Mom moved toward the door. "We need to hit the road."

"I'll clean up," I said. "Have a nice ride, you two."

"See you tonight," Reba called over her shoulder.

I wiped down the counter and took their mugs to the sink in our tiny kitchen area at the back of the shop. My phone started pinging off the hook, but I didn't have time to attend to any of it. I had an opening checklist to accomplish, and I was behind schedule.

CHAPTER 40

Orlean and Sandy hurried in together at exactly nine thirty, bringing a whoosh of fresh air with them. Orlean nodded her greeting and went straight to the mini fridge to stash her lunch. Sandy lingered near where I was arranging a new shipment of boxed helmets on a shelf.

"Mac, I'm sorry I missed work yesterday. I'm prone to migraine headaches. When one hits, I have to lay low in a dark room."

"Okay." I turned to face her. "A migraine must be painful. Do you take meds for it?"

"I have something, but it isn't very effective." Her hair neatly pulled back in a clip, she stood with hands in the pockets of a pair of khaki pants. She wore a green collared shirt under a black cardigan, looking like she was ready for a day in retail and customer service, albeit with bikes instead of fashion. "The drug almost makes me feel worse."

"I'm sorry to hear it." A couple of friends had described how bad a migraine could be, and I was grateful I wasn't prone to getting them. "I would appreciate hearing from you directly when you need to take a sick day. Do you agree to notify me?"

She didn't respond for a moment. Her body seemed to tense, and she gave me a look I couldn't interpret. I took a step back. I'd made a perfectly reasonable request as her employer, but Orlean had said Sandy had issues of some kind. I waited, not knowing if she was about to lash out verbally—or worse.

"Sure." She relaxed her shoulders. "What do you want me to do today?"

Whew. "You can finish putting out these helmets, and this box is full of shoes to shelve, too." I remembered the Chamber invitation. "But first, I have something to tell both of you. Orlean?"

"I'm listening." Orlean didn't glance over.

"The Chamber is throwing a memorial gathering for Wagner Lavoie this evening."

Sandy's nostrils flared.

"They've invited all the Main Street business owners and employees," I continued. "Do you think you'll both be able to make it?"

"What time?" Orlean asked.

"Five thirty."

"I'll go," Sandy said. "Nothing more I'd like to do than celebrate the fact he's gone." She turned away and set a helmet box on the shelf with a bit too much force.

I blinked. What a harsh thing to say. Think it, maybe, but utter it out loud?

"I'll go, too," Orlean said. "To pay my respects to the dead." Staring at her sister, she emphasized "respects."

"Good, then." We'd been closing at five all winter. The timing would work out perfectly. I lowered my voice and addressed Sandy. "It sounds like you had some unpleasant history with Wagner."

Sandy whirled to face me. "Oh, yes, I did. The man was a wretch of the first order, Mac. I'm not sorry he's gone." She clamped her mouth shut and returned to her work.

"Did you know him in Belleville?" I didn't want to let this go, and I kind of had her captive for the moment.

"Yes."

"How?"

"I don't want to talk about it." She slid the last helmet onto the shelf.

Three customers pushed through the door. A crash came from the repair area, followed by Orlean uttering a mild expletive. My phone rang in my pocket. I pulled it out to see a call from Corwin.

"Sandy, please help these folks." I smiled at them and hurried outside to connect the call. "Corwin?"

"Mac, sorry to bother you during the day."

"It's okay. I have a minute. I heard you stopped by the house yesterday."

"I did, but then I was out when you tried to get back to me."

I waited, but he didn't speak. "I'm outside. Nobody's listening, just so you know."

"Good." He cleared his throat. "I heard Sandy's working for you."

"She is."

"As you know, she was my sister-in-law."

"Yes."

"And she's a vet, like me."

I hadn't realized Corwin had served in the military. I did know he'd served time in prison.

"Were you in the service together?" I asked.

"Not at all." He barked a laugh. "I was infantry. Sandy was in an office handling the accounting. Somebody's gotta do it."

And maybe skimming money off the military? Not a smart move.

"Plus, she's older than me. Me and Orlie." His voice sounded wistful.

I'd never heard anyone call Orlean by a nickname. Not even her sister. It was my turn to clear my throat.

"You had something you wanted to tell me," I said.

"I do. Listen, I'm sure Sandy has changed her ways. But in case she hasn't, you might want to watch your cash, and don't ever let her watch you open your safe, if you have one there. She kind of has a history with wanting money belonging to other people."

Huh. "Can you give me specifics?"

"I'd rather not. At least, not over the phone," he said.

"I might have heard something similar about her from elsewhere. Do you know anything about her knowing Wagner Lavoie?"

"Mmm. Maybe." A voice sounded in the background. "Hey, I have to go."

"Corwin, you need to tell Detective Haskins what you know. It's super important."

"Mac, I—"

"I'm serious. I'm going to give him your number. You realize we're talking about homicide, right?"

A second went by. "Yes. All right. Catch you later." He disconnected.

Four tandems rode up. Eight people began to dismount. I plastered on a smile, stashed my phone, and did my best to ignore the fact that my newest employee might be an embezzler—or worse. *Wonderful.*

CHAPTER 41

By eleven, things were quiet enough in the shop for me to take a breath and retreat to my office for a few minutes' break. I first texted Lincoln, copying Penelope.

Corwin Germaine has info re Sandy McKean. She's working at my shop today.

I added Corwin's number and sent it before I could reconsider.

My gaze fell on the small safe. Corwin had seemed to imply Sandy could get into the safe if she saw me entering the combination. Did he think she could memorize the numbers I used to open it? He'd also said to keep an eye on the cash. Maybe I shouldn't let her work the register. Did she also memorize credit card numbers? At least these days nearly everybody's cards had chips, and they didn't have to hand them over to the clerk to pay.

As a merchant, I didn't much care for the system. It made it much easier for anyone to steal a card and use it. My card reader was set up to require a signature for purchases over fifty dollars, but those scribbled digital signatures were pretty much illegible.

I again felt the tangled mess this case was. It had so many connections. So many people had had conflict with the victim. Either Sandy or Kassandra could have accessed something lethal in a lab or research center. Yvonne, who couldn't stand Wagner, had known him at the Otis Air National Guard base. Wagner and Park had experienced a traumatic—possibly homicidal—event together as teenagers. Heck, even Lyle could have held a grudge against Wagner if he'd had an affair with Sandy during their marriage. Dentists had access to plenty of drugs.

Belinda might have had the worst grievances against her husband. Maybe it made me an ableist, but I couldn't see her poisoning Wagner in the bookstore and then pushing over a bookcase to finish him off. And I fervently hoped she hadn't enlisted Neli to kill him for her. I froze, a chill running through me. I'd read a suspense novel not long ago in which a guy in a wheelchair fooled the heroine. In a story that was definitely not a cozy mystery, this man had faked his disability and attacked her. I did not want to believe Belinda Lavoie would do such a thing.

The untidy scramble of facts and rumors made my skin crawl, especially when they were hard to sort out, to smooth and organize into submission.

Still, I needed to get back out front, ASAP. I tapped out a quick to-do text to myself.

Try to talk with Yvonne. Check out behind bookstore. Call Tim re Wagner memorial.

I sent it. I couldn't remember if Tim had said he had something going on this evening or not. I headed into my shop, nearly holding my breath at what would happen next.

By some stroke of luck, Yvonne herself stood in front of me. She was talking with Orlean, who was bent over Yvonne's sleek silver tandem.

"Hey, Yvonne," I began, summoning a friendly smile. "Bike giving you problems?"

She faced me slowly without returning my smile. "Yes."

"Nothing we can't handle," Orlean chimed in without looking up. She tightened one of the brake handles and squeezed it several times. "You're good to go."

"Thanks," Yvonne said. "What do I owe you?"

"No charge," Orlean said.

"I appreciate it." Yvonne pushed up her sleeves, revealing muscular forearms, and set her hands on the handlebars. "If you'll excuse me, Mac?"

Meaning, get the heck out of my way. "I'll grab the door for you." I hurried ahead.

We'd been friendly earlier in the week. Maybe it was Gin's questioning Uly, plus my friendship with Gin, that turned Yvonne cold toward me. I was about to push open the door when Sandy opened it from the outside. Where had she been?

"Thanks," I said to her. "Can you hold the door for Yvonne, please?"

Sandy stood back, her shoulders stiffening, doing as I'd asked. Yvonne wheeled the double bike out.

"What are you doing here?" she asked Sandy as she passed her.

This sounded interesting. I followed the chef outside, where spring was in the air. The day had warmed, and a brilliant red cardinal was singing his beautiful heart out in a tree across the street, letting all the ladies know he was available.

"I'm working for Mac." Sandy lifted her chin and headed into the shop.

After the door closed, Yvonne gave me a look. "Good luck with her."

"Why?" I asked.

"You might want to be careful with your money."

"Oh? What do you know?"

"I used to work with her, okay?" She climbed onto the front of the bike but kept a foot on the ground.

"Can I ask where?"

Yvonne gazed ahead of her for a moment, as if considering whether to tell me more. She turned her face toward me.

"We were both in the Air Force at Otis. I cooked. She did bookkeeping." Her mouth looked like she'd tasted a sour lemon. "I caught her more than once trying to do some fancy accounting with my kitchen orders."

Huh. "Wagner worked there, too. Did you overlap with him?"

"Yes. He was on base, too, and not as a civvy." She curled her lip. "He tried to hit on me, but I told him I played for the other side. I'm pretty sure he and Sandy had a thing for a while, though, and might have been up to a few financial shenanigans together."

"When was this, Yvonne?"

"Oh, it's been a few years. I got out and found work in restaurants. I think Sandy went to work in a lab or something."

"Thank you for telling me. Listen, I hope we can still be friends, you and me." I meant it.

"Yeah, sure, Mac. Whatever."

"Will you be at the Chamber thing for Wagner later today?"

"Um, no?" She pulled a face as if I'd made a ludicrous suggestion. "I'll be working."

"Right. Of course."

"I gotta run." She set her foot on the pedal and rode away.

At least I had mended that bridge. Maybe. And learned Wagner's extramarital fling might have been with Sandy.

I paused with my hand on the doorknob. All that business at Otis must have gone down at least five years ago, if not more. Clearly, past hurts and suspicions lasted a long time.

CHAPTER 42

After Derrick arrived and everyone had taken their lunch breaks, I slid into my jacket and slung on my EpiPen bag.

"Hey, gang, I have to do some business in town," I announced. "Derr, will you handle sales? Sandy can do rentals and restocking or whatever."

"Sure," he said.

I wanted to ask him if he and Neli Lavoie were a thing, but this wasn't the right time.

Sandy gave me a funny look, which I ignored. She wasn't going near the money if I had anything to do with it. I was the business owner. I could steer my employees where I wanted them. Well, except for Orlean. She had her fiefdom in the repair area, which was fine with me.

I headed out, soon enough realizing I barely needed the jacket. I gazed at a clump of inch-high future daffodils poking up their greenery in front of the gift shop. Spring growth was on its way, as happened every year. Thoughts of warm sunshine, late sunsets, sipping sangria, and wearing shorts should have made me feel more cheerful. Right now? Worrying if I had a murderer working for me was enough to dampen any seasonal joy. And if it wasn't Sandy, then the killer had to be one of the other persons of interest who lived right here in Westham. More than one had an intense dislike of Wagner, including Park, Kassandra, Yvonne, and possibly others I hadn't heard about. I shivered involuntarily.

My mood didn't improve when I walked into the Book Nook. Penelope, arms folded, feet slightly apart, faced Norland, who stood behind the bookstore's counter.

"With all due respect, sir, it appears you've been withholding information from the—" She broke off when she realized I'd come in.

"Hi, Mac." Norland's tone was somber, his gaze level. He addressed the detective. "With all due respect, ma'am, I have not withheld anything from the investigation. The information of which you speak came to my attention only in the last few hours."

I watched the two. What was going on? Surely a former police chief wouldn't have hidden important facts from Penelope and Lincoln. Why did she think he had? And what had he learned this morning?

"Very well," she said. "Please be in more immediate contact in the future, Chief Gifford."

"Yes, ma'am."

She strode past me and headed out. After the door closed, he put on a sardonic smile and gave a mock salute.

"What was that all about?" I asked.

A woman wheeling a toddler in a stroller came in, followed by another mom with not only a child in a stroller but also a baby strapped into a soft front carrier.

"Welcome to the Book Nook." Norland smiled at them, although his eyes still looked worried. "I'll tell you later, Mac," he murmured to me. "Can you stick around?"

"Yes." I moved out of the newcomers' way and moseyed back to the scene of the crime. I hadn't been in here since Saturday and was relieved to see L-braces securing the six-foot bookshelf to the floor as well as rods above attaching it to the ceiling. This unit wasn't going anywhere.

I perused the open space behind it. I knew it had been empty before, with only the shelves lining the wall, but now Norland had moved an easy chair and a round table into the area. The table displayed a dozen upright books and a sign reading, "Local Authors." *Good.* He'd probably wanted to distract anyone from imagining a dead body on the floor. It didn't keep me from those thoughts, though.

I blew out a breath. While Norland was busy, I could check out the parking lot. At the back door, I said, "I'll be out here for a few."

He gave me a nod and returned to helping the shoppers in the children's area.

I pushed through the door. I doubted any actual evidence remained out here, especially after the spring snowstorm we'd gotten. But it helped to visualize what had happened. Or try to, anyway.

Moving a few yards into the parking lot, I turned in a slow circle, pausing as I gazed at the side street.

It ran perpendicular to Main Street and was where I'd seen Park and Kassandra disappear after they'd left the bar. Had they gone to retrieve his car or to accomplish something nefarious?

I surveyed the backs of the row of stores and restaurants. The buildings were contiguous without even a passageway between them. They were old, though, and individual in a quirky kind of way. Above the Book Nook and Game's Up, the game store next door, were two floors of apartments. Yoshinoya, the Japanese restaurant, had a flat roof. On the Book Nook's left were two more stores with one floor of flats above, then the pizza and sub sandwich place on the corner, a single-story building.

Anyone could have headed back here to the parking lot and slipped into the Book Nook's rear door with Wagner—or followed him in. No, they would have had to agree to meet and go in together. Otherwise, why would the Chamber director, coming off his victory of a festival, be hiding out in the back of a bookstore? But . . . why go into the Book Nook at all?

I shook my head, bewildered. I ambled back toward the door, head down, still searching. For what, I didn't know. A small splash of red caught my attention. It was half under a dried leaf left over from the fall. I leaned down and reached for it. I pulled my hand back when I saw it was a Mac's Bikes keychain, the freebie we'd given out before the parade on Saturday. Instead, I rummaged in my jacket pocket and pulled out what I hoped was a clean tissue. I used it to lift the souvenir from the ground.

This could be anyone's. We'd given out dozens. But Wagner had gotten one. And if this particular keychain provided any clue to his killer's identity, I didn't want to pollute the evidence. *Wait.* I grimaced. I might already have ruined it. After one of the previous murders in town, Lincoln had mentioned it was better to leave evidence in place for an officer to retrieve rather than to move it, no matter how carefully. Too late now.

"What did you find there?" a man asked. "Anything good?"

I squeaked and whirled, shoving the tissue-wrapped item into my jacket pocket. Park Jenkins faced me. Wearing a blazer and open-collared shirt, his face was flushed. He wasn't glaring at me, but he didn't smile, either.

"Hi, Park." My heart beat like a jackhammer in my chest. How did he sneak up on me? I'd just been thinking about him and his daughter. I didn't believe in conjuring, but this seemed like a freaky coincidence.

He waited for me to answer. The parking lot was oddly quiet, with only a few cars in the lined spots. Usually shoppers would be coming and going back here. It was just my luck to hit it at a slow moment, with no one to call on for help if I needed some. I swallowed.

"I'm just picking up litter." I tried to keep my voice casual as I invented a story. "It's a family thing. Are you heading in to buy a book?" Maybe changing the topic would work.

"Not today."

I caught a whiff of stale alcohol on his breath. He must have had a liquid lunch at the Anchor again.

"Will you be at the wake?" he asked.

"Yes." Sidestepping around him, I said, "See you there." I hurried off toward the side street and a place, anyplace, where other people were. Friends, strangers, any other humans. I wasn't picky. I could talk with Norland later.

I would have loved to ask Park a few questions about Belleville. About Kassandra. About Wagner. But alone in a deserted parking lot? No possible way.

CHAPTER 43

I glanced behind me after I regained the bustle of Main Street. At least Park hadn't followed me. I halfway scolded myself for being spooked by him. On the other hand, I'd been alone in a deserted parking lot. It was entirely possible Park was innocent. And equally as possible he wasn't. Sunshine or no sunshine, bad things could happen when a murderer was nearby.

But now where? Getting back to my shop wasn't urgent. I didn't want to circle around and go back in the bookstore's front door in case Park had lied about his plans. I could stop in at Tim's bakery and ask if he was going to the wake, plus grab a quick kiss. I checked the time. Nah. He'd be closing now at two o'clock and busy scrubbing down the kitchen. Ahead I spied the Toy Soldier sign. What would June think if I casually dropped in again without buying a toy? If she seemed suspicious, I could always use the pretense of mentioning the wake.

Inside, June was ringing up a purchase for a man in a jacket and cap. She glanced up and frowned when she saw me. *Odd.* I smiled and held up a hand in greeting.

As I browsed the shelves, I moved past boxes of Playmobil blocks and tiny figures, the building toys, and the board games.

I came to a jigsaw puzzle area. Everybody seemed to be doing puzzles lately, and I had a sudden urge to buy one. Fitting five hundred or a thousand messy pieces into a tidy finished picture seemed like it would be supremely satisfying. I'd bet Tim would find it fun to work on one, too. We'd have to keep Belle away from the small flat bits of cardboard, though. It would be just like her to make off with one. A missing puzzle piece was supremely frustrating. Kind of like the current case, which had more missing pieces than assembled ones.

When I spied a puzzle box featuring dozens of different models of bicycles, I plucked it off the shelf and carried it to the register. The customer was turning away, holding a plush stuffed osprey, which was way cuter than the fierce bird of prey in real life. Ospreys were magnificent, but definitely not cuddly.

I blinked. "Hi, Corwin."

"Hey, Mac." He glanced at the toy in his hand and beamed. "I just became an uncle."

"Congratulations," I said. "Nice gift."

"Cape Cod and ospreys are like bread and butter, right? Can't have one without the other."

"Exactly," I said.

"Thanks, June. See you, Mac." He made his way out.

I turned toward June.

She still wasn't smiling. "Weren't you just in here?"

"Yes." I set the puzzle on the counter.

"I hear you've been poking around into my family, Mac. Doing your detective impersonation. I told you, the only person you need to look at for the murder is my ex."

"Yes, I remember. How long have you and Park been divorced?"

"A decade. Not long enough."

"You must be glad to have Kassandra back in the state," I ventured.

She cocked her head. "What are you trying to pull? You don't care about how I feel about my daughter. And I'll thank you to not butt into her business."

Fair, I supposed. I clearly wasn't going to glean any new information from her, and I wasn't about to argue with her in a toy store about a homicide. "Can I buy this puzzle, please?"

She rang it up without speaking. I paid.

"Thank you." I headed for the door.

Before I got there, Kassandra pushed through. "Mom, you wouldn't believe what I . . ." She let her voice trail off.

"Hey, Kassandra." I half turned so I could see both women. "I was just leaving. See you both at the Chamber gathering later?"

Kassandra nodded, but her gaze was on June.

"Maybe," June said.

The door opened one more time, letting in none other than Detective Johnson. She must be making the rounds. June muttered a string of swear words under her breath. They were enough to make a nun blush, if not a sailor.

"Mom!" Kassandra whispered.

"Afternoon, ladies," Penelope said. "Interesting to find you all together."

"Hey, Penelope." I held up my bag. "I just bought a puzzle. I assume you're not looking for me?"

"No, I'm not." She pointed two index fingers at Kassandra and her mother.

"Were you following me?" Kassandra demanded of the detective.

"I'll get back to my shop, then." I gave a little wave and hurried out before Penelope thought better of her decision, even though being a fly on the wall for the next few minutes would have been wicked awe-some.

CHAPTER 44

The next hour in the shop wasn't too busy, so I spent some time in my office paying bills. I left the door open, with instructions to my crew to grab me if they got shorthanded.

I took a second to tap out a text to Norland.

Sorry. Ran into a snag in the parking lot, had to clear out. Everything okay? New discovery?

He didn't respond immediately, and he hadn't written to the group. I hoped we'd find out tonight what he'd learned, what information Penelope had been accusing him about withholding. I hadn't picked up anything of substance to pass on to the Cozy Capers. I gazed around the little space. One wall held an antique poster of a woman in bloomers sitting upright and looking defiant to be riding a penny-farthing with its giant front wheel dwarfing the one in back. Atop the file cabinet was my favorite photograph of Tim and Cokey, getting ready to race on the beach, each crouched with a hand on their front knee. The top of a narrow bookcase near the door held a collection of toy bikes people had given me over the years.

But right now, right here? My job was keeping my business running. I focused on the work at hand.

By the time four o'clock rolled around, the accounts were all squared away. I had two envelopes stamped and ready to mail. They were payments to small businesses who didn't bill online, but the rest of what I owed was speeding its way along the cyber-highways of finance.

I heard two new—and familiar—voices out front, one very old and one very young. I closed down the laptop and ventured out. Reba and Helene stood talking with Derrick. A little blond bombshell hurtled toward me. I scooped up Cokey into a big hug.

"Titi Mac! Bizabo wants her friend to have a trike like hers and Abo Astra's," she lisped.

"She does? Then she shall have one." I set my niece down. "Welcome to Mac's Bikes, Helene."

I gave my grandma a kiss. Cokey skipped off to say hello to Orlean. My taciturn mechanic had a soft spot for Cokey and had already taught her the names and uses of basic bike tools.

"Are you taking care of Cokey?" I asked Reba.

"Yes." She smiled. "I kept her after school. Astra had a client, and your father won't be home until tomorrow. We're having a grand time."

"Did you want to look at a bike, Helene?"

"Mac, this lady insists I'll be able to ride a tricycle." Helene shook her head. "But one of my legs is shorter and weaker than the other. What do you think?"

"I think you'll do fine. I can add a lift to the pedal for your shorter leg or swap out a longer crank arm, if it would help."

"What's a cranky arm, Titi Mac?" Cokey, now back, asked. "Daddy says I get cranky when I'm tired."

I laughed and squatted to show her on the nearest bike. "The crank arm is this piece the pedal is attached to, honey. See? It's also attached to this wheel, so it goes around and around like a crank."

The girl nodded solemnly.

"You must give the trike a try," Reba urged Helene. "It's a different kind of exercise than aqua, you know, and it's very safe. You'll get fresh air, and you can ride with Astra and me on the trail."

Helene groaned, but it was a good-natured sound. "All right. Let me see what you have."

She was a lot taller than my grandma, for whom I'd had to special-order an extra-small adult trike.

"We have one in stock," I said. "Let's take it outside, and you can go for a test drive."

"Can I help?" Cokey asked.

"Of course. Come on." I wheeled out the periwinkle-colored cycle.

"I've actually never ridden a bicycle," Helene said.

"You should find this a stable ride," I said. "You squeeze these handles to brake. Just be sure to use both of them."

Helene climbed on and practicing squeezing the brake handles.

"But she needs a helmet!" Cokey looked alarmed. "We have to wear them for safety."

"She'll get one for when she goes in the street, querida." Reba stroked Cokey's head.

Helene pedaled slowly around the parking lot. She returned to us, smiling, braking to a perfect stop.

"I like it, Mac." She dismounted. "Can I take this one, or do you have to order it?"

"You can have it," I said. "Unless you'd like another color."

"No, I like this light blue."

"Sounds good. I'll have my mechanic give it a final once-over. She'll be able to figure something out for your right side." I glanced around. "Where's Cokey?" I had a sudden pang of alarm. She wouldn't have wandered away—would she? What if the murderer was looking for a hostage? What if they were watching and had nabbed our beloved five-year-old skipping down the sidewalk? I brought my hand to my mouth, whipping my head around.

"She ran inside to use the bathroom." Reba laid her soft hand on my arm and murmured, "She's fine, Mackenzie."

I let out a breath. That sweet little creature was more precious to me than my own life. I supposed it was how I'd feel about my own baby, once I got through the whole labor and birth thing. Should we ever get a baby started.

Helene ran her hand over the soft cushioned seat the trike came with. I was struck by June's resemblance to her, and Kassandra's by extension.

"You must be glad to have Kassandra back from Florida," I said.

She blinked. "Yes, I am. How do you know she lived down there?"

"She told me. I just saw her in June's shop, in fact. June is adamant Park must have been the one to kill Wagner Lavoie."

"She would be, wouldn't she?" Helene raised a single eyebrow. "Believe me, their marriage never should have happened."

"June said they'd been divorced for a decade, but she implied it should have happened earlier."

Helene looked away without speaking.

"Let's do the purchase," Reba said in a bright voice. "We all have to get ready for the wake, don't we?"

My abo was a master at the deft redirection. Helene was obviously done talking about her family. And it was true, the wake started in an hour.

"Sure." I set my hands on the handlebars. "Come back inside."

CHAPTER 45

As I walked up to the First Citizens' Federal Credit Union's building at five forty, Faye Lavoie stood—no surprise—smoking outside the door. The credit union had the only large non-restaurant meeting room in town, other than Town Hall and the high school gymnasium, and they'd made some kind of an agreement with the Chamber for regular use. It was where Wagner had held the pre-festival meeting, too.

"Good evening, Faye." I stuck my hands in my pockets. Oh! The keychain was still there in its tissue. I'd forgotten all about it. Lincoln would probably be here tonight. I could hand it over when I saw him.

Faye again dropped the cigarette on the ground but didn't return my greeting.

"I'm glad you were able to come to this gathering," I said.

"Wouldn't miss it for the world, Mac. I'm hoping to catch Wag's killer red-handed." She gave me a grim smile, pulled open the door, and disappeared inside.

I stared.

Gin hurried up. "Who was that?"

"Wagner's sister." I sniffed smoke. I glanced down. Faye had left the still-burning butt smoldering, as she seemed to every time. I ground it out with my foot. "She claims to be planning to catch Wagner's murderer all by herself. In the next hour."

"Seriously?"

"That's what she said. We'd better get in there, so we don't miss anything."

"No kidding. After you." Gin followed me inside.

Tulia stood behind a long table at the back, which was laden with appetizers. She must have been asked to cater the event. Another long table held cups and drinks, both alcoholic and not. Kassandra was stationed behind it, smiling, pouring wine, and schmoozing, as if she was jockeying for the now-open Chamber director's job.

I spied my mom, Reba, and Helene already sitting with plastic cups of wine and small plates of food at a round table near the front. Wagner had been Helene's neighbor, but I hadn't really talked with her about him in any detail. More tables lined the periphery of the room, but the chairs had been cleared from the middle of the space, which made room for people to mingle and talk. Park stood at the epicenter of a group of merchants.

"Shall we wade into the fray?" Gin asked.

"Absolutely."

Kassandra's smile faltered a smidgen when she saw

us approach, but she recovered fast. "Red or white, ladies?"

"Red, please," Gin said.

"What's the white?" I asked.

"Chardonnay or Sauvignon Blanc."

"I'll have the Chardonnay." I couldn't abide the acidity of the other choice. "Did you volunteer for this gig, or did the Chamber co-opt you to pour wine?" I kept my tone light.

"I'm always happy to help out." Kassandra poured for both of us.

"Thanks." I tried to figure out how to ask her what Penelope had wanted with her and June this afternoon, but an entry to that conversation didn't come to me. Gin and I turned away.

"Tim's not going to be here?" she asked.

"No. It's not really his thing, and he needed to make a call to his sister out west." His rather unstable sister, also mom to three young children, had sent him a disturbing text he wanted to get clarified over the phone. "Eli isn't, either?"

"Nah. He's not a merchant, and he never met Wagner. Also totally not his thing." She raised a hand to wave at someone across the room. "Catch you later, Mac. Walking tomorrow?"

"Let's do it."

Zane sauntered up to the food table and began talking with Tulia. I hoped Norland would show up, but so far I didn't see him. I'd also thought Lincoln would be here to observe all his persons of interest. If he'd already arrived, he was hiding out somewhere. Penelope wasn't in evidence, either. I headed toward my Cozy Capers friends, trying to think of the last time I'd spoken with Lincoln or even gotten a text from him. I supposed it was only yesterday when he'd stopped into the shop, but it seemed much longer ago.

"Hey, Mac," Zane said. "You have to try these." He pointed to tiny quiches on a platter. "Lobster. To die for."

"They look yummy. Thanks." I popped the quiche into my mouth. "So they hit you up to cater, Tulia?"

"They're paying me, of course," she said. "But Zane, I think we need to retire the phrase."

"To die for?" he asked.

"Yes. Because . . ." She waved her hand at the room and lowered her voiced. "We're here because someone died, and not peacefully."

"You're right." The smile slid off his face.

"I agree completely," I said after swallowing. "There are so many things we say mindlessly. 'She's brain dead' or 'He walks around like he's in a coma.' Just . . . no. If anyone has ever known a person in a coma, they'd never say that." Abo Alcindo, Reba's husband, had been in a coma for three months before he died, and it wasn't a condition to take lightly. "Tulia, do you know who's paying for tonight?"

"Nobody said. All I know is, I'm paid by the Chamber."

"I thought it was coming out of the Chamber budget," Zane said.

"They do charge us enough for membership." More than one disgruntled member had complained when the fee went up last year.

"I heard a rumor Park chipped in a big amount for the evening," Zane said.

So people would view Kassandra more kindly about replacing Wagner? Maybe.

"Did I tell you two I got a tour of his house?" Zane asked.

"How'd you manage a tour?" I cocked my head.

"He seemed to want to show it off." He shrugged. "The man has a killer woodworking setup in his basement. Next to the wine room, which is temperature and humidity controlled, of course."

"Of course," I agreed. "Sounds like an expensive thing to build."

"Do either of you know if something is going to happen tonight?" Tulia asked. "Like speeches or whatnot?"

"I have no idea," I said. "Maybe it's just socializing, ostensibly for us all to remember Wagner with great fondness."

Zane pointed with his chin to a door at the back. "Detective Johnson just slid in."

So she had, in her usual dark blazer and sensible shoes. "She looks super alert. She must be on the job." Should I give the keychain now burning a hole in my pocket to Penelope, or wait for Lincoln? It probably didn't matter. I followed Penelope's gaze to the main door. "It appears my employees are here, as well."

Sandy and Orlean stood to the right of the door. Orlean had changed out of her greasy mechanic clothes into cream-colored pants and a blue sweater for the occasion. I rarely saw her in what I thought of as civvies. She'd left her ever-present Fireball cap somewhere, too, and fluffed up her straw-colored hair. Sandy shifted from foot to foot, as if she'd like to make a break for it, despite just arriving.

The door opened again, admitting Neli Lavoie. She'd dressed in black leggings with ankle boots and a stylish thigh-length belted coat.

"Who's she?" Tulia asked. "Those are an impressive set of braids."

"They are. She's Wagner's daughter, Neli. Short for Nelinda."

"And you know her how?" Zane asked.

"She came into the shop this week. She and Derrick are apparently friends." I watched her stand there looking a bit unsure of where to go. She hadn't met Orlean or Sandy in the shop, and Derrick wasn't here. She probably didn't know a soul. "I'm going to go welcome her."

Before I took even a step toward Neli, Park beat me to it. He hurried over as if he recognized her, spoke to her, and pumped her hand. She looked a bit taken aback. Did she know about his youthful history with Wagner? I doubted it, but he certainly appeared to know who she was. Park steered her toward us, or, more likely, toward the drinks.

"Hi, Neli," I said when she drew close.

"Hey, Mac. Thanks for coming."

"Happy birthday." I smiled at her, but I was thinking how sad it was to have to attend your father's wake on your birthday.

"Thank you."

Park gave his head a shake. "How do you two know each other?"

"Well, I—" she began.

"She came—" I said at the same time.

Neli and I looked at each other, laughing softly.

"It doesn't matter," I said. "Neli, let me introduce

my friends, Zane King and Tulia Peters. King, as in King Liquors, and Tulia owns the Lobstah Shack."

Neli pressed her palms together in front of her chest. "Nice to meet you both."

Namaste hands again. I approved.

"Can I get you a cup of wine?" Zane asked.

"I'd love something white. Thank you."

He stepped over to the other table. Park looked deflated. Had he thought he would be the one to introduce the grieving daughter to the people here? Except she wasn't grieving, particularly. Also, she must know Derrick through classes and not AA, given the wine request.

"I'll let you all get acquainted, then," he said. "We'll start our brief program in a few minutes."

"Thank you, Mr. Jenkins." Neli's smile slid away. "I hope you'll understand I'm not able to speak publicly at this time."

"Of course, of course. But—"

Faye appeared at Park's side. "Well, if it isn't my little niece, all grown up. How's it shaking, Nelinda?" Tonight Faye wore a black top with little shiny bits sewn on in a swirl—the kind of shirt Walmart specialized in—and she'd applied red lipstick. It didn't go well with her complexion.

Neli cocked her head. "I go by Neli, *Aunt* Faye." She stressed the title. "Which you would know if you'd been in touch for, say, the last twenty years." When Zane handed her the wine, she thanked him.

Park stared at Faye with his mouth open.

I jumped in. "Park, do you know Faye?" I realized I wasn't sure if her last name was Lavoie or something else, but forged ahead, anyway. "She's Wagner's sister. Faye, this is Park Jenkins, Westham's lead selectperson."

"Parkie Jenkins? He was friends with Wag, back in the day." Faye peered at him. "And so it is. Well, you're a little worse for the wear, aren't you?"

Interesting. Life didn't seem to have treated her particularly well, either. Her appearance now couldn't match up with how she looked as a young woman, probably why Park been staring at her.

"Good to see you again after all these years, Faye." His voice took on a tremor.

Neli blinked, as if dazed by these connections.

"They ever nail you for what you did, way back then?" Faye's tone mocked Park.

"I have no idea what you're talking about." His color rose.

"Doesn't matter." Faye winked at him. "Bygones are bygones, right? I'm looking forward to delivering my baby brother's eulogy. When do the speeches and such start up?"

Park cleared his throat. "I'm not sure, uh, if we—"

"Oh, you have room on the program for me." Faye narrowed her eyes and raised her voice. "I plan to expose Wag's killer. Right here, tonight."

CHAPTER 46

The room stilled after Faye's announcement. Everyone's attention seemed to be on her. Neli took a step back. Park's eyes shifted right and left like a trapped animal's. Tulia looked worried, her dark brows low, her mouth pursed. I glimpsed my mom shooting me an inquisitive glance. Kassandra hurried around the table to her father's side.

Faye, looking satisfied with herself, popped a breaded mini crab cake into her mouth. "Mmm, good," she mumbled around the mouthful.

Penelope strode up.

"May I have a word, Ms. Lavoie?" She flipped open her blazer to reveal the badge. "Detective Johnson, Westham PD."

"Sure, lady. But I'm not the one you want to be talking to." Faye let her gaze drift over Park, Kassandra, and across to Sandy. Faye frowned. "Where's the cook who hated my bro?"

Yvonne, who was cooking at the Rusty Anchor. Did Faye have actual information about her?

"If you'll come with me, please." Penelope's tone to Faye harbored no discussion. She gestured toward the back.

"Back in a flash, Parkie-boy." Faye grinned at Park.

In a few seconds Penelope had her out the door. Park's face was beet red.

Zane and I exchanged a glance.

"What in h—?" Kassandra began to murmur to Park.

"Not now." He reset his shoulders, mustering a smile. "I think I might have a drink, after all." He tossed his water bottle in the trash—not the barrel labeled Recycling—and helped himself to a full cup of red wine. He lifted his chin and sauntered over to where Reba and the others sat.

I stepped into the gap. "Neli, have you met Kassandra Jenkins? Kassandra, this is Neli Lavoie, Wagner's daughter."

They nodded at each other.

"Jenkins. Park must be your father," Neli said.

"He is." Kassandra cast a worried gaze in his direction, then looked at Neli again. "And did I hear Faye is your aunt?"

"Yes. But I haven't seen her in forever. As you just heard, she's kind of a loose cannon."

A quartet of women approached the drinks table. Kassandra hurried back to her pouring.

"Who was the cook Aunt Faye referred to?" Neli asked me.

"Yvonne Flora," I said. "She's the chef at the Rusty Anchor pub."

"And she hated my father?"

"No, not really. They'd apparently had a few disagreements, but she never would have harmed him." I mentally crossed my fingers, hoping it was true. Yvonne hadn't liked the director at all, but the emotion wasn't virulent enough for her to commit murder.

"Somebody killed him." Neli took a sip of her wine and surveyed the room.

I did, as well. Orlean and Sandy no longer stood by the door. Had they split? I kept scanning. I finally saw they'd pulled up chairs to Astra's table. Park had moved on to chat up another table. Helene didn't look happy. Maybe she had asked him to leave. Interesting. June wasn't here. And Norland still hadn't appeared. I gave a quick peek at my phone, but he hadn't texted. Whatever. He could have gotten involved with a grandkid or two. Still, I felt a nibble of worry.

Gin walked up, accompanied by a good-looking dude. In his twenties, his black collared shirt and slacks would have been a conservative look except for the hot-pink and turquoise silk vest he'd layered over the shirt.

After I introduced Gin to Neli, they exchanged greetings.

"This is Uly Cabral, Mac, Neli," Gin said. "Uly, my friend Mac Almeida."

"It's good to meet you," I said. "You're the baker at the Rusty Anchor."

"I am."

He looked over my shoulder as he spoke, and I remembered Gin had said he wasn't good at making eye contact. His thick eyebrows reminded me of his grandfather Al's. Uly also combed his hair straight back from his brow, but his locks were all brown, unlike Al's snowy top.

"He wears black when he goes out, because at work he's always covered in flour." Gin elbowed him.

"Guilty," he said.

"So you work with this Yvonne, the chef who didn't like my father?" Neli asked.

Uly started. "Uh, yes, I do." He didn't meet her gaze, either.

Neli took a sip of wine, regarding Uly. "What do you know—?"

Just then Park stepped to the microphone at the front of the room. "Good evening, Westham—merchants and friends." He seemed to have recovered his usual complexion. He waited until the room quieted. "We're gathered here tonight to remember our dearly departed Chamber of Commerce director, Wagner Lavoie."

Gin made a sound in her throat, raising her eyebrows at me. He was laying it on thick, all right.

"Wagner's life was tragically cut short. But in his brief tenure with the Chamber, he had already made his mark and showed great promise." He ran his gaze over the gathering. "Mackenzie Almeida of Mac's Bikes, I'm sure you'd like to offer a memory. Please come on up."

Me? What in heck was he talking about? Park hadn't asked me to prepare any remarks. Maybe I was the only person he could think of who hadn't openly quarreled with Wagner. I swallowed. I couldn't very well refuse, with Neli standing next to me. But I hated public speaking. I'd barely gotten through my own wedding vows a few months ago, and we'd had nobody but cherished family and friends listening.

Gin gave me a little push and whispered, "You got this, Mac." Just like she had as we'd stood at the altar facing Tim.

I took a deep breath and made my way to the mike. I cast around frantically for what I could say. Reba flashed me a grin and two thumbs-up.

"Wagner Lavoie worked hard to encourage the well-being of Westham's Main Street businesses," I began. "He got a lot of pushback about last week's Spring Festival, but it was a resounding success." Which had been greatly helped by the weather, but we didn't need to go into that here. "He would have gone on to many more victories on our behalf. I know you all join me in extending sympathies to his family in their time of sorrow." Who was laying it on thick now? It was time to end this show. I'd brought my wine cup with me and raised it. "Here's to Wagner. May he rest in peace." I stepped away.

Voices murmuring, "To Wagner" and "Rest in peace" echoed around the room.

Faye strode up from the back and slid between Park and the mike. *Uh-oh.* Where had Penelope disappeared to?

"Excuse me, Ms. Lavoie," Park began.

"You're excused, Parkie." She kept a firm hold on the microphone stand. "Hey, everybody. I'm Faye Lavoie. Wagner was my baby brother. Parkie here doesn't want me to talk, but I have the right. I don't see a heck of a lot of people shedding tears for my bro tonight." She gave a gaping Park the side-eye. He closed his mouth.

"I know one of you killed him," Faye continued.

A buzz of scandalized whispers rose up in the previously quiet room.

"Maybe it was Parkhurst Jenkins, the *third.*" Her tone mocked his title. "Did you know he and my bro let a classmate die while they were in high school?" Faye looked around. "No, I didn't think so. Or maybe it was Parkie's dear daughter, who wanted Wag's job so desperately. Do they all know about the scandal in your past, honey?" She shot a dagger-filled look at Kassandra.

Kassandra lifted her chin and didn't return the look. Penelope still hadn't appeared. What had happened to her? Had Faye attacked her in the back hall?

"Coulda been the Rusty Anchor chef who hated my brother. Or . . ." Faye's voice trailed off as she pointed at Sandy.

Sandy stood, knocking over her chair in her haste. She looked like wild animal after the cage door clicks shut, trapping it.

Penelope strode up. She didn't look injured, but she sure looked mad. "That's enough, Faye." She took Faye's elbow and clicked off the mike.

As Penelope escorted her out, Faye raised her voice. "Maybe you Westham folks should hire some new detectives. These ones have let my brother's murderer roam free for near on a week."

CHAPTER 47

I made a beeline back to my friends, who blessedly still stood near the food table.

"Just . . . wow," Gin murmured.

I loaded up a plate with more of Tulia's appetizers, popping a fish fritter into my mouth. Conflict made me hungry.

Uly still stood next to Gin. "What she said was kind of shocking, no?"

I swallowed. "You bet, but Faye came here with a purpose. I ran into her on my way in. She said she planned to catch her brother's killer red-handed while she was here. Her exact words."

Uly gave a low whistle. "Brazen."

"You think?" Zane shook his head.

Kassandra breezed by, apparently recovered from being accused of murder in public. "Hey, Uly. Got everything you need?" She smiled and actually batted her eyelashes at him.

"Yeah, I'm good, Kaycie." Uly shoved his hands in his pockets and turned away.

Kassandra shrugged, moving back to the drinks table, where a cluster of people had started pouring their own second—or fourth—drinks.

"I can't believe she was actually flirting with me," Uly muttered. "I mean, we went to *middle school* together. Not to mention, she's totally not my type."

Gin shot me a look. "Maybe she's desperate."

"Whatever," Uly said.

I glanced around. "Did Neli leave?"

"No." Gin gestured toward where I'd last seen Sandy. "When you went up to speak, Reba motioned her over to join them."

"That makes sense. Helene lives next door to where Wagner was staying." And it was just like my grandma to welcome the only other Black person in the room. She'd told me once about being at a banquet during a big English teachers' convention where Walter Mosley was the guest of honor. He'd left the head table mid-meal and gone around to greet every Black teacher—of which there were only a couple dozen—in the hotel ballroom.

"Looks like Sandy and Orlean made a break for it," I added.

"Sandy rushed the door after Faye basically accused her of murder," Gin said. "Orlean followed her."

Uly gazed at me. "Gin was asking me earlier in the week about my boss and Lavoie. Aren't you a kind of detective, Mac? My granddad said you were a big help with what happened at the end of the year."

"I'm not a detective. Not really." I scrunched up my nose. "But when the police suspect someone whom I know is innocent, I don't like it. Not even when they are a person of interest, as they put it. I confess to have done a little sleuthing in the past, along with my partners in crime here." I pointed to Gin, Zane, and Tulia. "Including as recently as December."

"I get it," Uly said. "Loyalty is a good thing."

"How is Al, by the way?" I asked.

"He's good. Our family has managed to take back ownership of the assisted living place, so he's happy."

"I'm glad." I smiled at him before biting into a crab cake.

"Loyalty is fine, as long as it doesn't lead to false accusations," Zane said. "Faye hurled a lot of jabs just then."

"I'll say." Gin gave a little eye roll.

"I'd like to be loyal to my boss," Uly began. "But there was one more thing I saw. I just remembered it."

"Thing, as in an interaction between her and Wagner?" I asked.

"Yes." Uly knit his brow. "I told you, Gin, they'd known each other at Otis. She was active duty, working as a chef. He was a vet, too, so maybe he was stationed there. A few weeks ago, Yvonne was putting in a food order and muttering to herself while I was nearby. I asked her what was up, and she hinted at something Wagner had suggested they do with the accounting for food orders on base."

I waited, but he didn't go on. "Is there more?" She'd told me Sandy was engaging in the same shady practices. The two could have been working together.

"She said she refused to go along with it."

"Go along with what?" A woman spoke from behind me.

I whipped my head around to see Victoria. Where had she come from? She gave me a cold smile. She was definitely more full-of-figure than usual, and the color was high in her usually pale cheeks. Not in uniform, her blazer looked a bit big for her over an untucked dark blouse. I wasn't a medical professional, but I'd say there was no question she was either pregnant or had gained a lot of weight, fast. I wasn't about to ask about either.

"I couldn't help overhearing," she said. "Sorry to butt in."

I doubted she was sorry, but I kept my mouth shut.

"Mr. Cabral, isn't it?" Victoria asked him. "Victoria Laitinen, Westham chief of police. Might you have been talking about Yvonne Flora?"

Uly swallowed, going pale. "Yes, ma'am."

"I'd like a word with you in private, if I may?" She phrased the request as a question. It wasn't one.

"Yes, ma'am," he repeated. He followed her off to the far corner of the room where no one else stood.

Gin watched them go. "I bet he's afraid he'll lose his position at the restaurant by talking about Yvonne. He was working as an orderly at Westham Village. The job included emptying bedpans and changing residents' adult diapers. Uly baked on the side before he landed the Rusty Anchor job."

"I wouldn't want to do that kind of job, but somebody has to," Zane said.

"Indeed." I picked up my half-full wine cup from

the table. "I'm going to go chat with the ladies." One of whom was my grandmother, who at eighty-one could blessedly still manage all her bodily functions on her own. I knew I wouldn't hesitate to help her with them, should the time come. We were both glad it hadn't—yet.

"Mackenzie, honey, come sit down." My mom patted the one empty chair at their table.

"We've been having the nicest chat with Nelinda," Abo Reba added.

Neli smiled at me. Other than Kassandra, she was one of the few other people here under forty or even anywhere near my age. "You have a delightful family, Mac. And Helene has been telling me a few sweet stories about my dad." She'd hung her coat over the back of the chair, revealing a sunflower-gold tunic sweater that made her skin glow as much as Belinda's sweater had hers.

I pulled out the chair and sat. "Oh?" Somehow I wouldn't have paired "sweet" with Wagner.

"The man loved birds," Helene said. "He had a telescope on a tripod set up on his back deck, and he would sit out there with his binoculars watching birds for hours on end."

Neli gave a sad smile. "Looking at birds was something he and I did together when I was little. He taught me how to identify them, from song sparrows to bald eagles. We'd look at how they flew, their coloring and wingspan, their posture when they perched on branches, plus listen to their songs. Before he . . . I mean, when I was a girl."

"It's okay, hon." Reba covered Neli's smooth dark hand with her own, now old, veined, and gnarled.

"You hang onto those good memories. Nobody can take them away."

"Thank you. I will." Neli drained the last bit of her wine. "And I'll tell my mom how welcoming you all were to me."

Astra smiled at her. "I know you said you wished you'd made peace with your father, Neli. But you can rest assured. His spirit will sense the forgiveness in your heart."

I blinked at this uncharacteristic and entirely non-astrological pronouncement from my mom.

"Thank you, Astra." Neli swiped away tears as she stood. "It was lovely to meet all of you." She included me in her gaze. "I'm sorry about my aunt's outburst. She's always been sort of unpredictable."

"No worries," Mom said. "And, listen. I'm going to tell my boy in no uncertain terms to bring you to family dinner Sunday. You'll come, won't you?"

Neli's cheeks pinkened. "Thank you. I'd love to." She slid into her coat and made her way out.

CHAPTER 48

Tim and I nestled on the couch at eight thirty. He'd made us a big bowl of popcorn dusted with nutty nutritional yeast and freshly grated Parmesan cheese. I'd fixed a quick peanut butter sandwich after Zane dropped me off at home, but who could turn down hot popcorn? Especially in front of a cozy gas fire, another improvement we'd added in here after we'd made his house into ours three months ago.

I'd already given him the highlights of the memorial gathering. "And at the end, Mom invited Neli Lavoie to Sunday dinner." I munched a few pieces of popcorn.

"The murdered man's daughter is Derrick's new sweetheart?"

"Apparently. He must have talked to Mom about her."

"And you like her."

"A lot. When I first met her in my shop, she had seemed more angry with Wagner. Tonight, she was sadder, more wistful."

"The reality of his death has sunk in," Tim said.

"It appears so." I took a small sip from my glass of Scotch, rolling the flavor on my tongue. "I'll tell you, her aunt Faye is a loose cannon, hurling accusations here and there. Detective Johnson seemed quite interested in Faye."

"Why is the detective interested?" Tim's mouth drew down. "This Faye wouldn't have killed her own brother, would she?"

"Maybe all her posturing was an act to cover up her own guilt. She told me Tuesday she's out of work. She mentioned she'll be inheriting the family cottage. I wonder if it's true."

"Wouldn't the property go to his wife, or to Neli?"

"You'd think so, unless he'd made some special provision," I said. "Faye did seem interested in the prospect of selling the property. It's not in very good shape, but the location is great."

"You know what people do these days. They tear down the cottages and build expensive new places, even if they have to keep the same footprint."

"A big financial windfall is plenty of motive for murder." I shuddered. "Enough about town gatherings and homicides. Did you get through to Jamie?" Jamie being his rather troubled younger sister in Seattle.

He squeezed my shoulder. "Thanks for remembering, sweetheart. Yes. You know the older kids have a different father from the little one, right?"

I turned my head to gaze at him. "I thought all three had different fathers."

"No, although neither man has been involved in their lives. Nor sent child support, for that matter."

"But it's a legal matter, isn't? Can't Jamie make them pay? Get the court to enforce the law." I gazed at the flickering blue flames and sipped my drink.

"Sure, if she wanted to press for it. But my sister has never been careful, Mac." He winced. "That is, more than one man might have been the father of any of her children."

"So she would have to get the guys she suspects of being the fathers to give DNA samples and all of that."

"Exactly. Anyway, the father of the older two has reappeared. I mean, the man she's always claimed fathered them. And he wants back into their lives."

"What's wrong with that?" I asked.

"Maybe nothing." He scooped out a handful of popcorn and ate it, one puffy kernel at a time. "She's worried he'll take them away from her. She said she thinks he'll claim sole custody."

"But he can't steal them, can he? Just waltz in, say he's their dad, and abscond with two children?"

"He shouldn't be able to. But you know how troubled she is. She's had addiction problems, she's been fired from jobs, and her mental health is precarious."

All I could do was nod. Sadly, it was all true. Jamie had nearly died from an overdose in the fall in an attempt to end her life. Tim had rushed out to Seattle to watch the kids until his dad could drive up from San Diego to take over.

"Those poor kiddos," he murmured. "Jamie loves

them so much, and they know it. But Timmy, especially, has had to grow up way too fast."

"Your namesake. What is he now, eight?" I'd never met the kids. At the very last minute, Jamie had canceled out of bringing the children—and herself—to our wedding. Their absence had hurt Tim deeply.

"Yes. Nine in June." He yawned. "Oh, boy. Looks like I'm turning into a pumpkin, Mac."

I laughed. "Because it's nine o'clock. Off to bed with you. I'm going to stay up a bit longer. I still need to wind down."

He planted a luscious kiss on my mouth. "Mmm. I love you, Mackenzie Almeida."

"And I love you, Timothy Brunelle. Sweet dreams." I watched him head into our recently renovated bedroom suite, where we'd discovered a century-old skeleton in the wall when we'd opened it up in December to add a bathroom. Luckily, one long-ago murdered bride had been the only remains we'd unearthed.

As the door clicked shut behind my darling husband, I wrestled my thoughts away from the skeleton I'd first called Bridey, and away from three little children with a mom who wasn't quite up to the job. I focused instead on Wagner, a man who seemed to have made enemies wherever he went.

Who among the enemies had both access to poison and enough muscles to topple a big, heavy bookshelf? I ticked suspects off on my fingers.

Sandy was strong, and she had worked in a medical lab. Kassandra was young and had moved north in disgrace from a place specializing in tropical poisons. Her father could have had access to whatever toxins she had worked with. Park looked a bit out of shape, but he was a grown middle-aged man. Yvonne was strong, too, as any chef had to be, and could have cooked up something really bad. Or, as Tim and I were just talking about, Faye could be putting on an act to cover up murdering her brother. Wasn't such an act called fratricide? *Ick.*

It would help a lot if we knew what Wagner had been poisoned with. I wondered again why Lincoln had been AWOL tonight. I yanked out my phone and texted him.

Missed you at Chamber wake tonight, tho Penelope and V were there. Sis Faye made a scene. Any idea yet about Wagner poison? Thoughts on case?

I stared at what I'd written for a second. I felt like asking the detective if he was all right. I respected Lincoln and liked him personally, and it seemed odd he hadn't attended the event. But maybe asking after his well-being would be overstepping. He probably just had the night off. I sent the message.

I checked the group thread. Gin had texted a summary of the evening's shockers. Nothing from Norland. His non-appearance also bugged me. I tapped out a text to him, not the group.

Missed you at the chamber thing. All okay?

My phone did not ding with a return text.

I sat watching the fire, sipping whiskey, munching popcorn. All three were such ordinary, comforting, domestic things to do. What was Wagner's murderer doing tonight? Were they sweating, devising an escape route should the police come calling? Planning another homicide, heaven forbid? Or maybe sitting smugly in front of their own fire, confident they'd never be discovered.

I flashed on the keychain and swore quietly. It still sat nestled in my jacket pocket. Maybe it was totally innocent. I still needed to let Lincoln know.

Shivering again, I drained my glass. Time for this girl to put murder back in the locked mental cabinet where it belonged, at least for tonight. I had a hunk of a sleeping man to cuddle up with, ASAP.

CHAPTER 49

"Man, it's cold." I hugged myself the next morning at seven thirty, shifting from foot to foot as Gin retied one of her sneakers halfway through our walk. We stood on the boardwalk over a marshy area, and the air smelled salty. An egret lifted its bony legs high, one after another, to pick its way through the mucky reeds and grasses of low tide.

"It's partly the damp." Gin straightened. "You know it's going to pour rain starting at about ten this morning, right?"

"It is? No wonder the air is full of moisture." I laughed. "I totally did not check the weather this morning." I'd awoken when Tim's alarm went off at four thirty. We'd enjoyed a delightful marital interlude before he scooted off for a morning of baking. As a consequence, I slept until six thirty and barely made it to our walking rendezvous at seven.

"Race you to the bluff," Gin now said.

"Good. I need to get moving."

But before we could shift into our speed-walking gait, a bicycle bell dinged behind us. I stepped to the side and turned my head to see the cyclist.

August braked to a stop and set one foot down. Next to him rode Kassandra, who also stopped. I winced at her squealing brakes. Her thermal leggings looked warm, and a neon-green jacket and gloves were perfect for biking. Not so much the lack of a helmet.

"We have to stop meeting like this," he said to us, smiling.

His sister didn't smile. She kept her hands gripping the handlebars and her gaze on the path ahead. The ponytail she'd pulled her hair back into made her look younger than usual.

"Good morning, you two," Gin said. "I haven't seen you out here on a bike before, Kassandra."

"It's because Mac's shop *still* doesn't have mine ready."

I opened my mouth to reply but shut it again. I didn't have to defend Orlean's work schedule.

"And then my brother forced me to go with him this morning on a borrowed bike," Kassandra went on, her mouth in an unpleasant curl. "Even though it's wicked cold." Her knee jittered.

Whiny much?

"It's good for you, Kass," August said.

"Yeah, well, then let's get it over with." She pedaled away, picking up speed fast.

"She's not really a morning person," August said in an apologetic tone. "Take care, ladies."

I lifted my hand, but he was already whirring away

after her. Gin and I resumed walking, turning off the rail trail onto the extension. We picked up the pace, striding and swinging our arms, not speaking. I'd told her about Tim's concerns with his sister and her children, but we hadn't gotten into the weeds of the homicide yet this morning, nor rehashed the wake. We made it to the bluff in a close finish and stood stretching for a couple of minutes.

"Kassandra is in shape," I began. "Did you see how fast she rode away from us?"

"I did. I also saw she didn't want to stick around and schmooze, not even for a minute."

"I noticed."

"I wonder why not."

"Could be for a number of reasons." I gazed out at the miles-wide bay, where the wind whipped up waves, the water today an angry shade of dark green. "You know, if either she or Park—or both of them—killed Wagner, it'll be devastating to August."

"Poor kid. And him being in law enforcement, no less."

"Their mom and grandmother would be hit hard, too, if Kassandra did it. Not so much if Park were guilty, I'd guess."

"Not from what you've said," Gin agreed. "Brr. Let's head back. I need to wear more layers next time."

"Fine with me. Hardly seems like spring, does it?" I began retracing our steps.

"Not in the least." Gin kept up. "But, hey, at least it's not snowing."

"Which it was less than a week ago." I laughed. "I'm appreciating that blessing, for sure."

We made it back to Salty Taffy's and started in on our last stretches.

"I'm a little worried about Norland," I said. "He didn't show up for the wake. And as of nine thirty last night, he hadn't responded either to the thread or to a text I sent him."

"Mac, didn't you hear?" Gin stared at me.

"Hear what?"

"He wrote this morning. He's in the hospital with a broken ankle."

What? "OMG. Seriously?" I asked.

"Yes. He checked in with the thread this morning. He was horsing around with his grandkids yesterday. He's still in Falmouth. Apparently they found something on his heart monitor they want to check out."

"That's terrible. Both parts. And no wonder he didn't reply yesterday." I let out a sigh. "Yeah, I was running late this morning. It was all I could do to get Belle up and fed and get myself dressed and out the door." I finished my last stretch. "I'm heading home. After I get my shop open, I'll see if I can run down to the hospital and visit Norland."

"Give him my love."

"I will. Catch you later, Gin."

I continued my speed walk until I was home. As I showered, threw on clothes, put in my contacts, and did all the things, I kept reflecting how glad I was Norland was in the hospital because of an accident, not an attack.

CHAPTER 50

I parked Miss M at the far end of my shop's lot at eight forty. If it was going to rain soon, I wanted her on the premises, especially since I planned to visit Norland in the hospital a few towns away. I unlocked the door and hurried about my opening routine. I was running late again and didn't like the feeling.

Or maybe it was the feeling of too many loose ends in the case of Wagner's murder. They flapped at my brain like the shredded edges of a tattered boat flag in a strong onshore breeze.

I got the register ready to go and started a pot of coffee. After I hung out the Open flag at nine, I fronted a few of the new bikes into a better display. We often set several outside to catch the eye of shoppers, but not today, not with rain on its way. Once all was in order, I poured myself a mug and settled on a stool with my phone.

Sure enough, there was Norland's text about his accident and his continued stay in the hospital. No wonder he hadn't replied to my message last night. He'd sent the text to the group at six this morning. Hospitals were good that way—not—waking you up early in the morning after you'd barely slept during the night. I'd somehow gotten through my life without a single surgery or broken bone, but I'd visited friends and family in hospitals, including Reba after she'd had a health scare last fall.

I quickly added to the thread.

Heal up soon and easily, Norland. Will stop by to see you sometime today.

I almost pulled out a sheet to jot down all the loose threads. Instead, I opened a text to myself and began to dictate.

SECRETS. Know K's. Know Park's, maybe. Not sure about Yvonne's. Sandy's? Faye's?

I sent it, then reread the words. Could I do a quick bit of research right now while things were quiet? Maybe.

Faye Lavoie was not a common name. I tapped it into a search bar. I blinked at the results. She'd been convicted of assault and battery fifteen years ago. She'd done time for the crime at the state correctional institution now called MCI-Framingham, the only place women were incarcerated in Massachusetts. Spending time in prison for assault was certainly a secret, and maybe a reason Faye was having trouble finding and holding down a job. I hoped she was offered conflict resolution training for violent inmates during her incarceration, but she might not have been.

No wonder Faye hadn't been in Neli's life. Belinda wouldn't have wanted her daughter exposed to an aunt prone to lashing out physically. I wondered if Neli knew about Faye's past, or if she thought her aunt just hadn't been interested in her.

This was so frustrating. I was missing vital pieces of information. I had my finger poised to call Lincoln when the door swung open.

Aha. "Just the man I want to talk to," I said to Lincoln himself.

"Uh-oh." He kept his hand on the door. "Maybe I should leave."

"Don't you dare. Can I pour you a coffee?"

He held up a purple metal travel mug. "All set, but thanks. Got a minute?" He moseyed in.

"I have minutes either until an employee or a customer follows you through the door. Have a seat."

"I take it neither Orlean Brown nor her sister is here?"

"Not yet. But they should be soon. At least, Orlean will be here, for sure."

"I think you said a few days ago Sandy isn't so reliable." He peered over the top of his glasses.

"I did. So far she hasn't been. I'm hoping she'll change." I sipped my coffee. "What can you tell me about the substance they found in Wagner? Do you know any more?"

"You always were direct, Mac."

"What can I say?" My available time to talk could be cut short at any minute. "I think it's important."

"It is, in fact. As of now, the pathologist thinks it was something biological." He drank from his own cup.

"Which means it could be animal-based or botanical, right?"

"Yes."

"Kassandra dealt with tropical animal and plant toxins at her job in the Everglades, and Sandy worked in a medical lab in Providence," I said. "I don't know what she did, though."

"We're looking into Sandy's role at the lab," he began. "Since Kassandra is currently living with her father, you're thinking Park Jenkins might have made off with a toxin she secreted home with her."

"Right," I said, stretching out the word.

"I know you're friendly with Yvonne Flora. Unfortunately, she, along with the others, has not a shred of an alibi at the time of Lavoie's murder."

"Too bad." I ran my finger around the rim of my mug. "Um, did you get my text about last night? You missed Wagner's sister putting on quite a show."

He lifted his heavy eyebrows. "I heard."

"What do you think about this—maybe Faye was accusing everyone in sight because she herself killed Wagner." I saw him wince, but I forged on. "I know it's a horrible thing to think about a sister killing her brother, but worse has happened, hasn't it?"

"Sadly, yes."

I again flashed on the keychain. "Hang on, there's one more thing." I hurried over to where I'd hung my jacket. "I found this yesterday in the parking lot outside the Book Nook." I handed him the tissue-wrapped freebie.

Lincoln laid it on the counter and unwrapped the tissue. "And this proves what, Mac?"

"Um, well, we handed out quite a few. But what if

Wagner's killer dropped it? Maybe it has fingerprints or DNA on it."

"You should always leave evidence in place." He exhaled with an exasperated sound. "But you know that."

I nodded, feeling sheepish. I did know.

"Since you didn't, how about giving me a business envelope. I am currently without an evidence bag on me."

I found an envelope and watched as he labeled it, slid in the little package, and sealed the flap.

Orlean pushed through the door, followed by three dejected-looking cyclists. Sandy was nowhere to be seen. I let out a sigh. Lincoln gave me a sympathetic look.

"Early rental returns," Orlean murmured, heading straight into her shop.

"My cue to exit right," Lincoln said. "Be in touch, Mac."

"I will." I mustered a smile for the bikers. "How can I help you?"

"Rain today, and we have to leave tomorrow," the woman in front said. "Thought we'd better return the bikes now before they get wet."

"I appreciate it. I'll come out and help you with them in one second." I turned toward Orlean. "I don't suppose you know where Sandy is?"

"Said she had to run an errand." She didn't meet my gaze as she tied on her heavy repair apron.

Whatever. I'd either be shorthanded, or I wouldn't. What I did need to do was start looking for a new employee.

CHAPTER 51

Sandy didn't come to work. I kept glancing at the door, but she didn't appear. Orlean and I made do all morning without her. The heavy rain never let up, and business was slower than sludge. Being shorthanded wasn't as bad as it might have been, and I was able to get some ordering done.

"You have no idea where she is, Orlean?" I asked during a quiet moment, leaning on the doorjamb next to the repair room.

"Nope. She said she was running an errand. Appears to be an extra-long one." She glanced up from the wheel she was truing. "I told you I'm sorry I recommended her. I can't say more."

I nodded my understanding and turned away. Orlean was faithful, competent, and on time. I didn't want to alienate her on account of her errant sister.

Abo Reba pushed through the door at about eleven,

rain dripping off her rainbow-striped jacket, which she'd bought at a high-end children's store. Helene followed her, wearing a more conventional dark blue—and adult-sized—raincoat. She pushed back her hood, but stayed near the door, looking tentative.

"Hey, ladies," I said. "Come on in."

Reba beckoned to her friend, who shook her head.

I headed over to join them. "Are you here to pick up your tricycle, Helene?"

"No." Helene's voice was low, somber. "I told Reba we shouldn't stop in, but she insisted."

"We're on our way to the police station," Abo Reba murmured.

Why? My breath rushed in, but I coughed to cover it up and waited.

"Nobody's listening." My grandma elbowed her friend. "You can tell her."

Helene cleared her throat. "I overheard a disturbing exchange between my granddaughter and Wagner Lavoie. It was one of those warm days a few weeks ago. I was sitting on my deck, and he'd been birdwatching from his back patio. I have a sheet of latticework between the end of my deck and his property, so I'm primarily hidden from view. But I can peek through, and I hear everything, for better and for worse."

"What was the exchange about?" I asked.

"My grandgirl was asking him to step down from the Chamber directorship. He threatened her with exposure about what happened at her last job. She became agitated and mentioned something her father knew about him. They yelled at each other, and

I heard more accusations." She clamped her mouth shut.

Again I waited. The rain rapped on the western-facing windows. A tool clanked against metal in the repair area. Reba hummed an almost imperceptibly low melody. Helene gazed into the far corner of the store.

Finally I spoke. "Did you hear what she said Park knew about Wagner?"

"No. It was before the yelling."

"I understand. What happened then?"

"Kass had enough smarts to leave. She came around by my front door to say hello, pretending she hadn't been next door."

"I'm sorry to ask," I began. "But do you know what went on at her job in the Everglades?"

Helene gave her head a sharp shake. "No, and I don't want to. I love my grandgirl, and I know whatever it was, she didn't murder Wagner over it." She raised her chin. The move was one of defiance, but her lip wobbled, and her eyes brimmed. She turned her face away.

Reba tucked her arm through her friend's. "We should get along."

"Thank you for sharing with me, Helene," I said. "Telling the police is the right thing to do."

"I hope so." Helene didn't sound optimistic.

"Be sure you ask for Detective Johnson," I added.

"All right." She stared at me. "I just wish this whole mess was solved and over with so no one else is hurt or falsely accused."

"Mac's working on it." Reba hurried Helene out.

Poor Helene. She was clearly worried Kassandra

had done something bad. Killing Wagner would qualify. And the way she'd stared at me? Reba must have been feeding her stories about previous homicides I'd helped solve. *Great.* Now I felt responsible for clearing Kassandra's name. But what if she was guilty?

I needed more information. I glanced into the repair area, where Orlean seemed focused on the task at hand. The shop was empty. I made my way to the far corner of the retail area and searched for the number of the Everglades Tropical Research Center. Tapping it, I held my breath. I wove my way through a bit of a phone tree before reaching the department where Kassandra had worked.

"This is Ms. Wagner from Woods Hole Oceanographic Institution in Massachusetts." I crossed my fingers, mentally if not physically. "I understand you employed a Kassandra Jenkins not long ago. She has applied for a pelagic research position with us, and I wondered if someone there can recommend her."

"No, we cannot under any circumstances provide her with a recommendation," the woman on the other end of the line said. "None of us would. Are you aware, Ms. Wagner, we believe she stole valuable specimens of biological toxins from us?"

"Goodness, no. Was she arrested for her theft?"

"The evidence was not conclusive, more's the pity. Some of us also believe she poisoned a colleague, who later died."

The newspaper article had mentioned the person's death had been accidental. No, they'd *believed* it had been an accident, which were two quite different things.

"Again, the authorities declined to press charges," she went on. "If I were you, I would stay well away from Kassandra Jenkins, both personally and professionally." She disconnected with a click.

I stared at the phone in my hand. Just . . . wow. I'd conjectured about Kassandra bringing something poisonous back from Florida, but this call confirmed it. I sent myself a quick text about the research center woman's name and saved the number, in case Lincoln could use it.

Should I also tell him about Helene's news? No, she was reporting it right now to the WPD. They would relay it to him.

But the Cozy Capers group would want to know. I had my finger ready to open a new text in the thread. Instead, I put my phone away. If I passed along what Helene had told me, I would feel like I'd violated a confidence, even though she hadn't asked me not to tell anyone about seeing and hearing Wagner and Kassandra exchange threats.

The door opened and a pack of fit-looking older women bustled in. Rain or no rain, I had customers. Murder would have to take a number.

"Welcome to Mac's Bikes." I mustered a smile. "How can I help you ladies today?"

CHAPTER 52

Derrick arrived at noon, on time for his shift, so I thought I could step out for a few minutes of sleuthing. And the rain had lightened up, so I wouldn't get soaked.

"I'll bring back lunch for everybody," I announced to him and Orlean.

I grabbed a Rusty Anchor menu from our stack of local restaurant offerings and took their orders. I entered the order and paid online, adding a mushroom cheeseburger for myself, then suited up with EpiPen bag, raincoat, and umbrella. I was unlikely to get stung by a bee or a wasp during a March rain event, but I no longer took chances. When your throat starts to swell seconds after you feel a sharp barb, you don't mess around.

Main Street was mostly deserted. Tim's bakery had the most foot traffic. Shoppers walked out carrying white paper bags and happy expressions. From the heavenly aromas drifting out with them, I knew why. My stomach growled, but I knew I'd be biting into the best burger around in a few minutes.

I slowed as I passed the darkened windows of the Book Nook. Poor Norland. I was a little surprised the owner hadn't arranged for a backup employee to keep the place open. On the other hand, late March—mud season—was one of the slowest times for Westham businesses. He probably couldn't justify the paycheck for a second staffer. I'd get over to visit Norland in the hospital this afternoon, unless he was released, in which case I'd find him at home. Or at his daughter's, more likely. He lived alone and would probably need extra care for at least a few days.

The florist was next on my path to the pub. I snapped my fingers. Who didn't love fresh flowers to look at in a place as depressing as a hospital room? A few minutes later, I walked out with a lovely arrangement of tulips in a simple vase, all wrapped up and ensconced in a handled bag.

My phone said the takeout order would be ready in ten minutes, so I steered myself into the Rusty Anchor. I'd expected it to be hopping, with a Friday lunch crowd eager to get in out of the weather. Instead, things seemed fairly quiet. I spied the greeter seating a party of four. Rather than stand around waiting for the bag of lunch, I thought I'd see if Yvonne had a minute to chat, if she was even working this shift. Maybe she would open up to me a bit and talk about what went on at Otis between Wagner and Sandy.

I wove back to the kitchen and poked my head in. A cook's hands flew as he flipped burgers, sausages, and chicken breasts on the grill. Someone else did plate prep, toasting buns, scooping coleslaw, adding pickle spears, and sliding lettuce leaves and tomato and onion slices into ready burgers. My stomach rumbled as I took it all in.

I didn't see Yvonne, and hadn't met the two cooks currently working, but Uly Cabral was pulling out a sheet pan of thick brownies from the oven. I moved inside, keeping to the edges of the busy space.

"Hey, Uly," I said. "Is Yvonne around?"

He glanced up, frowning when he saw me. "No. She won't be on until three. You shouldn't be in here, you know." He set the pan on a cooling rack.

"Sorry. It's a bad time, I guess."

"You think?" He flipped open his hands and jutted his chin forward. He lowered his voice. "Plus, I got in major trouble for talking on the job with Gin. So, if you'll excuse me?" He turned his back.

I took the hint and pushed back through the swinging doors, barely missing a busperson heading in with a tray full of dirty dishes. *Ack.*

"Hey," she muttered. "Watch it!"

"Sorry," I said, but the door had already swung closed behind her. Uly had been right. I had no business invading a busy restaurant's kitchen. What had I been thinking?

The tables seemed to have filled in the few minutes I'd been in the back. I blinked at the two people I saw perched on bar stools. Shades of last Saturday. I'd never been known as a timid person, so I pointed myself at Kassandra and her father.

"Hello, Jenkinses." Standing next to Kassandra, I smiled as I spoke.

Her hand gripped the stem of a full wineglass. She twisted her head to see me. She didn't speak—or smile.

Park hoisted his glass of something amber. "Cheers, Mac. Can you join us?"

"Thanks for asking," I said. "I'd love to, but I can't. I'm only here to pick up a takeout lunch for my crew at the bike shop."

"Those flowers for me?" Park winked.

Very funny. "Sorry, no." I thought fast. Did I have any way to ask Kassandra about what had gone on in the Everglades? No. Not even remotely. But I had something else I could bring up. "Kind of a shocker, what Wagner's sister said last night, wasn't it?"

"Her?" Kassandra scoffed. "She's a BS machine. She was spouting pure fantasy. That's all it was." She took a healthy swallow of wine and stared straight ahead.

I would reserve judgment on whether Faye had spoken fantasy or truth.

"It's a shame Chief Gifford is laid up," Park said. "He was such a dedicated public servant."

"How do you know about Norland's injury?" I asked. "Are the two of you friends?"

"The news is going around. I don't have to remind you I am head selectman, Mac."

I didn't correct Park and his smug expression. The Westham select board had retired the term "man" from the title almost ten years earlier.

"The only thing Norland has wrong is a broken ankle." I smiled. "He's not dying or anything."

"Of course not." Park swigged his whiskey.

"Well, I'll let you two enjoy your meal. Mine is ready and I need to get back to the shop." I wanted to ask so many questions of the father and daughter over their liquid meal, but it wouldn't be wise. Not now and probably not ever. Plus, had I ever been hungrier?

CHAPTER 53

While Orlean and Derrick ate their takeout lunches, I was ready to devour an energy bar, paper wrapper and all. Or maybe my arm.

Instead, I checked in a family's six rental bikes. I sold three helmets, a pair of shoes, two pairs of biking gloves, and a tool kit. I used my hungry nervous energy to fill an online order for six biking shirts branded with Mac's Bikes, Westham, and printed out the mailing label to Vancouver, British Columbia. The customer hadn't blinked at the cost of international postage.

And I reassured a nervous dad his fifth-grader would do fine riding in the ten-mile Science Ride the middle school had planned. I said he could bring in the bike—and the kid—for a safety check during the week before the ride, but that I was sure she would be safe for the duration. It was a school event, for goodness' sake. If his anxious hovering was an example of helicopter parenting, I didn't want any part of it. I was positive Tim didn't, either. I also checked the Cozy Capers thread, but no one had added anything new.

After my staff finished eating, I popped my now-cold cheeseburger into our tiny microwave for a quick warm-up before I took a bite. Nothing had ever tasted so good.

I hoped I could get out to the hospital to visit Norland. I shook my head, remembering what Park had said. He'd made "He was such a dedicated public servant" sound like a eulogy for Norland. *Too soon.* Yes, the former chief's public service was in the past, but he was still a lively and contributing member of society and of our town. He worked at the free food dinners, he served as a consultant to Victoria and the WPD, and he was a loving and much-beloved grandfather as well as a book group member.

And speaking of the Jenkins family, Kassandra hadn't looked happy to see me come up to her and her father at the Rusty Anchor bar. She couldn't know of my digging into her past—could she?—but something had gotten her back up.

By the time I finished the burger, the pickle, and the little container of coleslaw, the shop was full of customers. Sandy never did make an appearance. I would have to figure out how to legally terminate her employment and what I owed her monetarily. After that? I'd have to find a new part-timer. Advertising for a position and interviewing people wasn't a fun prospect. But needs must, and tomorrow would do for all of it.

I washed up, then put on my best business owner's smile and waded into the fray.

As I replenished our stock of headlamps an hour later, Derrick rang up a customer and was handing him his bag and receipt when the door opened. My brother's face split into a wide smile. I glanced over to see Neli venturing in. She held the door for the customer, then made her way to Derrick. She didn't smile in return.

Something was up. I kept restocking and arranging items on shelves. I also checked out of the corner of my eye as the two conferred in low voices. I hoped it wasn't a glitch in their relationship. If it was, I didn't want to intrude. I turned my back and kept working.

Neli appeared at my side. "Can I talk with you for a sec, Mac?" she asked in a low tone.

"Of course." The store was currently empty of customers. "Do you want to sit in my office?"

"No, but . . ." Her voice trailed off as her gaze wandered to the repair area.

"Let's go over there." I took her to the far corner where I'd made the call to the Everglades earlier. Neli clearly didn't want Orlean to hear us. "What's on your mind?"

"For one, I keep thinking about my aunt," she began, after we stood among the rental bikes.

"Faye?" I asked, keeping my voice gentle.

"Yes. She's my only relative, since Mom doesn't have any sisters or brothers. Faye was super off the rails last night." Neli fiddled with the pull on her jacket zipper. "She was such a fun auntie when I was little, but then she changed and went away."

To prison is where she went. I kept quiet so Neli could continue.

"Last night was the first time I'd seen her in years. This morning she sent my mother an email asking for the keys to the cottage, saying she knows it's hers now."

"Is it?"

"We don't know. Mom's meeting with the lawyer in an hour to look at Dad's will and talk about everything. But Mom thinks the property is common, so it will go to her."

"Your parents weren't divorced?"

"No, but they hadn't lived together for a couple of years." She exhaled. "There's something else I think you need to know. I told Mom she should just call you herself, but she didn't seem to want to."

I gave Neli what I hoped was an encouraging smile and waited without speaking.

"Mama's the Belleville town clerk, as I think you're aware."

I bobbed my head.

"So she hears pretty much everything." Neli took in a deep breath and blew it out through her lips. She continued in a whisper. "She told me Sandy stole money from her husband's business, had an affair with my father, and might be dealing drugs. Mama thinks Dad was going to expose Sandy—and she killed him so he wouldn't."

CHAPTER 54

What a shocker Neli's message from Belinda had been. I'd had a hundred questions ready to ask when a ten-person British biking club had trooped in, followed by five college students wanting rental bikes for the weekend, topped off by a regular customer needing a new chain, ASAP.

All I could do was thank Neli. She blew a kiss to Derrick and left. I didn't have a moment to dwell on what she'd said. My crew and I ran our little butts off for the next hour. And then the shop grew quiet again as quickly as it had gotten busy.

I perched on one of the stools behind the counter to think. Was it true Sandy was dealing drugs? Was Orlean aware of what Sandy was doing? I didn't think she could know. Otherwise, Orlean would never have recommended her sister to work here. My mechanic was nothing if not a straight arrow.

And, yes, I'd heard rumblings about Sandy and Wagner, and about Sandy's hand in the till of her husband's business. But to murder Wagner? That was a step too far. For Orlean's sake, I hoped it wasn't true.

The part about Faye expecting she would inherit the cottage hadn't shocked me as much. She'd said as much to me directly. It seemed more in character with what I'd seen of her in the few times we'd spoken this week. It seemed she felt others owed her more than they did. That others were to blame for her situation in life, not her own actions.

I had my thumbs on the phone to text Lincoln and Penelope about what Belinda had heard when I paused. "Hey, Derr?" When he looked up, I beckoned him over.

"What's up?"

"Neli told me something kind of shocking when she was in. Do you know about it?"

"No," he said in a low voice. "She only said she needed to talk with you. But she sounded worried."

"It's about her father's murder."

He nodded as if he expected me to say that.

"I think she needs to speak with Lincoln or Penelope, but I didn't have time to mention it," I said. "Do you think she'd be willing?"

"She kind of has to, doesn't she? Whether she wants to or not." He pulled his mouth. "I'd sure like not to be involved, though."

"Don't worry, you won't be. But can you text me her cell number?"

"Yes. First I need to tell her I'm doing it."

"Thanks, and take your time." I composed the text

to Lincoln and Penelope but waited until I got Neli's number before I sent it.

Derrick disappeared into the restroom. Orlean clanked something into place. The *psst* of pressurized air filling a tire sounded as I considered what Neli had said.

Why would Sandy steal money? For drugs? In my dealings with her, she'd seemed not exactly shifty, but not particularly open, either. She also dressed conservatively and looked healthy enough. Were those traits of a drug addict or someone searching outside her marriage for intimacy and companionship?

Actually, I had no experience with extramarital affairs. Maybe people were just looking for new and exciting sex, or escape from a relationship they felt trapped in. In my own marriage, I hoped never to find out. My union with Tim was young yet, but we were both mature thirty-somethings when we'd met, and I couldn't imagine ever wanting anyone else.

Neli had also said Belinda thought Sandy could have murdered Wagner under threat of exposure. Had Orlean's sister been driven to such desperation she would have poisoned him and then pushed the bookshelf over to finish him off? I shivered at the thought. I'd seen her strong arms, though. She was physically capable of the push, for sure, and she'd been AWOL from the bike shop at the time.

I checked my phone. Nothing new. I frowned at the slim rectangle. Poisoned. That part of the murder was still a mystery. Whoever had given Wagner the poison—or tropical toxin, as the case may be—how had they administered it? Had he accepted the offer of a doctored cup of coffee? Had a bit of poisonous frog fluid been pressed onto his eyes or forced into his mouth? These were questions I should have thought about days ago. I could only hope the detectives were on top of it.

"Hey, Mac?" Orlean called. "Can you come look at this rear derailleur? I think it's shot, but you're the one who's going to have to explain to the customer why they need to shell out for a new one."

"Be right there." I shoved my phone in my back pocket and joined Orlean. "Yes, I'd agree. This part is never going to work right. What did they do to it?"

"She claimed the friend she lent it to piled something heavy on the bike, but I'm not sure. Anyway, the front derailleur is bent, too."

"And look how rusty the chain is," I said. "This cycle has been stored under bad conditions. Do you think the owner can afford a new bike?"

Orlean peered at me. "How should I know? It belongs to the Jenkins girl."

Oh! I peered at the bike. "I guess I didn't look closely when I helped her unload it from her car, when, a few days ago? I remember it did look pretty beat up, but I was focused on the tires."

"It's going to need a lot more than new tires."

"I'll send her a text." I cleared my throat. "Orlean, about Sandy. I really need someone reliable. I'm going to have to terminate her as an employee."

Orlean fiddled with the bike, not looking at me. "I know."

"Do you think she needs help?" I knew I was inserting myself into my mechanic's personal life, but I had to ask. "Like, does she have an addiction problem or anything?"

"My sister has problems, all right. Believe me, Mac, the two of us are on rocky ground right now. But I can't talk about it." She turned her back.

I waited a beat. "Okay. I'll let Kassandra know her bike is in bad shape."

Orlean gave a nod. I headed into my office.

After I sent the text, I grabbed my bag. It was three forty-five and time for me to take tulips to Norland.

CHAPTER 55

At the Falmouth hospital, I checked with a nurse on the floor. He directed me to Norland's room, where the door was partly ajar. I gave a little knock and pushed it open.

"Mac, come in." His voice creaked.

I made my way to his side. Under the covers, one foot was a lump raised higher than the other. Norland, pale and looking pinched with pain, lay back on pillows with the bed's head elevated. A whiteboard on the wall had the date, plus the names of the nurse, the nursing assistant, and the hospitalist neatly scribed in blue.

"How do ya like this?" He gestured toward his foot. "All I was doing was playing. Guess I'm too old for the monkey bars. Broke the fool ankle."

"I am really sorry about that." I lifted out the vase full of yellow and red tulips from its bag and set it in a spot on the windowsill where he could see them. I shrugged out of my raincoat and draped it over a chair under a wall clock reading four fifteen. My wipers had been going double time on the way here, and the traffic had been the usual Friday afternoon congested.

"It's good to see you." He pointed with his chin. "Those are pretty. Thanks, my friend."

"I got here as soon as I could." Not a passing spring shower, the heavy precipitation had resumed after my walk and showed no signs of letting up.

"Would you mind handing me that water bottle, please?" he asked.

I gave it to him, waiting until he drank through the straw. I set it back on the bedside tray.

"Thanks." He winced as he lay back. "Heard I missed quite the show last night."

"You did."

He barked out a short laugh. "If I hadn't tried to hang from my knees on the kids' climbing structure, I would have been there. Turns out I'm not quite as nimble as I was sixty years ago." He tried to shift positions and winced. "And they tell me my bones won't heal as fast nowadays, either."

I perched on the visitor's chair. "Gin said something about your heart. Is it all sorted out?"

"I'm waiting for the doc to come in, but she won't be around until five, they tell me. Apparently nobody else is authorized to say a thing about my condition. I'm fed up with it, Mac, but I'm kind of helpless here. All I want to do is go home."

"It sounds like you'll have to stay until tomorrow."

"Yes, more's the pity." He let out a breath, as if after a pang of pain. "Don't suppose you have any good news to tell me about the homicide investigation, do you?"

"Not really, no."

"Too bad. You know, I seem to remember I got another message from my pal in Belleville. Did I tell you?"

"No." My eyes widened. "What did he say?"

"Well, that's the dang thing about it. I don't think I brought my phone here with me. I'll have to call my daughter and ask her to bring . . ." His voice trailed off as his eyes drifted shut.

The poor guy. He was probably taking heavy-duty painkillers. He needed his rest, to heal. Still, what had Norland's cop friend told him? It had to be about the high school incident involving Park, Wagner, and the friend who'd ended up dead. Faye had claimed they'd let their friend die. I so wished I knew the friend's news.

I waited another minute, but he didn't rouse. I whispered, "Get well soon, my friend," and turned to go. I was at the door slipping on my raincoat when he said something, his voice low and slurred. I hurried back to his bedside. "What did you say, Norland?"

With eyes still shut, he murmured, "Tell Jenkins thanks for the visit." He resumed sleeping.

As I made my way down the hall, I wondered why Park had come to see Norland. Because he was head selectperson? I didn't think the men were friends. It would have made more sense for someone from the police department to have stopped by to see how their former chief was, or another Cozy Capers member.

When the elevator door dinged and then swooshed open, Victoria stepped out. She was alone. She extended her arm to hold the door open for me. *No way.* I wanted to tell her what Norland had said.

"Hi, Victoria. Thanks, but you can let the elevator go."

"Were you visiting the chief?" After she pulled her arm back, the lift went on its way.

"I was. He fell asleep mid-sentence, so I left."

"How does he seem?"

"Pale, frail, and in pain. He must be on some pretty good meds. You're on your way in to see him, I assume."

She nodded.

"As he was drifting off," I went on, "he told me to thank Jenkins for visiting him."

Victoria's pale eyebrows came together. "He did?"

"Yes. I don't know why Park would be stopping by. It kind of worries me."

She gazed down the hall, then back at me. "Be brief. Why?"

"I've told Lincoln all this—or maybe it was Penelope—but Norland knows someone who was on the force in Belleville years ago. Park and Wagner either murdered a classmate one night while they were in high school or let him die after he slipped off a cliff. They apparently didn't inform the authorities until the next morning."

"That's bad." Victoria looked stern. "Go on."

"When I was in his room just now, Norland said he thought he'd gotten another call from the guy, but he can't find his phone. He said he was going to call his daughter to bring it."

"But maybe Park stole the cell."

My eyes flew wide open. I hadn't thought of that. "Right." I drew out the word. "I spoke with him and Kassandra at the Rusty Anchor at lunchtime. Park seemed cheery. He must have already been in here."

"I'll check it out," she said. "They have cameras everywhere."

"Do you also know there's a possible anomaly with Norland's heart?"

"I heard they found something suspicious." Victoria gave a slow nod.

I swallowed. I didn't usually propose theories to Victoria. In the past she had not reacted well to my suggestions. But Norland was my friend. I had to.

"What if Park brought him coffee or a drink this morning and put poison in it?" I asked. "A toxin could have caused his reaction." A tropical toxin, in fact.

She let out an expletive. "I have to get in there, Mac, and quiz the nurses." Her voice caught. "Make sure he's all right."

I gave her a sympathetic smile. "He was your boss for a long time."

"And my friend. I didn't get to my position as chief without a lot of struggles, being a woman, and a petite one, to boot. He always went to bat for me. Had my back." She swiped a tear from the corner of her eye.

"He's good people, for sure."

She started to walk away.

"Victoria?" I called after her. "I brought him the tulips in his room just now. There's nothing toxic to check out with them."

She gave me a thumbs-up without turning around. I pressed the elevator button again. The woman was definitely pregnant. For her to get so emotional was a hundred percent out of character. And when she'd stretched her arm out to hold the door for me? There had been no mistaking the baby bump.

CHAPTER 56

I stared through the rain at Miss M's front tire on the driver's side. It was flatter than stale beer. I swore out loud. The slumped rubber couldn't support either the rim nor the weight of the prettiest little sports car ever made. How had the tire gone so thoroughly airless so fast? I knew it hadn't been low when I'd left Westham. I'd had the car serviced in the fall, and the tires were fine. Miss M was only three years old, for goodness' sake, and I didn't put very many miles on her.

A chilly precipitation continued to pour down, splashing up from puddles and beating a different rhythm on each vehicle roof. My nose was cold, and so were my fingers. I could call AAA, but they always took forever to arrive. I was perfectly capable of changing out the flat for the spare. And I could dry off once I was home.

I slid into the passenger seat and took a moment to send two texts. The first was to Derrick. **Bad flat tire at hospital. Lock up the shop for me? Feel free to send Orlean home and close now. Thx.**

I thumbed out the next one to Tim. **Visited Norland at Falmouth hospital. Miss M has flat tire. Will be home as soon as I change it. XXOO**

There. I left my bag on the passenger seat, then opened the trunk and dug out the tool kit, the jack, and the donut tire. I'd been astonished the Miata didn't come with a spare. The manufacturer apparently thought an emergency pumped-in sealant would serve until one could limp to a service station or dealer, but a sealant didn't seem a reliable solution to me. I'd supplied my own small spare tire and lug wrench after I bought the car.

I stuck the kit's handy orange wedge under the other front tire before I knelt next to the flat and got to work. The work of pumping the jack handle enough to take the weight off the tire warmed me, but my hands were freezing from the damp cold. I wouldn't want to spoil a pair of gloves with this grimy work, not that I had brought any.

Pa had taught me how to change a tire when I was a curious girl of eight. I hadn't done the job in a long time, but the method was still stashed in some part of my brain. I stopped pumping before the wheel was high enough to turn freely. I fitted the lug wrench on the first nut. It was too tight to turn with my hands, so I stood and placed my foot on the heavy tool, then lifted up and brought my weight down.

I swore as the tire iron slipped off the nut and my foot crashed down, scraping my knee against the side of the car. I bent down to retrieve the tool and froze, staring at the part of the tread facing front.

A slim metal handle stuck out from the dark rubber. A handle that looked like it belonged to a razor-sharp woodworking tool. I stared. The side of the tire also bore slash marks.

I swallowed, jumping to my feet. Someone had pierced my tire. Someone with a woodworking studio in their basement? It had to have been Park. Or Kassandra, who spent a lot of time at his house. My heart pounding, I gave a quick glance around. While five o'clock was nowhere near sundown at this time of year, the glowering clouds made it much darker than if it'd been sunny. The parking lot had been nearly full when I'd arrived, and I'd pulled into one of the spots farthest from the facility's buildings. With the change in shift and end of the day, the lot was much emptier now. Miss M sat alone in her row next to the band of woods on the perimeter.

My feet were blocks of ice imprisoned in concrete. I realized I still grasped the sturdy wrench. Should I run for the hospital entrance? Set down the tool and call nine-one-one? But what if my attacker was watching? My hand numbed and I gripped the tool even harder so I wouldn't drop it. I'd never be able to make a phone call with my fingers like this. I should make a dash for safety. But my bag was in the front seat.

I forced myself to move around the car to the other side. I awkwardly pulled open the passenger door with my left hand, never relinquishing the tire iron.

"Need some help?"

What? I whirled. A smirking Park faced me from a

yard away. The color was high in his face and the rain had plastered his thin hair to his head. His eyes glittered.

"No, I'm good," I croaked. I thought furiously about how to get around him.

"Too bad about the flat tire." He held up his right hand, which gripped another carving tool, its sharp edge glistening in the rain.

I swallowed, hard. "You need to put your tool away, Park."

"Actually, I don't." His smirk morphed into a narrow-eyed glare.

"There's no wood to carve out here, is there?" I gave a little laugh, trying to sound casual. "If you'll excuse me, I'm just going inside to call AAA and wait for them out of the rain." I took a step toward him.

"No, I won't excuse you." He moved in and set his left hand on the car roof, effectively boxing me in between the car and him. He bent his elbow and held up the tool, waggling its lethal blade. "I knew you were getting close to my girl and me, you and Gifford in there."

"Getting close to what?" I knew very well what, but I needed a second to figure out how I was getting out of this predicament. A fatal one, if I didn't act fast.

"Everything that's been going on around here. Plus stuff in the way-back past."

"By things that have been going on, do you mean like Kassandra stepping into Wagner's shoes?"

He stared at me, then snorted. "As if."

"What happened in the past?"

"Shut up, Mac Almeida. Your buddy Gifford is now out of the picture. Like you will be soon. You're not going inside. Never going to happen."

I knew what wasn't going to happen—letting him attack me. In one move I tightened my core and brought the lug wrench up under his elbow. His sharp tool went flying as he cried out. I stepped back, bent my arm, then backhanded the wrench flat across, hitting his neck with all my force.

Park fell back and to the side. His head hit the pavement with a thud. I leapt over him and sprinted toward the building.

CHAPTER 57

"Mac?" Victoria hurried toward me as I jogged, her coat flapping behind her. "What's going on? Why are you running?"

I slowed, my bad knee screaming at me to stop. "Park Jenkins slashed my tire. He tried to slash me." Breathless, I bent over, leaning my left forearm on my thighs.

She glanced at the tire iron I still held in a possibly literal death grip. "But you put him away handily, would be my guess." She smiled, even as she pulled out her phone.

"Yeah." I straightened. "Enough to get free, anyway. It sounded like he hit his head when he fell."

"I'm on it." She peered at me. "Are you all right?"

I blew out a shaky breath. "I will be."

"Why don't you go wait in the lobby?"

I nodded, swallowing.

She scanned the parking lot. "That's your red Miata, right?"

"Yes." My voice wobbled.

"Go. And Mac? Nice job." Victoria turned away and began a string of orders into her phone, using terms like homicide suspect, emergency treatment, and more.

I pointed myself at the hospital. I hadn't even reached the main building when a siren sprang to life somewhere in town. It whooped closer and closer. Two people in blue scrubs with coats thrown on over them burst out of the Emergency Department doors pushing a yellow stretcher on wheels with a big red bag atop it. Three cruisers screeched into the lot and headed for Victoria.

Me, I slipped through the automatic doors and sank into a chair away from the entrance. My teeth chattered. I gazed at the lug wrench. Nice wrench. Handy wrench. Now what was I supposed to do with it? I set it on the next chair. Would the police want it as evidence? Maybe.

The kindly senior-citizen volunteers who always sat at the information desk during the day had gone home. I wanted to call Tim, but my phone was in my purse. Which was in Miss M. I thought of going in search of a blanket, but the effort seemed impossible. I was the only person in here. I couldn't even ask a fellow human for help. So I sat, arms wrapped around myself, shivering.

A young woman in maroon scrubs hurried in from a side hall. "Ms. Almeida?" She carried a cardboard cup with a lid and a folded cream-colored package.

I held up a finger. "Me," I croaked.

"Hot chocolate, extra sugar." She handed me the cup. "You poor thing." She unfolded one of the blankets and wrapped it around my shoulders from the front.

The blanket was warm. With my free hand, I snugged its comfort around my neck and glanced up at her. "Are you an angel?"

She laughed. "No, only an ER nurse who was told you'd be here. Now, sit forward for me." She unfolded the other blanket and tucked it behind me and over my head like a hood. "Now, take a drink. It would be better with brandy, but they don't let us stock it for some reason. And here's something to munch on if you get hungry." She squatted next to me and handed me an oats-and-honey granola bar.

"Why am I so cold?" I could barely speak for my clacking teeth. I took a first sip of the hot, sweet drink, which helped.

"It's the adrenaline ebbing. Were you injured in the attack at all?"

"No."

"You'll be fine, then. I was told someone from the police will be in soon to speak with you." She straightened. "Is there anything else I can do for you?"

I thought for a moment. "I don't have my phone. Can you please call or text my husband for me? His name is Tim Brunelle."

She nodded.

"Tell him I'm fine, but I need a ride home."

"Of course," she said. "But my phone's back in the ED. Tell me the number."

After she slid a small pad of paper and a pen out of her pocket, I recited Tim's number. It was one of the few I knew by heart. I didn't need my phone's contacts list to remember it for me.

"I'll do it right now." The angel smiled. "Take care now." She swished away on rubber-soled clogs.

CHAPTER 58

I sipped and thought, as I gradually grew warmer. Park must have followed me from the bike shop. Or maybe he was lurking, hoping to dose up Norland with more poison. *Norland!* I prayed he was all right. I wasn't the only victim of an attack today.

I also hoped I hadn't killed Park by whacking him with the wrench and making him fall. I'd had to defend myself, but I didn't want to have caused another death.

My teeth finally stopped chattering. I dropped my shoulders when I realized I'd had them hunched around my neck in an effort to keep warm. My ED angel deserved a medal for knowing exactly what I needed.

When the sliding doors from the outside began to open, I tensed, shrinking into my blankets again.

Would this be Kassandra coming to finish off what Park had started?

Except it was Penelope who hurried in, not a vengeful daughter. I let out a whoosh of air as my shoulders relaxed. She glanced around, then strode over to join me, pushing back her raincoat hood.

"Are you all right, Mac?" She perched on a chair across from me, leaning toward me with her elbows on her knees.

"Yes, thanks to some angel who brought me hot chocolate and blankets."

"Good. For the record, I'm sorry you had to go through what you did."

You and me both, honey. I didn't voice the thought.

"Park was high on our list for the homicide," she said. "But it was taking us way too long to amass sufficient evidence."

"Is he alive?" I asked.

"He is, but you hit him pretty hard." Her gaze fell on the wrench. "Was the wrench your weapon?"

"Yeah. I happened to be holding it when he came up behind me. He threatened me with a very sharp tool, so I had to do something. I'm just glad I didn't kill him."

She pulled out a small tablet from her jacket pocket, folded open an attached keyboard, and tapped it on. "I'd like you to give me the thumbnail of what happened. What he said, and so on. We'll get a full report later. Are you up for a quick retelling?"

"I guess." I scrunched up my nose. "It's kind of the last thing I want to be thinking about."

"I understand."

"But I know you need it." I took another sip of the now-cooling drink. I didn't care. The sugar in it, along with the blankets, were restoring my energy.

"Thanks. We do."

"I came over to visit Norland Gifford. Brought him some flowers. It was four fifteen when I got to his room."

"How was he?" she asked.

"In pain and groggy. I thought it must have been from pain meds, but I think Park must have slipped him something when he stopped by this morning." I stared at the floor, remembering.

"Go on, please," the detective said in a soft voice.

I glanced up. "Right. So, when I left, I ran into Victoria in the hall and told her Norland said Park had visited him earlier."

Penelope nodded as she typed.

"She looked worried and hurried away to check on him. Then when I got to my car, the left front tire was completely flat. I was starting to change it when I saw the handle of a tool sticking out of it."

"What kind of tool?"

"Zane King said Park has a woodworking shop in his basement, so I expect it's some kind of carving tool." I swallowed, remembering. "I went around to the passenger door to grab my phone and call it in when Park showed up behind me. He was holding another blade with a handle. It looked lethally sharp."

"What did he say?"

I pressed my eyes shut, thinking. I opened them.

"He said he knew Norland and I were getting close to his girl and him."

"Kassandra."

"I'm pretty sure she's his only daughter."

"Did you see her with him?" Penelope glanced up from the tablet.

"No."

"And then?"

"Then I knocked the blade out of his hand and hit the side of his neck with the wrench. I didn't stay to see how he was. I needed to get out of there as fast as I could."

"You're a brave person, Mac, and you think fast on your feet. Ever thought of joining the police? We could use someone like you, and we always need more women."

I gave a little laugh. "Thanks, but I like my life just the way it is."

Tim burst through the doors, looking frantic. After he spied me, he hurried over and wrapped his arms around me.

"Oh, sweetheart," he murmured in my ear. "I was so worried."

"Hey, you're all wet," I protested, laughing. "I just got dry."

My sentimental husband straightened, his eyes full.

"You remember Detective Johnson," I said.

He turned, nodding at her.

"I ate one of your splendid scones in your kitchen a few months ago," Penelope said. "Wasn't that the morning of your wedding?"

"It was," Tim said. "Are you done with my bride? Because I'd like to take her home."

"Absolutely. Mac, do you have any questions for me?"

I stood and unwrapped the blankets. "Do you know how Norland is? Has anyone figured out if Park poisoned him?"

Tim frowned but didn't ask. I would have to catch him up on all the news after we got out of here.

"Let me check." Penelope stashed the tablet and swiped through her phone. "Yes. Here's a report saying the chief is doing well. They found the cup Jenkins brought him this morning, and it's at the lab."

"I'm so glad. Thanks for keeping this brief, by the way," I told her. "Do you need the lug wrench for evidence or anything?"

"Yes, if you don't mind." She rose and slipped on a pair of purple gloves before taking hold of the wrench.

"I'd like it back eventually. It's a great tool, and it saved my life."

"Mac, you saved your own life," Penelope said. "If you ever want to reconsider and train to be a detective, you let me know."

"I will." But I knew I wouldn't. I glanced up at Tim. "Let's go home."

CHAPTER 59

"Are you sure you're comfortable?" I asked Norland at four the next afternoon. We'd convened a meeting of the book group to wrap up details about Wagner's murder. I'd invited Lincoln, but he hadn't showed yet, and Tulia couldn't make it. And, because Norland had been released from the hospital, it made sense to meet at his house. He'd refused his daughter's offer of her spare room, insisting he could manage on his own.

"I'm fine. Sit down, Mac." Norland smiled from the recliner in his living room, where he sat with his feet on the attached—and now raised—footstool of the big cushy chair. The broken ankle was wrapped and in a removable cast. A pair of crutches lay on the floor next to the chair.

I sank down next to Gin on the couch. Zane brought us each a glass of wine, then sat in an armchair with his own. Gin had brought a platter of cheese and crackers, which took center place on the coffee table. I'd sent around a quick summary on the group text thread last night and promised to give details today.

"First, here's to Norland for getting sprung." Zane lifted his glass.

We all joined in. Norland raised a glass, too. His held ginger ale, since he was still taking pain medication, although he'd said he was off the heavy-duty stuff.

"And for surviving whatever Park put in your coffee yesterday," I added.

"Thank you." Norland smiled. "We still don't know what it was, though."

"Here's to Mac for putting away Park Jenkins," Gin added.

"It was kind of a close one." I relayed the details of finding my pierced tire and of Park's threatening me. "If I hadn't been holding my lug wrench, I'm not sure what I would have done. I feel like putting a ribbon on the wrench and giving her a name."

"You would have figured out something," Norland said.

"Maybe. Do you remember when I visited you yesterday afternoon?" I asked him.

"It's kind of fuzzy, actually," he said. "I know Victoria came in after you and woke me up with a great deal of effort. She was quite agitated with concern for my well-being."

"Did your daughter have your phone?" I helped myself to a piece of goat gouda and a cracker.

"No," Norland said. "As a matter of fact, Victoria discovered it in Jenkins's pocket. What a fool he is.

You steal a former police chief's phone, and you don't take out the battery and smash it?"

"Why did he take it?" Zane asked.

"It had another message from a Belleville police buddy of mine," Norland said. "He confirmed there had been a strong suspicion Jenkins had killed their high school friend and Lavoie had helped him cover it up. Maybe in my fog I mentioned the call to Park when he stopped by to see me."

"Wow," Gin said. "And then Park murders again, after all these years."

"We still don't know why he killed his friend, though," I said.

"My buddy dug that up, too. You might not be surprised to learn it was stupid teenage BS. Park's girlfriend had dropped him for the boy he murdered."

I gaped. "That's it? A puppy love quarrel?"

"Apparently," Norland said.

CHAPTER 60

"Knock, knock?" Lincoln poked his head around the corner. "I don't know, Gifford. Leaving your place unlocked? Any old trash could walk in." A smile played on his lips.

"Come on in, Haskins," Norland said. "I told you I'd leave the door off the latch for you."

Lincoln strolled in and first shook Norland's hand. "Glad you're doing well, sir." He greeted the rest of us.

Zane stood. "Sit here, Detective. Can I pour you some wine or a soda?"

"You know, I might have a half glass of white, thank you. There is much to celebrate today."

I blinked. Lincoln didn't usually drink alcohol. "Do you have something to celebrate beyond Park Jenkins being in custody, or in hospital custody, I guess?"

Zane handed him a glass and drew up a straight chair for himself.

"I do." Lincoln inclined his head.

Was he blushing? Did he have a love interest I didn't know about? He'd said when we first met he wasn't currently married.

"So, dish, already," I demanded.

"I just passed my first Wôpanâak unit." Lincoln stretched out the last vowel in whatever he'd said.

The others looked as bewildered as I felt.

"We're trying to bring my people's language back as a living tongue," Lincoln added.

Aha. "You're studying Wampanoag?" I asked.

"Yes. As is my tribal sister Tulia, along with many folks younger than us. Another sister, Jessie Little Doe Baird, is a linguist, and she's leading the project. One goal among many is to have children once again speaking our tongue as their first language."

"Didn't Baird get a MacArthur genius grant some years ago?" Zane asked.

"She did, for this exact work," Lincoln replied.

"That's very cool, Lincoln," Gin said. "Can you say something for us?"

"*Wuneekeesuq.* Which means, 'hello.' " He grinned. "I'm a toddler yet in my studies."

"Tulia hasn't talked about the classes at all," I said.

"We don't want to flaunt the project. And it's early days yet." Lincoln sipped the wine and set the glass down. "Now, I suppose you all have questions about Lavoie's murder. I'm sure you in particular, Mac, have unsettled threads."

Several pairs of eyes turned toward me. "I do. Park

said something about Norland and me getting too close to, and I quote, 'his girl' and him. Was Kassandra involved in Wagner's murder? I saw the two of them leave the pub and head behind the bookstore at about the right time on Saturday."

"Sadly, it appears she was." Lincoln's expression was somber. "We have her in custody. The shock of discovering her father had tried to attack Mac and then hearing he'd been injured in return seems to have sent her into confession mode. She told us she knowingly supplied Park with the frog toxin she'd stolen from the lab in the Everglades." He pointed at Norland. "You're lucky, my friend. Jenkins wasn't aware the poison's effect is lessened by both acid and cream."

"As in the drink he brought?" Norland asked.

"Exactly." Lincoln looked around at the group. "What else?"

"This means Yvonne Flora is in the clear," Gin said.

"She is. Just because she didn't get along with Lavoie doesn't mean she killed him." Lincoln gazed at me. "Same with Sandy McKean, Mac. She apparently has other issues, but being a murderer isn't one of them."

Whew. "I'm glad for her sake, and even more for Orlean's."

Gin patted my hand.

"How did the Jenkins pair administer the poison to Lavoie?" Norland asked.

"Good question. There's no doubt the homicide was premeditated—and sneaky. Which is a technical term, by the way." Lincoln winked at me. "They lured Lavoie into the bookstore saying they had the hush money he'd demanded. Kassandra pulled a bank envelope out of her purse, but her father stepped out from behind the children's section and pressed a poison-laden cloth against Lavoie's face. They then both pushed over the bookcase on top of the poor man."

"Were there fingerprints on the bookcase?" I asked.

"No, because gloves. But those Jenkinses scattered their DNA all over the place."

"I wonder how they would have pulled it off if I hadn't stepped out front to watch the parade—and left the back door unlocked," Norland mused.

"I'm sure they'd have figured out something," Lincoln said. "An attack on you might have been part of the package."

"I feel bad for August," I murmured. "He's an officer of the peace, and here his father and his sister are both guilty of murder. Thank goodness for Helene and June. He still has a family."

Norland shifted in his chair and grimaced.

"I think we've stayed too long." I drained my glass and stood. "How do you say 'thank you' in Wampanoag?"

Lincoln beamed. "*Kutâputush.*"

I did my best to copy what he said. "And I'll add this. *Santipaaph*, which means 'peace' in Thai."

"I can get behind that," Norland murmured. He tipped out a pill from a bottle at his elbow and downed it with the rest of his ginger ale. "Now if you'll all excuse me, it's nap time for this peace-loving old man."

As I walked home, I was grateful for one more case solved. Another bullet—or blade—dodged. No more murderers roaming the streets of our quiet Cape Cod town. And peace among us.

CHAPTER 61

On Sunday at four thirty, Tim and I set out hand in hand to walk to dinner at the parsonage. We'd taken a day of rest together, after the long, fraught week. It was finally now over. The rain and cool temperatures were over, too, at least for today, and the late afternoon air was a feathery brush of spring on my face.

Where the path from the Shining Sea Trail came out to Main Street next to my shop, we ran into Derrick, Cokey, and Neli. They had the same destination as we did. Cokey skipped in the middle, holding hands with both her father and Neli. The little blondie let go of their hands and ran to grab ours.

Derrick introduced Neli to Tim, and vice versa. They shook hands. I'd told Tim about her and Derrick, so he wasn't surprised.

"Let's skip," Cokey urged Tim and me.

"Let's," Tim said.

I let go of Cokey's hand. "I'm too tired, querida. You go on with Tio Tim. We'll meet you at the parsonage." In fact, my bad knee was still aching from my spurt of panicked running on Friday. But it choked me up to watch the tall and the short of them, one in a yellow shirt and one in pink, skip away down the sidewalk like two happy flowers.

"Tim's a natural with her," Derrick murmured.

"I know," I said.

He took Neli's hand, and she gave him a shy smile.

I glanced at them. "So, where did you two meet?"

"At the college," she said. "But I'm also doing my student teaching at Cokey's school. Derrick and I were surprised to run into each other there, too."

"It was a match made in heaven." Derrick leaned over and kissed her temple.

I wasn't sure if I could stand all this sweetness. But, hey, their love was young yet. Who knew, maybe the affection Tim and I showed for each other struck people the same way.

"Mac, are you okay, I mean, after Friday?" Neli's expression turned somber. "I heard what happened, with Park Jenkins attacking you and everything."

"I'm fine. Thanks for asking. It was pretty shocking—and scary. And could have been a lot worse."

"There's one thing you can count on," Derrick said. "My baby sis knows how to take care of herself."

So far that'd been true, although I'd had a couple of close calls with people intent on stopping me, or worse.

"But how are you, Neli?" I asked. "I mean, Park

and his daughter were responsible for your father's death. Does it feel good knowing they're in custody?"

"Of course," she said. "I didn't want anyone else to be hurt, for one thing."

I nodded. "You're not alone in that."

"Also, my mom called after her meeting with the lawyer," she continued. "He said Dad did leave a will, and he wanted me to have the cottage. In fact, Dad had already put the deed in my name."

Derrick nodded, as if he already knew. Wagner must have wanted to make sure the rift between him and his daughter was healed, even if only after his death.

"How wonderful." I meant it. "It's in such a pretty, quiet spot, and Helene will be a great neighbor. Will you live there?"

"I think so." She gave Derrick a shy smile. "I want to take up birding again, as kind of a tribute to the good times with my father."

I smiled at her. "You'll have his scope and everything."

Faye wouldn't like hearing the cottage wouldn't be hers, but she couldn't very well contest the inheritance if Wagner had already transferred the house to his daughter. We walked in silence for a few moments. I wondered if Neli knew about Wagner's part in the decades-old death. I wasn't going to bring it up. She and Derrick were in a happy bubble I didn't want to burst.

"Hey, Mackie?" Derrick asked.

"Yes?"

"Remember when you asked me to look into what Sandy was up to?"

I nodded.

"She contacted me yesterday. She wanted to let me know she was leaving to check herself into a long-term rehab place."

"Seriously?" I asked.

"Yes. Not for drugs or alcohol, but for stealing. She said even as a child she would lift small things from the convenience store, the drugstore, wherever. It's like a compulsion with her. And when she saw money for the taking in her husband's accounts, she went ahead and took it."

"Wow." The issue Orlean had mentioned. I kind of wished Orlean had let me decide if I wanted to hire someone with a history of stealing. "I guess I'm glad I kept a close eye on my shop's money while she was working there. I don't think I ever heard if her husband brought charges against her."

"He was about to," Derrick said. "By then Sandy had decided to seek treatment. She's already paid back half the amount and signed a written agreement with him she'll pay back the rest over time."

"Good." I hoped Orlean also approved of Sandy's trying to get help with her problem.

We reached the big white UU church where Pa ministered.

"Your father delivered an amazing sermon this morning." Neli gazed at the wide wooden doors.

"You went to the service?" My voice rose.

"We both did," Derrick said. "I mean, all three of us, except Cokey was in Sunday school."

"You sound surprised, Mac," Neli said.

"Um, no." *Um, yes.* That is, I had fallen away from regular attendance on Sunday mornings, as my brother also had for a while. I didn't realize Derrick had resumed going. It made sense he wanted his daughter to have a broad-minded religious education.

"Mom and I were regulars at the Belleville UU," Neli added. "Now I usually go to services in East Falmouth."

As we moved on toward the parsonage, Neli slowed her pace. I glanced over to see a worried look on her face.

"I bet you're apprehensive about meeting the family," I murmured.

"How'd you know?" she asked. "I mean, I met your mom and grandma last night, but that was at a public event. Family dinner is different."

I laughed. "I had to meet Tim's parents for the first time the day before our wedding in December. I was a wreck, but it turned out I loved them, and they were both so kind and gracious toward me. I promise you, Neli, our family is going to adore you. As you say, you've already met most of us, anyway."

"Exactly what I told her." Derrick squeezed her hand. "Come on."

"Just remember." I smiled at her. "If Astra starts spouting astrological stuff, you have our permission to ignore it."

A minute later we were in the kitchen amid the chaos of family. Mom welcomed Neli, hugged her, and handed her a jelly jar full of red wine, then resumed slicing a crusty baguette. An apron-clad Pa smiled and shook Neli's hand. Tucker barked and charged at us. Tim collared the pup and took him outside to chase a stick. Cokey tugged at Neli's hand and dragged her into the sitting room to greet Reba. Derrick followed. I gave Pa a kiss and welcomed him home, then lifted the lid of a big, fragrant pot of beef stew.

"Mmm." My stomach grumbled as I inhaled.

"You've had quite a week, I hear," Pa said. "But everything's all settled now?"

"It seems to be. And I'm thinking we have a new addition to the family," I added in a whisper, pointing to the living room.

"One who fits right in, too."

I nodded. "She does."

Derrick seemed to be entering a new chapter in his life, and a happy one. Who knew? Maybe we'd be raising cousins the same age soon. Or not. Either way, I hoped homicide wouldn't again insert itself into the lives of Westham residents. We'd had quite enough mess and more than enough murders. Nobody needed anything else to go wrong around here.

Recipes

Spring Cocktail

Zane hands out recipes for a spring-inspired cocktail at the festival.

For one drink:

Ingredients
6 strawberries, sliced
6 mint leaves
2 tablespoons simple syrup
1 ounce gin
1.5 ounces tonic
Juice from 1 lime wedge
Three drops orange bitters
Ice
Additional mint and whole strawberries for garnish

Directions

Add strawberries, mint, simple syrup,` and gin to a shaker and muddle gently for approximately 15–30 seconds to make sure all of the flavors are combined.

Fill a glass with ice and pour the strawberry mint mixture over the ice. Add in the bitters and lime juice and top with tonic.

Garnish with a sprig of mint and a whole strawberry.

Curried Shrimp and Vegetables

This easy dish is one Tim threw together for a dinner at home.

Ingredients

2 tablespoons cooking oil
1 onion, minced
1 clove garlic, minced
1 green pepper, seeded and diced
1 teaspoon finely grated fresh ginger
1½ teaspoons curry powder
2 tablespoons tomato paste
1 can coconut milk
1 carrot, peeled and sliced
1 cup snap or snow peas, de-stringed
1 pound frozen raw shrimp, thawed and peeled
Juice of one lime
Fresh mint leaves

Directions

Heat the oil in a skillet or wok. Sauté the onion until translucent. Add the green pepper, ginger, garlic, and curry powder and cook, stirring, for one minute. Stir in tomato paste and cook another two minutes until slightly darkened.

Add coconut milk, carrots, and a pinch of salt. Bring to a simmer and cook several minutes until carrots are cooked. Add peas and shrimp and cook, stirring, until shrimp are barely opaque.

Squeeze lime juice over the sauce. Serve hot over rice, garnishing with fresh mint.

Spring Rolls

Yvonne puts Thai-inspired tastes of spring on the menu at the Rusty Anchor.

Ingredients

Peanut sauce

½ cup natural peanut butter, unsweetened
2 tablespoons soy sauce
1 tablespoon rice vinegar
2 tablespoons brown sugar
1 teaspoon chili garlic sauce (omit if you don't like spicy food)
1 tablespoon fresh lime juice
1 garlic clove, minced or put through a garlic press
1 tablespoon ginger root, finely grated (or one teaspoon ginger powder)
2–4 tablespoons warm water

Spring rolls

1 package wonton wrappers
1 cup peeled and finely shredded carrots
1 cup finely shredded cabbage
1 inch peeled and finely grated ginger

Directions

Peanut sauce

Whisk together all ingredients except water. Whisk in water, one tablespoon at a time, until desired consistency is reached.

Set aside.

Spring rolls

Mix vegetables, ginger, and lime juice in a bowl.

Lay a wrapper on a damp dishcloth. Spoon two tablespoons vegetable mix along one side. Fold in the ends, then roll and set join-side down on the towel. Repeat.

Serve at room temperature with peanut sauce.

Cheese Bread

Tim bakes these pull-apart breads full of cheese.

Ingredients

2¾ to 3¼ cups flour (half whole wheat and half unbleached white, combined)
1 tablespoon sugar
1 envelope or 1 tablespoon yeast
1 teaspoon salt
¼ cup water
⅓ cup milk
1 cup shredded very sharp cheddar cheese
1 cup shredded mozzarella
1 egg white, beaten with 1 tablespoon water

Directions

Grease a 9-inch cake pan and set aside.

Combine 1 cup flour mixture along with the sugar, yeast, and salt in large mixer bowl. Heat water and milk until very warm (120° to 130°F). Gradually add to flour mixture. Beat 2 minutes at medium speed of electric mixer, scraping bowl occasionally. Let rise for 10 minutes.

Add cheeses and ½ cup flour; beat 2 minutes at high speed, scraping bowl occasionally. Stir in enough remaining flour to make a soft dough and incorporate with dough hook, if you have one.

Turn it out onto a lightly floured surface. Oil the bowl and set aside. Knead dough until smooth and elastic, about 8 to 10 minutes. Return to bowl.

Cover and let rise in a warm place until doubled in size, about 40 minutes. Turn out onto surface and form into a ball. Cover and let rest 10 minutes.

Cut dough into 8 equal pieces. Form each into a smooth ball, pulling the cut edges into the middle. Pinch the connections.

Place each ball pinched-side down in greased 9-inch cake pan. Don't worry if the rolls touch. Cover and let rise until doubled in size, about 30 minutes. After about 15 minutes, preheat oven to 375°F.

Brush rolls with egg white mixture. Bake at 375°F for 30 minutes until lightly brown. The rolls should sound hollow when you tap them. Remove from the oven and the pan. Cool on a wire rack.

Try to wait until cool before tearing apart or slicing, but it's not a crime to eat one warm from the oven.

Mushroom Shallot Risotto

Chef Yvonne serves this for her vegetarian and gluten-free customers.

Ingredients

4 tablespoons good quality olive oil
½ pound shiitake mushrooms, cleaned and sliced
3 shallots, finely minced
Fresh thyme
1 cup short grain brown rice
2½ cups vegetable stock
Salt and pepper to taste.

Directions

In a small skillet, sauté mushrooms and shallots in two tablespoons oil until tender. Add one teaspoon fresh thyme leaves. Remove from heat.

Bring stock to a boil in a small pot. In a heavy-bottomed saucepan over medium-high heat, add two tablespoons oil and the rice, stirring until well-coated and heated through. The rice should start to turn opaque.

Reduce heat to medium. Ladle in boiling stock, a half cup at a time. Stir constantly until stock is absorbed, then add another half cup and repeat four times. Add the vegetables to the pot without stirring. Ladle the last half cup of stock into the skillet and scrape sides and bottom, then add to saucepan. Reduce heat to low, cover, and simmer without stirring until all liquid is absorbed (tilt pan to see if any rises up at sides), about 20-40 minutes. Stir all together and adjust with salt and pepper to taste.

Serve hot with a sprinkling of thyme leaves and a grating of Parmesan cheese, if desired. For non-vegetarians, you can use chicken or beef stock, and serve next to a piece of grilled fish or meat.